I0719757

Dragon Fugue
Coddiwomple: Book 2

By Lea Carter

ISBN 978-1-951248-03-1

Learn more about the author at
leacarterwrites.wixsite.com/flinch-free-fiction

Chapter 1

The wooden ax handle was roughly as long as Neba's arm, smooth and worn from years of use. He ran his dark brown thumb along the sharpened edge of the ax head, listening to the ringing sound it made as his skin stroked the burr. There was a familiarity to the feel of the tool and he swung it experimentally.

CRACK. The ax bit into a log of seasoned odol wood, splitting it to reveal the dull red of the wood beneath the bark.

Neba whistled softly and looked at the ax with new respect. Odol wood was dense and thick, making it an excellent choice for firewood on the cold bruma nights the others assured him were coming. Placing another thigh-sized log on the chopping block, he raised the ax and let it fall.

He split another log. Another. When he'd volunteered to chop firewood for his new best friend—and doctor—he hadn't actually been sure he could do it. But like so many of the skills he was discovering, it was just a matter of trying. It could be extremely frustrating, at times, to have no idea who he actually was.

The impact of the axe head against the wood jarred his arms and shoulders. The raw force required and the repetitive motions felt good. It gave him something useful to do with his pent-up anxiety. They were leaving in the morning for Ibilia, the Lurrakian capital. He planted the ax in the chopping block with minimal force and began stacking the wood he'd just split.

He'd turned up on the outskirts of Herrixka

almost a lunar ago with little more than the clothes on his back and a cut in his side. Unable to access his memories, he'd nevertheless demonstrated a handful of skills. Leuna had treated him, taken him in. Now she and her apprentice, Sati, as well as a local man named Jartz, were all going with him to Ibilia to try to find the solution to his missing memories.

Wiping the sweat from his face, he finished working his way through the heap of logs, which he restacked as firewood. His next task was to haul water from the well in the backyard, so he started by dumping a bucket of it over his own head. Refreshed, he resumed his tasks with a will. Helping set Leuna's house in order for the winter was the least he could do.

The last two buckets he carried to the house, pausing just outside the back door for a moment to listen to Leuna humming. He didn't have to recognize the cheery tune to enjoy it. She'd been humming all morning while she chopped this and measured that, graceful white hands moving with speed and precision. Her humming was no doubt meant to reassure her anxious young apprentice, Sati.

"Does this look right to you, Miss Doctor?" Sati asked for the dozenth time, holding up a jar of amber-colored tonic water. She felt a little silly for asking, especially when Leuna was doing most of the preparation, but she couldn't seem to help herself.

Leuna shrugged. "Does it look right to you?" She shared a quick smile with Neba, who was just coming in from the garden, laden with brimming water buckets. If Sati was a little more cautious today, a little more uncertain of things, it was understandable. They were leaving in the morning, Sati's first time outside her hometown of Herrixka, and that was enough to addle anybody's brain.

Sati bit her lip, looking younger than her nineteen years. "I…I think so."

"Then seal the lid with wax and set it with the others to cool," Leuna advised gently. Using the rag tied to her arm, she dabbed at the sweat on her forehead. Even with the front and back doors of the cottage open to the breeze, the kitchen seemed to cling tenaciously to the heat the way the five-year-old flowering mahat vines clung to the brick chimney outside.

"I've topped off the wood pile," Neba reported, setting the buckets within easy reach of the two women. Leaning against the wall for a moment, he watched Leuna's nimble white fingers line up a row of dried fruits to be chopped. "Remind me what you're making?"

"Fire tonic," the women answered in unison. At Leuna's nod, Sati explained.

"Fire tonic is a concoction of herbs, hot fruits, vinegar, and honey that, taken regularly, can help prevent sickness during bruma, the cold time." Sati relaxed a little at Leuna's approving nod.

"It needs a few months to reach full strength," Leuna added, using her knife blade to slide freshly chopped hot fruits into a basket. "So we always make it in uda, when the temperatures are just beginning to cool."

"How can I help?" Neba shifted to a standing position, arms folded across his chest.

Leuna saw his closed posture and tried not to

frown. What was bothering him? He was half the reason they were in such a rush to make the fire tonic. If Neba didn't need her help getting his memories back, she could've waited until after taking Sati to Ibilia for her entrance examinations to come back to Herrixka and make the fire tonic.

"We're bumping into each other as it is," Leuna did her best to laugh. An idea struck her. "Maybe you could go check on Jartz? See if he needs help packing the supplies?" He nodded and left her wondering at the sudden change in his attitude. All morning he'd been cheerfully keeping himself busy with one thing or another. Had she said or done something to upset him? She couldn't think of anything.

Chopping the next line of fruits with slightly more force than necessary, she shook her head. Maybe she expected too much. After all, how well could she really know him? Their dramatic meeting (wherein he'd saved her life) was still less than a lunar ago. And he'd spent three of those weeks—fifteen days!—in the forest and beyond, working with an orphaned dragon. Since his return after releasing the dragon on Firedrake Crags, he'd been keeping his distance. Including bunking over at Jartz' instead of in her spare bedroom. It was the proper thing to do, of course, yet she found that she missed his company.

"Alright." She meticulously washed off the minak residue and wiped her hands on a clean towel. "I've finished chopping. Let me help you fill the bottles."

Leuna added the herbs and hot fruits, then Sati poured in warm vinegar and honey. Tired of the terrible smells and heat, Leuna began humming a cheerful tune to take her mind off it. With a shy smile, Sati joined in with the lyrics in her sweet soprano and soon they were both singing about the fun they would have skating on the sheets of ground-ice that would cover the land in bruma.

"The trees will glow in the sunshine," sang Sati as she heated enough wax to seal the last half-dozen jars. The tips of her fingernails had absorbed some blue dye from the wax, but she shrugged it off. She'd trim her nails soon anyway so they wouldn't hinder her while she was working. "And cheeks will glow in the cold…"

Leuna stopped to stretch and survey their work. She seemed to feel every moment of effort in the muscles of her lower back—harvesting, drying, scrubbing, chopping, *everything* it had taken to put together the three dozen jars. She wasn't even thirty springs old yet, but she could feel every one of those, too.

"There." Sati set the last jar in place and beamed at the rows of amber-colored jars with their flat, silver tops and ring of rich blue sealing wax. She'd helped in the past, of course, stretching as far back as when she fetched and carried for Miss Doctor's father, but this was the first time she'd been in charge.

Leuna's discomfort faded in her own pleasure at Sati's happiness. Which reminded her… Removing the apron she'd worn to protect her clothes, she hung it on a peg and smoothed the front of her shirt.

"Sati, now that we're done, let's sit a minute. Alright?" She put on a smile, though she was rather dreading the conversation she was about to initiate. There was nothing for it, though. She couldn't stall any longer or they'd be discussing this while on the trail to Ibilia.

Leuna took her father's chair, as she had so many times since his death, and the leather sighed a little as she curled up in it. Sati was just settling into the other chair when Leuna cleared her throat.

"There's something I need to ask you." Leuna ducked her head, embarrassed at how serious she sounded.

Sati looked up from where she'd been about to relax against the tall, soft back of the other chair. The skin around her soft brown eyes crinkled a little at the corners.

"Have I done something wrong?"

"No!" Leuna reached out to put her hand on Sati's. "No, it's just the opposite." The deepening crinkles on Sati's face warned her that she wasn't making sense. She took a deep breath. "Sati. Tomorrow we're leaving for Ibilia, where you'll take the entrance examinations for the university."

"You don't think I'm ready?" Sati interjected, her fingers closing tightly around Leuna's. "Oh, I knew it! And after you've worked so hard to teach me!" She closed her eyes, thereby completely missing the stunned expression on Leuna's face. "You even promised that I could stay with your grandparents if I got into the medical program." She gasped, her eyes opening as abruptly as they'd closed. "If I go and fail the test, we'll have to tell your grandparents and…"

"Sati, Sati!" Leuna jiggled the hand she still held while adopting her most soothing doctor-voice. "Listen to me, please! You're putting words in my mouth. Yes," she nodded to encourage the faint light of hope in Sati's eyes. "I have every confidence that you will pass the examinations." She smiled and let that sink in for a moment. "If you really want to."

The puzzled look returned to Sati's face. "If I want to?" she repeated.

"I never asked you if you wanted to be a doctor." Leuna dropped all pretense of a casual conversation in favor of the bald truth. Worse than her admission was that she'd never have given it a second thought if Neba hadn't brought it up. "You began your training with my father when you were just ten years old, Sati. I continued training you after his death, yet I never asked you if that was what you wanted." They stared at each other, both of them temporarily without words.

"It's your choice, Sati. I needed to make sure you knew that."

Sati smiled. "Thank you for asking, Miss Doctor…but I choose every day. To follow you into the woods to harvest medicinal plants. To spend hours copying your father's journals. Even to practice my sewing skills in case I must suture a wound." She squirmed a little at that. "I want to go to Ibilia. I want to pass the exams."

"Then that is exactly what is going to happen." Leuna started to get up, intending to hug her student, and stopped to laugh when they both winced. "Here, let me show you another stretch."

Across town, Neba was still trudging over to Jartz' two-room cabin, which was located on the far side of the colorful village from Leuna's. He didn't expect to find Jartz there, but that was alright. He needed time to think. About everything. So far as he knew, this would be his first visit to Gertuk, the busy port town five days walk from Herrixka. Jartz hadn't learned anything during his last visit, which they all agreed was due to the Lurrakian soldiers' strange behavior.

Neba kicked a rock and watched it bounce away, then lifted his eyes to the squat cottage at the end of the lane. All of the houses in Herrixka were built from the colorful local hardwoods, so he could predict that the family living there was large. The main wall in this case was purple morea wood, while the new rooms on either side were made with green and blue woods. *What is my home like?* he wondered.

A friendly whine brought him back to the present and he looked down in surprise at the village dog walking beside him. No one person owned the village dogs; rather, they all shared the responsibility, setting out leftovers and water, and so forth. In return, the dogs kept a constant vigil, alerting the townspeople to new arrivals. Like the day Neba arrived.

"Hey, Akur." He bent to pet the mutt, his brown fingers sliding through its rough gray fur. Their first meeting hadn't been quite as friendly, but by now he'd accepted Neba.

Ordinarily, a larger town like Gertuk kept at least a few secrets from the local law. Now, however, the soldiers were turning over every rock, poking into every hidey-hole, and arresting everything that moved in a concerted effort to stop the smuggling of illegal dragon goods. It was hardly the best time to admit to knowing…anything. Especially to a stranger like himself. That was where Leuna came in.

"She's the key," he told the dog. He supposed that was better than talking to himself. Probably. "She can find out who the mind manipulators on record are, and where they are." With Leuna's help, he'd been able to remember just enough of what happened to identify the manipulator as a woman. If there were as few female manipulators as Leuna believed, it should be as simple as looking her up in the university records.

Once they found out who had taken his memories, he'd be on his own again. He'd have his bow, steel-tipped arrows, and the few remaining gold arranos he'd accumulated by selling meat to the local butcher. But Jartz would come back to his trapline. Sati would commence her medical courses. And Leuna? She might be as reluctant to part company as he was—they hadn't actually spoken of their near-kiss in the woods—yet she'd be duty-bound to return to Herrixka as its one and only doctor.

Patting the dog on the back, Neba straightened and resumed walking, this time heading straight for Jartz' fur shack. It was the most likely place to locate Jartz at this time of day.

The shack was a smallish construction that looked somewhat like a wooden beast with a fondness for adorning itself with animal pelts. There were no windows, just four well-built walls, a tight roof to keep out the rain, and a door. The door was open now while Jartz worked and daylight struck the dozen or more gleaming new traps Jartz had bartered for during his last visit to Gertuk.

"Need a hand?" Neba offered, eyeing the stack of kastore pelts at Jartz' knee. He wasn't sure why he offered. He didn't know anything about processing hides.

Jartz looked up from the one he was stretching on a wooden board. "You any good?" he asked bluntly.

"No idea." Neba grinned a little. His amnesia was no secret here in Herrixka. What kept astonishing him was how many things his muscles remembered how to do. Carving, camping, training a dragon… His grin faded as he thought of Sparks, the orphan dragon he'd recently rescued and returned to the wild. He'd done the right thing, but sometimes he still caught himself looking around for the pesky creature.

"Sure, c'mon and give it a go." Jartz' hands continued moving expertly, centering and securing the pelt he was working on. "'s not like you can hurt 'em. Kastore pelts ain't worth much to begin with. Wasn't for the bounty, I wouldn't even bother with the sharp-toothed vermin." He didn't object to getting paid twice for them, naturally—a bounty for each head and a pittance for each pelt.

"Looks like you're keeping busy," Neba remarked as he turned a bucket over and seated himself on it. Jartz had spent almost two weeks away in Gertuk, trading furs for supplies and keeping an ear open for information about a missing Marroi man matching Neba's description. "Despite having your trap lines robbed." He sighed and picked up a pelt. That was how they'd found Sparks, a scrawny little thing that ate the carcasses from Jartz' line to keep from starving.

Jartz shrugged. "Kastore always run thick through these parts. The village dogs keep 'em out of town, but they're plentiful elsewhere." Jartz kept an eye on Neba as he clumsily tried to spread the pelt on the wooden board. He chuckled a little upon realizing that Neba was watching him from the corner of his eye, trying to figure out what to do next. "Never mind, never mind," he waved away Neba's chagrin at getting caught. "Put that down before you catch your finger on a pin."

"I guess I'm not a fur trapper." Neba managed a small smile. The closer they got to leaving, the tighter the knot in his stomach became. "Did you know I thought I was a Dragon Soldier?" Jartz silently raised his eyebrows and Neba kept talking. "Jerl Karruan, Dragon Soldier of the first order."

"Sounds mighty convincing to me." Jartz reached for another pelt.

"It did to me, too." Neba's shoulders slumped. "I'd still believe it if Leuna hadn't known better."

Jartz shook his head. "She don't talk about her patients." Deftly, he secured the pelt and set the frame aside. "I guarantee she had good reason, though, if she told you that you wasn't this Jerl somebody-er-other."

"She did." Neba nodded. He'd collapsed under the strain of a mind fever when confronted with the truth that what he'd 'remembered' was false. He still sometimes had to use the words she'd taught him—*I control my mind. No one else.*—to ward off a relapse. "She sure did."

"Well, then." Jartz set another pelt aside and stretched as he rose, popping his back. "Why don't you tell me what's really botherin' you whilst we get the supplies packed and ready to go?"

Neba rose and walked over to the small pile of supplies stacked by one wall. They would each carry their own personal items, extra clothing, blankets, that sort of thing, and divide the food stuffs between them. Shaking out a bag made from the waterproof lehorra cloth, he loaded it with half of the flour, dried beans, and other dense items.

"What if we figure out who manipulated my mind, get my memories back, and it turns out that I'm a poacher?" Neba asked, his back still to Jartz.

Jartz studied him a moment. "Might be." He held steady when Neba swung around to look at him, his brown face contorted with anger and fear. "And might not."

Neba swallowed hard. "Every minute that I spend wondering is like a starving eltxo fly whining in the dark, taking bites out of my peace of mind."

Jartz scratched his chin and shoved a strand of brown and white hair back out of his face. "The longer you sit in one spot, the more eltxo flies gather, the worse it gets."

Tying off the second heavy bag, Neba considered the statement.

"I can't say as I know what you're goin' through," Jartz admitted, arranging the cook pot and pan for easy transport. "But I reckon the only way to kill this fly is with the truth."

Neba almost laughed at the simplicity of it. He'd always intended to follow-through, to find the 'doctor' who'd deprived him of his memories. However…

"It's…hard." Neba fought for the words to express what he was feeling.

"Bein' around Leuna?" Jartz winked knowingly at him. "I'm right proud of you two. It's a tough situation, no two ways about it. Handsome young man, purty young woman." He shrugged and reached for the fishing poles. Carrying smoked fish would lighten their packs as well as simplifying mealtime on the trail, so he figured to use what daylight there was to lay in a supply.

The packing done, Neba squared his shoulders. "I care too much to offer what may not be mine to give."

"I know that already." Jartz nodded approvingly. "Reckon you'll be glad to learn the truth of whether or not you're bound to another." Handing Neba a rod, he headed toward the stream.

"If I'm not…" Neba hesitated. Leuna's parents were both long dead, yet he knew Leuna planned for them all to stay at her grandparents' home while they were in Ibilia. Jartz seemed the closest thing Leuna had to family in Herrixka. Or should he wait and speak to her grandfather? He shook his head ruefully. How could he possibly explain his situation to a stranger?

I don't know who I am, but your granddaughter calls me Neba. We're going to get my memories back and if I'm not already bound to someone else, I'd like your permission to seek her favor.

Jartz chuckled. "How about we take things one at a time, huh?"

Neba grinned sheepishly. "Sounds like good advice." After a clean bait and cast, he asked, "Who'll take care of your trap line while we're gone?"

"Zoli has agreed to keep an eye on things for me,

but there ain't much to be done this time of year," Jartz shrugged. "Kastore have already started moving toward their bruma home near the sunbelt. Too soon for the fancy furs, like bisoi or azeri. They won't be ready till after the snow falls."

Neba nodded, feeling better about having Jartz along now that he understood he wouldn't be interfering with the man's livelihood.

They took turns cleaning the fish they caught and keeping a small smoke fire going until the light began to fade. Two of Jatorri's three moons were full that night, but they packed it in anyway, knowing that it would be an early morning for them all.

Chapter 2

As the pale pink light from Argia, the third moon of Jatorri, peeked through windows all over Herrixka, it struck the clear bottle Leuna had set out. The dark liquid inside quickly became agitated and began to bubble. The building pressure was too much for the bottle, and the vaporized gas escaped through a tiny, fluted vent in the bottle's neck.

In her bedroom, Leuna groaned as the intermittent, high-pitched whistle emitted by the bottle roused her from a deep sleep. It wasn't that she minded rising early. She simply preferred allowing the sun to rise first. Reaching for the nearest candle to light it, she climbed out from under her warm blankets and did a few knee lifts to wake herself up. It was time.

After a light wash, she dressed for the day in comfortable leggings, a hip-length tunic, and sturdy boots. Mindful of her companions, she added a few freshly-cut lotai leaves wrapped in damp cloth, in case of blisters, to her travelling medical case. Breakfast was as simple as reheating what was left of the delicious meat pie her friend Ama had brought to share with her the night before.

Giving the cabin a final once-over, she settled her pack on her shoulders and stepped out the front door, listening to the bittersweet sound of the alert bell tinkling. How long had it been since she'd gone a day without hearing it announce someone's entrance, even if it was just her own? Shoving her hands into her pockets, she turned away, leaving the door unlatched so Ama and the other villagers would have easy access in case of an emergency. And tripped.

"What was…?" Her words trailed of as she whirled around and found herself face to face with a sleepy dragon. "Sparks?" She took a hasty step back when the dragon hissed at her. The pink moonlight had fooled her, for this was no iridescent blue gailen, it was a yellow dragon of quite a different kind. At least…she thought it was yellow. As she squinted at it, it looked rather orange, but surely that was a combination of yellow and the pink moonlight?

Something nudged her elbow and she nearly fainted. Was she surrounded by dragons? A friendly chuff prompted her to look. Weak with relief at finding Sparks beside her, she leaned on his neck.

"You're not supposed to be here," she reminded him inanely when she was able to speak. She stayed close to him even as she turned to get a better look at the yellow dragon. "You're supposed to be," she flinched at the increased volume of hissing from the yellow dragon, "flying with the wild dragons on Firedrake Crags."

Sparks responded to the persistent hissing by spitting a dab of liquid fire on the ground between Leuna and the wild dragon. Leuna caught her breath at what the light revealed—for the wild dragon's scales were the brilliant yellow of the sun as it rose in a fiery dawn. *So beautiful…*

"Hello, you old trap robber." Neba's voice came out of the shadows, causing Leuna's heart rate to spike in surprise and sending Sparks into wriggling spasms of joy. "I suppose you think you're clever, following me here." He somehow kept his feet despite Sparks' enthusiasm and looked over at Leuna's home. "Or did you?"

Confused, Leuna stared at him. "Did he what?"

"Did he follow *me*?" Neba wondered aloud. "Or did he follow you?"

Leuna gasped and sat down on the chair by her front door. "You can't be serious."

"Can't I?" Neba watched as Sparks pranced over to her and laid his head in her lap. "He wants you to tickle his ear feathers."

Numbly, she complied.

"I was here just yesterday," Neba reminded her. "I grant that he had to follow my scent here from somewhere in the woods, but he stopped when he reached your home."

"What're you insinuatin'?" Jartz stepped out of the shadows, walking stick in hand.

"I'm not sure," Neba admitted, shrugging slightly. "I took him to the crags and released him. I watched an old aitak accept him into the kabi." The frown on Jartz' face reminded him that he was unwittingly using Marroi terms. "Aitaks are older dragons responsible for keeping the kabi, or group of dragons, safe."

"So as far as you knew," Leuna ventured, "Sparks was settled on the crags."

"Yes, except…" Neba drummed his fingers on his belt. "There was a mob of young males nearby. Close enough to hear, anyway."

Jartz nodded sagely. "You figure Sparks didn't know better and tried to get friendly?" Male animals tended to get combative, particularly with a male they'd never seen before.

"Something like that," Neba agreed. "Although, if he was driven away, I don't think the others would've allowed her to leave with him."

"Her?" Leuna repeated. Looking back and forth between the two dragons, she asked, "Do you mean Sparks has found a mate?"

"A friend for now," Neba corrected, leaning on his staff. "But yes. When they're ready, they'll have a splendid hatching." By that time, the dragon in question had stopped hissing and retreated sulkily into nearby shadows.

"What're we going to do?" Leuna asked, suddenly remembering the real reason they'd gathered. "We can't take them to Gertuk!"

"Why not?" Neba grinned. "Sparks has clearly chosen you over the kabi."

"Why not?" Leuna sputtered, choosing to ignore the rest of what he'd said. "Gertuk is much larger than Herrixka, it's true, but it is definitely not big enough for two dragons!"

"'Specially not a wild one." Jartz nodded at the female.

"No need to worry about her," Neba assured them. "If she decides to stay, she'll get used to us. If she doesn't, she knows where the crags are."

Leuna, mouth already opened to respond, snapped her lips shut and tried to turn away. Unfortunately, the dramatic effect was ruined by Sparks, whose head was still planted in her lap.

"Oh…my." Sati stepped into the light and stood there, staring back and forth between the dragons, for even the shadows couldn't properly hide the glistening yellow scales. "Are those dragons?" she squeaked.

"Harmless dragons," Neba said quickly.

"Is that possible?" Sati asked, looking to him in wide-eyed innocence.

"Well…" Neba cleared his throat. "Sparks," he pointed, "is as friendly as a kaleko, just a lot less furry."

"Presa, on the other hand, is a wild dragon straight from Firedrake Crags," Leuna countered.

"Presa?" Neba quirked an eyebrow at her. "You've already named her?"

Caught, Leuna scowled at him. "Presa, in the old tongue, is the word for an animal mother."

He couldn't help smiling broadly at that. She'd named him the same way. 'Neba' meant 'brother' in the old tongue. He didn't know what the word for 'suitor' was, but he felt that more accurately described his feelings toward her, if not his actions.

"Alright." Jartz, tired of standing around when he could be walking, thumped his stick on the ground. "You two grab this gear," he held out two, roughly equally-weighted sacks to the women, "and let's get a move on."

"What about the dragons?" Leuna asked, still worried.

"Seems likely Sparks'll come along of his own accord. I reckon Presa can do the same if she's a mind to." Jartz shifted his pack and started off. "As for what to do when we get there, we'll have plenty of time to discuss it on the trail."

Reluctantly, Leuna tied the bag of shared gear in place on her pack and nudged Sparks off her lap. Unwilling to chance that he'd stay behind in Herrixka out of curiosity, she tried to coax him into coming along.

"Unless you're carrying fresh fish, you're not going to have much luck with that," Neba advised her.

"What do you suggest?" she asked tightly, annoyed with him on general principle. The faint smile playing around the corners of his mouth did nothing to improve her disposition.

"Follow the others. The village is still asleep, so we're the most interesting thing around right now. Besides," Neba gently took her by the arm, "he's going to have a much harder job convincing her to come along while we're standing here."

"Fine." She tugged her arm free. "We'll walk."

Neba waited until she was a few strides away before muttering to Sparks, "I hope you have better luck with Presa, pal."

In her irritation, Leuna walked faster than she knew was wise and soon caught up with the others, leaving the dragons behind in the process. Sati had been only too happy to get a little distance between herself and the dragons, so now she cast an anxious glance over her shoulder. Relieved at not being able to see the dragons, she smiled at Leuna.

"Put these where you can get at them," Jartz advised, handing out packets of smoked fish. "We likely won't stop for a midday meal, so these'll be good for nibblin'."

"What about rest stops?" Leuna asked forthrightly, acknowledging his self-appointed role as group leader.

"We'll stop as needed," Jartz replied affably. "Don't wander off by yourself, either. Drink freely for now as there's a stream a few hours along. If you need to stop a'fore then, just give out with a whistle."

"I suggest we plan to pause a while at the stream," Leuna proposed sensibly. "That will allow us to adjust our gear, tend to any other needs, such as emptying rocks out of our boots, and so on." She went for a light-hearted approach to reminding the others that they were travelling in mixed company.

Jartz chuckled and nodded his understanding. He flattered himself that he'd taught her everything she knew of woodcraft and considered himself a sort-of-uncle to boot.

From where he walked at the rear of the group, Neba watched their easy interaction a little enviously. He told himself that it was a good reminder, though. He was different from them, a stranger. Take his clothes, for example. Unlike the straight-cut style of Lurrakian clothing, the loose fabric of his shirt sleeves and pant legs bounced as he walked, then narrowed around his ankles and wrists via many pleats. He supposed that must be popular Marroi style, given that they were the clothes he'd been wearing when he woke up outside of Herrixka.

He straightened his shoulders and walked tall, even though he wasn't really sure what it meant to be Marroi. All that he knew was what little Leuna had told him.

The Marroi Empire reaches as far as the distant shores of Baketsu Waters and stretches south into the wild Izutu plains... Though much of their lands lay wild and empty of man.

Full of dragons, perhaps? Such as the ones he could sense following along behind them?

Leuna had also detected the scratch of scales on rocks and casually looked around as if to check on

Neba. Easily spotting the shimmering dragons amidst the shadows, Leuna looped her arm through Sati's.

"Is that a memory bracelet?" she asked, nodding at the new bracelet on Sati's left wrist.

"Oh. Yes." Sati held it out so Leuna could see it better. "My parents gave it to me last night after supper."

Leuna smiled and touched each of the five stones lightly. The two largest (one orange, one purple) represented Sati's parents. The three smallish stones were rough-cut spheres. Sati would polish them when she missed her family and remember that her little sister and brothers were still growing and changing, too.

"I still have mine from when I left for university." Leuna smiled.

"Did you miss Herrixka very much?" Sati felt quite bold for asking.

"Every day at first," Leuna nodded. "The snug homes built of many-colored planks. The one road through town." She chuckled. "Knowing every single person."

"There must be many, many people in Ibilia," Sati observed uneasily. She was confident in her ability to learn and become a doctor. The prospect of being surrounded by strangers, on the other hand, made her stomach twist.

"That's true." Feeling the tension in Sati's arm, Leuna gently squeezed it. "Students come from as far away as the Arrotz kingdom, clear across the Heze Sea, to attend university there. But you get used to the people and the noise. If you're anything like me, it's the countless buildings, all looking so much the same, that will cause most of your trouble."

"Countless buildings?" Sati's voice trembled slightly. She knew every house, every shack in Herrixka.

Kicking herself mentally for adding to Sati's trepidation, Leuna shrugged dismissively.

"I had to have my grandfather's servant go everywhere with me for quite a while," she laughed, offering a solution to the intimidating picture she'd painted. Only when Sati's muscles relaxed under her hand did she continue. "In Ibilia, most of the large buildings are made of granite. The gray buildings are always stuffy businesses, banks and that sort of thing. Some of them stretch so high into the sky that they throw shadows almost until the sun is at its zenith." Sati's eyes grew quite round and Leuna stifled a chuckle. "Brown buildings are usually trade houses, where craftsmen practice their arts."

"But not all of the buildings are made of stone," Sati interrupted.

"No, you're right." Leuna accepted the hint easily. "The shops and stores are made of wood, as are the food carts that move up and down the main streets."

"Are there a great many food carts?" Sati asked, wondering why she'd never before thought about what Ibilia would be like. Leuna rarely spoke of her time there, though she often shared amusing snippets from her grandparents' letters.

"Dozens! Their wares fill the air with the most mouth-watering smells." Leuna shook her head at a memory. She'd been one of the few students in her class whose family could afford to provide spending money for her. She'd managed to spend all of it at the food carts two weeks running! "You must ask Dari, my grandparents' cook, to send you with a treat in your pocket, or you will be tempted to stop at every cart."

Sati touched Leuna's arm lightly. "My parents and I wish to thank you for arranging for me to stay with your grandparents."

"It's my pleasure," Leuna reassured her. "Theirs as well. Tonight after supper, I'll let you read the last letter they sent. They're *so* excited to meet you."

"What if they ask me about your home in Herrixka?" Sati asked. She paused a step and then began to walk more quickly, nearly knocking Leuna off-balance. "What shall I tell them? That you chop your own wood and hunt your own food and draw your own water from a well?"

Leuna patted Sati's arm before the girl could get a second breath and continue.

"Yes! Yes, tell them all of that. Tell them anything that is true. But don't just talk about me," Leuna laughed. "They will be delighted to hear about all of Herrixka. The people, the children, the plants and animals." She hesitated, remembering something else.

She remembered waiting…for letters from home. At first, she'd naturally relied on her parents for advice and guidance. Not until her father—and then her grandfather—had gently suggested that it might be wiser to ask the people actually *living* in Ibilia had she realized her folly. It was so much simpler and faster to talk with her grandparents, who were right there under the same roof. They gave wonderful advice, too, on every subject from dating to finding the best shop for her lab equipment.

"Whatever you care to tell them about, they will listen. Including your classes." University students were under a great deal of pressure to succeed and she wanted to be sure Sati knew from the beginning that she didn't have to endure the stresses alone.

Sati heard the sober tone and nodded, tucking that information away for later, when she was more familiar with what would be her new home.

Jartz had pulled ahead by then, just enough to give them some privacy as they talked. Unlike most of Herrixka's citizens, he spent most of his time in the forest. He knew every tree and rock around his trapline and for half a day's walk in any direction around it. He could tell within a few feet of stepping into the forest if something was wrong. And while he hated leaving it, he knew that what he'd stumbled onto during his last trip would have far-reaching consequences.

He'd barely gotten three days out from Herrixka before he'd encountered a group of Lurrakian soldiers. Dispatched from Gertuk by some bureaucrat Jartz had never heard of, they'd swept through the forest, almost as far as Herrixka, burning every structure that wasn't on their map. Feigning disinterest, Jartz wrangled an invitation to ride with their cook when they headed back to Gertuk, but he'd never gotten a decent look at that map.

Not that he needed a piece of paper to tell him they'd disturbed the two-legged shadows that prowled the woods. Displaced them. That they, like most predators, would range uneasily over their territory, quicker than usual to attack. So, whilst he kept an ear open for a whistle from behind as he strode along, he mostly concerned himself with the forest that lined one side of the path. The rolling meadow to his right didn't worry him near as much as the forest, where anybody with half a brain could conceal themselves while waiting for a small party such as theirs.

The sun was high overhead when Neba quickened his pace and overtook Jartz. Speaking in a conversational tone, Neba observed, "Your head is going to come unscrewed from your neck if you keep looking around that hard."

"Might be." Jartz shifted his pack over from where the strap had started bothering his left shoulder. "Might be I prefer unscrewing it to having someone knock it off my shoulders."

"Fair point." Neba looked behind him as though checking on the dragons' progress. "Do you really think we're in danger this close to Herrixka?"

"No telling." Jartz shook his head. He'd already told the others about the soldiers, so he didn't bother repeating himself. Neba surprised him by chuckling. "Something funny?"

"I was just thinking. Maybe having a couple of dragons along isn't such a bad thing." Naturally possessed of scales hard enough to shatter any ordinary arrow, it would take a trained dragon killer to pose a threat to these animals.

Jartz laughed with him at that. "Hadn't occurred to me," he admitted.

On his way to the back of the group again, Neba checked to make sure that the others still had water and snacks, then devoted his attention to Sparks. It didn't take much to revive their camaraderie, much to Presa's disgust.

Chapter 3

The morning of the third day, Leuna woke to a strange sound. Thumping? Thudding? Rolling onto her stomach, she propped herself up on her arms and listened carefully. It was…stomping. Careful not to disturb Sparks, who'd insisted on herding her over to sleep with himself and Presa (who thankfully hadn't objected!) she slipped out from under his wing and looked toward the sound.

On the other side of a charred wall that used to be part of a traveler's shelter, stood Neba. He seemed to have something in his hands, but she had to blink a few times and squint against the gloom before she was able to tell that he was holding his staff.

Forgetting to worry about waking Sparks, she leaned against him and watched as Neba moved from offensive to defensive positions and back again, practicing against an invisible opponent. Muscles she'd forgotten she had began to ache in empathy as he worked through a particularly intricate sequence. She could almost hear her university instructor warning her about the position of her elbows, which always seemed to be up too high, or in too far, or something.

"Egun ona," she greeted when he'd finished.

"Good day to you," he returned, still breathing rapidly from his exercise. His eyes were already adapted to seeing in the near-darkness and he took his time looking at her. Her sleep braid had done a pretty good job of keeping her hair tidy, but he could see a few stray blades of grass in it, which made him smile.

"You're very good with that," she observed, indicating his staff. "I've never seen anything close to the moves you were doing."

He used one end of his staff to flip his water skin up in the air so he could catch it.

"Moves like that?" he grinned as he uncorked it.

"Not exactly." She laughed softly, not wishing to disturb Sati, who had fallen asleep without supper the night before.

"But you have seen someone practicing with a staff before?" he clarified.

"Yes, when I was at university. I was already a decent archer thanks to Jartz, so I wanted to learn something new." She did her best to shrug it off. It had been years ago, more than she cared to admit.

Neba took another sip, then offered her his staff. "Here. We have some time before we leave if you'd like to practice." He liked the idea that they had something concrete in common, a shared skill.

Leuna eyed the staff uncertainly. Part of her was curious. She'd only survived that class by becoming an expert at mixing ubel cream to treat numerous self-inflicted bruises. And yet, she'd improved enough to pass her evaluation.

Neba surrendered the staff to her and took her place by Sparks while she moved off to a safe distance. He nodded his approval when she started with a simple rotation of the staff, in front, then on either side. The staff, which he'd made for himself, was too tall for her to use easily in the full range of movements, but it would probably be alright for a simple practice session.

She stepped forward and made a waist-high thrust

with the staff. Blocking left, she followed with a head strike and a reverse jab at a second imaginary opponent attacking from the rear. She continued through the order of positions at a restrained speed, her whole being focused on getting them right. As she whipped the staff around her body for a final overhead strike, she managed to catch herself on her extended knee with the opposite end of the weapon.

Neba sprang to his feet and rushed over to her. "Are you alright?"

"Sure." Grimacing, she rubbed the sore spot. "This sort of thing happened all the time in class." Handing back the staff, she turned away only to be scooped into his arms. Her arms automatically circled his neck for support and she vaguely noticed that he'd left the staff behind. "What're you doing?" she asked after recovering from her surprise.

"Nothing, really." He seated her close enough to Sparks to lean against his folded wing. "We've got a long way to go still and that bruise isn't going to make it any easier for you."

"True." She tried not to smile as he began riffling through her medical case. "Looking for anything in particular?"

"Yes." He lifted a bottle to his nose, shook his head, and set it aside. "Roll up your pant leg, please."

While he delved deeper into her case, she did as he asked, stopping just above the knee. Not surprisingly, there was already discoloration.

"Here." Neba held up two bottles triumphantly.

"What're you going to do with those?' she asked, suddenly apprehensive.

"Um…" Looking into her bag again, he pulled out some gauze and a narrow roll of cotton cloth. "Let's find out." He winked.

She bit her lip against the reflexive urge to snatch it all away from him and find the ubel cream on her own. It would've been a lot easier than it was to watch him mix liquid mehe with lasaitu balm until they'd formed a sort of runny poultice, then slather it on the gauze.

"I…" She finally spoke up when it looked like he was ready to apply the gauze to her knee. "Let me." Sitting with her leg stretched out had slowed her heart rate and allowed the bruise to cool, but she still took care as she gingerly spread the gauze across her knee.

Neba began unrolling the cotton bandage, expecting her to object to that as well. Their eyes met and she smiled. Gently, he wrapped the bandage around her knee, leaving a long tail once he was satisfied with the job. Deftly, he tied a simple knot down near her skin, tore the rest of the tail in half lengthwise, and used the two attached strips to secure the bandage around her leg.

"I've learned two things this morning," she remarked, tugging her pant leg back down. "A new poultice for bruises." Assuming it worked, of course. She let him take her hands and pull her to her feet. "And a quick way to tie off a bandage." She tested her weight on her leg. "You're quite a good nurse."

He smiled down at her, trying to stay as unaffected as she appeared to be. Her white skin was warm against his brown fingers, but she didn't seem to have taken any notice at all. The contact had distracted him enough that he'd barely been able to tie the last knot. Now he continued holding her hands, curious to see how long she would allow it.

"I suppose we could've woken Sati, given her a little hands-on experience." She chuckled. And spared her Neba's disconcerting touch, efficient as it had been. "Except that I'd rather let her sleep as long as possible. I've never seen her so exhausted."

"And now your knee is injured." He cocked his head to the side thoughtfully. "I'll speak to Jartz about a short day when he gets back from hunting. He mentioned that there's a stream about halfway along today. It sounded like the perfect place to rest and clean up before we reach Gertuk."

"Yes, of course." She kept smiling even as she took a half step back. He didn't release her hands and she began to wonder what to do. "I know the place well. There used to be a few small huts and some chairs there. I suppose they're gone now, though," she tugged ever so slightly on her hands, "since the soldiers Jartz saw were destroying everything."

"Not everything," Jartz corrected, entering camp with three untxi's in his game bag and a barely subdued smile on his face. He had to clear his throat to keep from laughing out loud when they stepped abruptly apart. *Fool kids, tormenting themselves like that.* "Just whatever wasn't on that fancy map of theirs." He shoved the bag at Neba so he'd have something else to do with his hands. "I caught and cleaned 'em, so you get to cook 'em, dragon expert." They hadn't had to gather firewood once on this trip, thanks to Sparks' cooperation at mealtime.

Neba laughed out loud at Jartz' bluntness. "Fair enough." Taking the bag, he headed over to the fire pit he'd dug for supper the night before.

"I know." Leuna sighed once Neba had discreetly taken himself out of earshot. "I didn't mean for it to happen." Stooping, she began repacking her case.

"Let's not get ahead of ourselves," Jartz cautioned, frowning at how awkwardly her left leg was working. "If we knew for certain sure he was bonded, you'd both be in the wrong." He shrugged with his hands. "Bein' as we know no such thing, I reckon what I walked up on was as innocent as holdin' hands."

Leuna groaned aloud. "That's because that's precisely what we were doing!"

"Alright, then." Jartz patted her arm. Neba already had one untxi spitted for roasting and he wanted to get started on properly working the hides. Untxi's were larger than the rabbits that ran wild to the south and had thicker pelts, too. "You'd best wake Sati up. She'll need time to get ready before breakfast."

"About Sati." Leuna caught hold of his shoulder to keep him from leaving. "We've done some camping out, she and I, but nothing like this. I'm worried about her," she admitted. "Last night she was so tired she could barely stand, let alone walk, by the time we made camp. We have to slow down."

"I didn't realize." Jartz scratched his side where an eltxo fly had bitten him while he stalked the untxi. "We'll, umm…we'll take our time getting to the stream. Then a long lunch and we can take turns washing up for the city."

"Thank you, Jartz." She leaned in and kissed his scratchy cheek. A movement in the forest caught her eye as she turned away to go wake Sati. "Jartz? Neba?" Her voice rose as four men burst from the trees, weapons drawn!

The nearest man was almost in position to attack Neba, who'd slipped and fallen in his haste to rise. Jartz loosed an arrow, taking the villain neatly in the throat. The others stepped around their comrade's body like water flowing around a rock.

Neba lunged to his feet, belt knife in hand and already dirty from working with the untxi. A wild-eyed bandit charged him, short sword in hand.

The largest man attacked Jartz, which left the remaining man leering at Leuna.

Forcing herself to breathe, Leuna assessed her options. The staff was yards away on the ground. She could never reach it before he reached her. Neba's bow was closer, but she dismissed it at once because she already knew she wasn't strong enough to draw the bowstring back. Putting her hand on her shoulder strap, she prepared to use her precious medical case as a blunt object…and was struck by a thought.

Ignoring the disgusting kissing sounds her enemy was making at her, she shoved her hand inside her case, where she unsnapped a special side pouch. Her fingers closed around a cool glass jar, pulling it free. Her eyes locked with his and she hesitated for an instant, confirming his evil intent, then she popped the cork with her thumb. Taking three quick steps toward him, barely registering his shocked expression, she threw her hand forward, emptying the acid from the bottle into his face.

Everything around her seemed to stop as his scream rent the air. Her vision narrowed until all she could see was him. His shrieks filled her ears so that she could feel her heart pounding in her chest, but couldn't hear it. Then Sparks howled in response and was joined by Presa. And everything began moving again.

Her now-pitiful enemy ran off into the forest, clawing at his eyes as he stumbled over his own feet and bounced off trees. Neba's attacker slid slowly off Neba's belt knife and onto the grass, eyes wide open. Jartz likewise dropped his assailant to the ground, where he lay lifeless, his neck turned at an unnatural angle. The attack was over and it had barely begun.

"Are you alright?" Neba asked, looking anxiously at Leuna. He'd been desperate to get to her sooner, but had his hands full with the very smelly thug.

At the same time, Jartz wiped the sweat off his forehead and muttered, "Bones and ashes, girl. What'd you do to him?" He ignored the cut in his own arm; it wasn't deep.

Before she could answer either of them, Sati was beside her, taking hold of her hand and inspecting it in the faint light. White-faced, she grabbed the nearest water skin and used it to rinse the back of Leuna's hand, where an angry red welt was already starting to rise.

Leuna stared dully down at her hand. She hadn't even felt the pain of the acid sloshing over her skin.

"Need to get some hozte salve on that right away," Sati muttered to herself. She deliberately turned her back on the men—and the bodies—in favor of focusing all her attention on treating Leuna's burn.

"Where did they come from?" Neba asked Jartz, jerking his head toward the bodies. "Why?" He held his bloody hands away from his body, hating how easily he'd taken care of his attackers and the questions the fight raised about his identity.

"Why?" Jartz shook his head. "Maybe they wanted our food and gear. Maybe they wanted Sati and Leuna. Most likely they had their own stuff burned by those blamed soldiers, were driven off their hunting grounds, or the like." He shouldered Leuna's pack. "Whatever and wherever or why-ever, it's time to go."

Neba rinsed his hands quickly, then retrieved his and Sati's equipment. Pausing just long enough to stuff the untxi back in the game bag, he hustled over to the others.

"We can't leave now," protested Sati as she treated Leuna's burn.

"Anybody and everybody within a mile around heard those screams." Jartz darted a look at Leuna. It was hard to tell in the waning pink moonlight, but he thought she was turning green. "We have to move on."

"I've got to finish dressing and wrapping this hand!" In her agitation, Sati slopped the soothing cream on much too thickly and had to wipe some off.

"You can do it while you ride," asserted Neba. Catching Leuna around the waist, he lifted her slowly onto Sparks' back. "Easy, fella," he soothed, patting the dragon's neck with one hand while he steadied her with the other. "Jartz, you've got Leuna's blankets, right?" He'd noticed last night that she hadn't bothered to get them out, probably because she knew

Sparks' body heat would keep her warm. "Drape them over Sparks' shoulders."

"Are you sure that's a good idea?" Jartz interrupted. "I seem to recall you telling me that he really doesn't like blankets." He watched approvingly as Sati braved a dragon to bandage her mentor's hand.

Neba blinked. He'd completely forgotten about the time he'd accidentally—and very temporarily—caught Sparks in his blankets. The damage to his blankets had been irreparable, and he'd wound up sacrificing them for Sparks' target practice once the dragon's fire was lit.

"Just don't make any sudden moves," he instructed Jartz. "Let him see exactly what you're doing. And then you," he pointed at Leuna, "shift forward so that you're sitting on them. They'll provide a little protection against these rock-hard scales." Seizing Sati's blankets, he positioned them behind Leuna as soon as he could.

"Oh no." Sati retreated from him, her hands raised to ward him off. "You're not putting me on that," she squealed as he twirled her around, picked her up, and plopped her unceremoniously on her blankets. "Dragon," she finished in a squeak.

"Easy Sparks." Leuna rested her uninjured hand on his shoulder, willing him to feel her warmth. "You know me, big fella." She caught her breath when Sparks turned to look, his long neck allowing him to come nose-to-nose with her. "We need your help, please."

"Come, Sparks," Neba commanded, stepping out onto the trail. He ignored Presa, who was stalking in circles between the bodies of the brigands and Sparks with his unusual load. "Come on," he repeated. Inspiration struck him and he dug the freshly-skinned untxi out of the game bag. "All yours, Sparks. Just come and get it."

Sparks took a few tentative steps forward. He barely felt the weight of the non-dragons on his back, but one of them was making noises that he didn't like at all.

"Sati, shhhh." Leuna couldn't turn and hug her apprentice, so she reached back until she found where Sati's hands were gripping the tops of two of Sparks' scales. "Deep breaths now." She patted the ice-cold fingers. "Deep breaths. And count. As high as you can!"

Sati whimpered wretchedly and closed her eyes. "One." Deep breath. "Two." She screeched a little when Sparks took another step. "Three."

"Well done." Leuna spoke to both the girl and the dragon as she broke a stick off a conveniently-located branch and used it to scratch Sparks' neck. "Keep going," she encouraged, still speaking to both of them.

Sparks, liking the sound of Leuna's voice—while remaining completely oblivious to her efforts with the stick—moved onto the trail. Ignoring Neba's bribe, he looked to his right, then his left, uncertain as to which way he should go.

"I'll be a plume-tailed scuriday," Jartz muttered to nobody in particular as Sparks decided to go in the direction they'd been travelling the day before.

Neba looked over Jartz' shoulder to where Presa was getting a little too interested in the bodies. Dropping the gear he was holding, he circled around the edge of the camp and came at her from the side, shooing her toward the path. Jartz didn't have to be warned to get out of the way of the unpredictable dragon and they were on their way moments later.

Jartz jogged ahead to take the lead and Neba trotted beside Sparks. Both of them kept their eyes and ears wide open in case of trouble. They kept on that way a good hour, until Presa began hissing at the girls.

"I think she's ready to go hunting," Neba informed the others.

"I'm certainly ready to eat." Leuna smiled bravely and lifted her good leg over Sparks' back.

"You're not leaving me up here alone," Sati whispered fiercely.

"Here." Neba held out his hands. "Lean toward me a little." He'd no sooner started to lift her down than Sparks bent his knees in a four-legged squat of sorts. "A little late there, pal," Neba grunted as Sati tumbled into his arms.

Leuna slipped off the other side and took a moment to stroke Sparks' muzzle. She was always taken by surprise by how soft it was. Sparks demonstrated his affection for her by butting her gently in the chest. Satisfied that his work was done, Sparks shook the blankets off his back and ambled over to Presa.

"Will they come back?" Leuna asked, watching as the dragons spread their wings and lifted off.

"Best guess?" Neba was already busy shaking out the blankets and rolling them up. "Yes."

Hampered by her injuries, Leuna allowed Jartz to help her into her pack.

"How long until we reach the stream?" Neba asked as he assisted Sati with her pack.

"An hour at the outside," Jartz answered. "We covered a lot of ground."

"Think you're up for it?" Neba slipped his arm around Sati's shoulders. She'd slept through most of the attack, but hadn't bounced back nearly as quickly as Leuna. Jartz he'd worry about later, if at all. The tough old bird was actively scanning the forest for threats while the rest of them were trying to catch their breath.

"I'm going to have nightmares tonight and I think a few teeth rattled loose about a mile ago, but," Sati sighed, "I can do it." She'd had a chance to think over what had happened at their camp while bouncing around on Sparks' back. Even criminals had friends and she absolutely did not want to meet any friends of the men they'd left behind. "I have to."

"We'll all do it together." Leuna smiled and squeezed Sati's free hand.

Chapter 4

They heard Gertuk before they saw it. Peddlers calling their wares, dogs barking, and even the faint clanging of ships' bells. After days in the forest, the noises were deafening.

"I'll stay here, with the dragons," Neba offered, stopping at a curve in the road. "You go ahead and book passage."

Jartz frowned sourly at him, then at the dragons. He'd half expected the dragons to abandon them a few miles outside of Herrixka. Since that hadn't happened, he was stuck with the decision the others had made over breakfast.

"You're sure they'll follow the boat?" Jartz was still skeptical.

"If they want to, yes." Neba ran his hand through his hair. "If they don't want to, they'll have no reason for staying around here. Too many people in the city and their movements too restricted here in the forest." He didn't really mind repeating himself, particularly since Sati seemed to need the reassurance, too.

"What if a patrol comes by?" Leuna asked suddenly. They all turned to look at her. "It wouldn't surprise me if they've started patrolling the forest, given everything else they've done lately."

"She's right." Jartz blew out an exasperated breath. "I better stay, too, just in case."

Leuna nodded. "Good idea. Sati and I will buy the tickets."

"We will?" Sati sighed and shrugged out of her pack. Of course they would.

"We'd better clean up a little," Leuna suggested, mostly to give Sati some time. "Over here."

Taking her water skin and pack, she walked over to where two small trees were positioned close enough together to allow her to string up a blanket as a curtain between themselves and the road. Once they'd washed up a bit and changed into clean clothes, they brushed and braided each other's hair.

"That feels so good," Leuna sighed as Sati ran the brush through her hair.

"So did washing up," Sati giggled. She felt lighter all over now that the top layer of travel dust was gone.

"Mmm." Leuna couldn't nod, but she certainly agreed. "I always appreciate a proper bath so much more after a trip like this."

They were still smiling when they entered town, passing by a group of soldiers unchallenged. Sati hung back a little, eyeing the way before her with trepidation. Of a necessity, the streets in Gertuk were wide and straight, allowing wagons and handcarts to more easily transport the goods and passengers that the boats carried.

"What if we get lost?"

Leuna tipped her head to one side and nodded slowly. "That could happen," she admitted. Linking her arm through Sati's, she began walking slowly. "But we can always ask for directions." Sati jumped when a peddler shoved a tray of roasted erre nuts toward them.

"No, thank you." Leuna smiled and kept walking. "Let's see," she thought aloud. "We need to book passage on a boat. Boats will be by the river."

"Of course." Sati gave herself a little shake,

determined not to let Gertuk's size or population intimidate her over much. "By the river."

Together, they walked through the town, the forest to their backs. The buildings changed slowly, from private homes to two- and three-story inns—*with real beds!* Their noses told them what each public eating house was serving for lunch, but they moved doggedly forward, at last reaching the point where they could see the tall masts over roughly built warehouses.

"We're definitely in the right area." Sati didn't know how Leuna could stay so calm with so many strange men looking at them. A great many more men were milling about, engaged in the necessary physical activities of a dock area. A train of empty handcarts was just leaving one warehouse, heading inland toward the shops, while a heavy sled arrived at another. Oddly, the sight of the massive draft animals that were pulling the sled made her feel better.

Her cheeks pinked instantly when one of the drivers looked up, caught her staring, and winked at her.

"There." Leuna had spotted what she'd paused to look for: a warehouse with chairs outside for public use. The three rocking chairs were occupied. "Come on."

The men in the chairs looked up as they approached, revealing weathered faces and eyes fixed in a permanent squint. They each gave the women the once-over, strictly for business purposes. Better-dressed travelers were usually willing to pay more. These two, now... They weren't fancied up like some as came through Gertuk, but they were neat and tidy looking.

"Where you ladies bound?" the man on the far end asked, his voice grating like an old gate.

"Upriver," Leuna answered vaguely. "We need passage for four."

"Expensive." The middle man grunted, snorted, and spat between the slats of the porch.

"How expensive?" Leuna drove straight to the heart of the matter and all three pairs of eyebrows twitched.

"Four arranos per person might do it."

Sati had all she could do to keep from gasping. *Four* arranos? Making a total of *sixteen* arranos? Herrixka functioned primarily on an exchange or barter basis. Many of the children there had never seen a coin in their lives!

"We're not bank robbers." Leuna put a faint emphasis on the word 'robbers,' which was exactly what she thought of these three...gentlemen. "Nor have we lucked into buried treasure."

"Ain't much call to go upriver lately," defended the first man huffily. "Passenger transports only come through now and again fer students."

"Yep." The third man spoke for the first time. "You missed the last one by, oh," he pretended to think, "two lunars."

Leuna squeezed Sati's arm when the girl swayed slightly. Bargaining was hardly Leuna's favorite activity, but she got the point. The harder it was to get tickets, the more they would cost. Or, in other words, the men figured to make a profit on this sale.

Something kept tugging at her, though. Distracting her from the conversation. Tilting her head to one side, she inhaled deeply. She smelled dust, tar, wood baking in the sun, the sweat of man and beast... There were all these scents and a hundred others, including rich foreign cargos of spices and soaps.

"How's the fishing?" She smiled sweetly, as though she hadn't just completely changed the subject. Again, six eyebrows twitched.

"What fishin'?" the middle man grunted.

"Ain't had a decent haul o' fish come through here in quite a spell," grumbled the third man.

"That's a fact," averred the first man. "Place smells better without 'em, don't it?" He guffawed, tickled at his own joke about the snooty miss and her air-sniffing ways.

Leuna smiled at her own private joke. "Oh dear me. What has happened to all the fishermen?"

"When the hauls started comin' up short, the smart ones took off, headin' fer other ports." The middle man spat again. "A few stuck around. Not many."

"Yeah, and them as stayed on went into debt to do it!" the first man sneered. "Gonna lose their boats, too."

"How dreadful!" Leuna shook her head and pressed one hand to her mouth. "Those poor men. Where would we find them?" The men blinked at her, almost in unison. It was positively eerie.

"Umm... Most of 'em hang out at the Brewer's Beacon. But," the third man cleared his throat delicately, "you don't wanna go there."

"A tavern? I should think not," Leuna agreed.

"Might find one or two at the wharf," suggested the middle man, automatically pointing at its location.

"Who'd be at the wharf this time of day?" snickered the first man.

"There's still one or two what goes out of a mornin'," insisted the middle man.

The other two scoffed and began talking over their crony, so that they were almost immediately engaged in a full-blown argument.

Leuna waved a farewell that they missed completely and walked off, pulling Sati with her.

"We," Sati had to hurry to keep up, "didn't get what we need!"

"No, not yet." Leuna smiled. "We may have to strike a deal with those three yet, but I think we'll do well to check with the fishermen first."

"What? Why?"

"Simple." Leuna stepped up from one boardwalk to the next, still walking briskly. "If you were out of work and needed money, wouldn't you jump at a paying job? Even if it wasn't what you regularly do?"

"Oh." Sati smiled and sped up. "Oh!"

Passing the larger cargo vessels and the long piers that stretched out between them, they ducked and dodged their way along. Bells pealed and whistles shrieked while all around them men and women shouted instructions and insults. One large group of swarthy sailors sang loudly as they ran up and down the gangplanks with bundles of goods balanced on their heads.

The colors. The sounds. The smells. Sati clung to Leuna, all her senses assaulted at once, but kept her chin high.

"Almost there," Leuna promised, ducking to her right to avoid an oncoming cart.

"Look out!" A dozen voices chorused warnings at the same time as the women were grabbed by the arms and hauled unceremoniously to one side.

Sati nearly fainted with fright when an immense cargo sling, laden so heavily with boxes that the wooden jib arm bowed under the weight, thudded onto the dock where they'd been standing.

"Thank you," she whispered.

"Yes." Leuna forced herself to let go of where she'd taken hold of their burly rescuer's arm. "Thank you very much."

"You oughtn't to be here," barked the man. "Civilians ain't allowed on the docks while we're unloading."

"Our apologies." Leuna smiled weakly. "We're looking for the fishing boats."

He scratched his head, then jerked his chin to his left, the direction they'd been travelling. "Over that-away. Only stay to the left of the road, will ya?" He thrust them off to the far side of the road from where they were standing and turned his back on them. "What're ya staring at, ya lubbers? These boxes ain't gonna walk themselves into the warehouses!" he bellowed at the workers who'd dared to stop.

The gawkers leapt into action, swarming the pile of boxes like ants on piece of berry pie.

"This way." Leuna let Sati lean on her despite the wobble in her own knees. Still a bit numb, she plowed along, refusing to give way before the carts and runners, who always seemed to wait until the last second to swerve around them.

"Maybe we should've just paid the sixteen arranos," Sati quipped. She made eye contact with a clearly astonished Leuna and shrugged. "It wouldn't have been this exciting, but actually, that could be a good thing."

Leuna laughed aloud, delighted by Sati's quick recovery. They were still laughing when the chaos of the freight docks fell behind them.

On the fishermen's wharf, empty boats glumly rode their mooring lines. Here and there the tail of a carelessly furled sail flapped in the breeze. While there wasn't a fish in sight, the potent odor lingered, rising from where it had seeped into the wooden decks and wafting along wherever the wind carried it.

"I don't see anyone to hire."

"Neither do I," Leuna agreed. "But I think I hear someone."

They followed the sound of someone humming softly until they found a spry old man on his knees, scrubbing the deck with a block of sandstone while his graying fisherman's braid fell forward over his shoulder. He lithely crabbed to the side once he'd worked an area to his satisfaction.

Leuna took her time looking the boat over, noting how tidy it was. Freshly polished brass gleamed in the sunlight. The nets were neatly folded and stowed. Even the faint creaking noises emitted by the boat as the current gently rocked it resembled sighs of contentment.

"What kin I do fer ye?" he asked, never looking up or pausing in his work.

Leuna smiled. "Is your boat for hire, sir?"

The tan, wrinkled hands paused in their movement. Slowly, his face lifted and he studied them with his vivid blue eyes.

"Well now." He rose gracefully and set the sandstone aside, dusting off his hands in the process. "Ye don't look like criminals." He folded wiry arms across his stained shirt. "Or is Zigor that desperate these days?"

"He probably is." Leuna shrugged dismissively. "But he's no concern of ours. We simply want to travel upriver to Auzo."

His leathery brow wrinkled. "The two of ye?"

"Four of us," Leuna corrected. "Our friends are waiting for us outside of town."

"Hmm." He shook his head slowly. "Be a might crowded with six of us aboard."

"And our baggage," Leuna inserted sweetly. "We haven't much."

"I'd like to help ye." Picking up an empty bucket, he lowered it into the river by the rope attached to its handle. "But it's at least three days hard sailin' to Auzo. Plus two days back. Can't leave my fishin' fer that long."

Leuna waited until he'd hauled the full bucket up, taking care not to let it bounce off the side of the boat.

"The return trip would take a lot less time," she pointed out. "And we are offering to compensate you for your time. Say, an arrano apiece."

He shrugged and shook his head.

"Two." She narrowed her eyes at him. If he was one who had gone into debt to stay on, eight arranos should seem a fortune.

He picked the piece of sandstone back up, but hesitated. "I'd need at least one man on the sails."

"Whom did you have in mind?" Leuna asked,

tilting her head to the side.

"Well." He picked up a length of rope, shook it out, and re-coiled it exactly as it had been before. It was the first indication he'd given of how serious this job was to him. "My grandson's a bit young. I reckon he knows port from aft, howsomever."

Something clicked in her mind and Leuna smiled. This man was after more than keeping body and soul together. He had family to think about, including seeing that his grandson got experience when and where possible. Suddenly, she no longer cared about getting the best deal. She couldn't rescue Gertuk's entire fishing community, but she could at least help this family.

"Three arranos apiece. My final offer." From the corner of her eye, she saw Sati's jaw drop.

"Done." The fisherman bobbed his head at them, then leaned over the forward railing to shake hands with her. "I'll have you in Auzo in three days, given a fair wind, or me name ain't Ginte Abizenak."

"Half now." Leuna didn't immediately take his hand. She couldn't let him think she was *too* soft. "And half after you've landed us, bag and baggage, at the dock in Auzo."

He chuckled, hand still extended. "Can't ask for a fairer bargain than that."

They shook on it then and Leuna produced the six arranos she'd been surreptitiously working free from the bag on her belt. Of course, the bag was still the most likely place for a traveler to be carrying their funds, but she didn't have to be obvious about it.

"When do we leave?" she asked after the coins had changed hands.

"Could leave as soon as yer friends got here." He looked up at the sky and shook his head. "Too late to get far, though, a'fore we needed to drop anchor fer the night."

"First thing tomorrow?" she suggested.

"Aye, that'll do fine." He nodded. "Be here a'fore sunup. We'll get a jump on the other ship's captains and have the river to ourselves fer a bit."

"Agreed."

Sati managed to hold her tongue until they were out of earshot, but not a step further!

"Do we even have six more arranos?" she squeaked.

"Mmm, not exactly." Leuna slipped her arm around the younger woman's shoulders. "Sati, I'm going to tell you something about myself that most of Herrixka doesn't need to know. Will you promise to keep my secret?"

Sati pinched the bridge of her nose between two fingers and stopped walking. Everybody knew everything about everyone else in Herrixka! Didn't they? She'd certainly believed she knew all about Leuna. After taking a couple of deep breaths, she lowered her hand, looked Leuna in the eyes and nodded.

"I promise."

"I come from a wealthy family." Leuna waited for that to sink in.

"Wealthy," Sati repeated. Her right hand started waving in small circles of its own volition. "How wealthy?"

"That doesn't matter," Leuna demurred. "What matters is that we can definitely afford to pay a good man to take us up upriver to Auzo."

Sati closed her eyes hard, giving her face a pinched expression. "We probably could've booked passage with those…those rocking-chair-pirates for less!" she asserted. "And then we wouldn't have had to risk our lives winding through that awful dock." Her voice began to fade out as she realized aloud, "The dock we have to go through *again*."

"I'm sure you're right." Leuna waited for both of Sati's eyes to open. "In fact, I'm sure I could've offered Ginte less than I did and still persuaded him to take us."

"Then why didn't you?" Sati's frown hadn't completely cleared.

"Because it was more important to me to help him out of a bad situation." Leuna tugged on her braid, wondering if she was making sense.

"You mean," Sati hesitated, gathering her words, "like the time our neighbor gave my mother five quarts of milk per day instead of the four quarts they'd agreed on in exchange for part of the cheese and butter she would make with it?"

"Yes." Leuna couldn't believe she'd forgotten such a perfect example.

"He kept saying it was because he wanted the richer cheese and butter she could make," Sati smiled at the memory, "but I always thought it was because we had so many children at home."

"Sati." Leuna hugged her. "You amaze me. That is exactly why I don't mind paying Ginte so much."

"I shouldn't have called them that." Sati pinked, embarrassed that she'd casually insulted someone in her frustration.

"Nor should I," Leuna agreed, happy to take a

lesson so humbly given. "Now. I think if we take that little trail there," she pointed at a line of worn grass that led up a nearby hill, "we can skirt the dock. From there we can find a bank and get some food to take back to the others. Alright?"

Chapter 5

Jartz woke up from his nap, stretched and yawned. It felt good to sprawl in the sun for a few hours after walking all day for almost five days. He was using a handy stick to scratch his back when his smile changed to a frown. He had intentionally positioned himself so that the shade would fall over him while he slept, but he was almost completely in shadow. Glancing around, he confirmed that it was still just himself and Neba.

"They're not back yet." Neba didn't bother turning to look at Jartz. Presa had been diligently ignoring them both since Jartz rolled onto his side and stopped snoring. The only logical reason for her to be glaring in their direction now was that Jartz wasn't sleeping anymore.

"Wonder what's keeping them," Jartz muttered. His tongue didn't move easily in his dry mouth and he took a swig from his water skin. The water was tepid, but wet.

"Maybe they're having trouble finding a boat to hire." Neba groaned inwardly when his knife cut too deeply into the staff he was making. He was supposed to be smoothing the shaft, not weakening it. Perhaps if he carefully shaved off just the damaged wood, he could salvage the project.

"Hope that's all it is." Admittedly, Leuna with her medical credentials and apprentice shouldn't have trouble with even the fussiest of city guardsmen. Nevertheless, Jartz felt responsible for their safety and hated that he hadn't gone with them. Noticing Presa just then, he glared right back at her. If not for the dragons, he'd have gone into Gertuk and gotten the tickets himself.

"Hello the camp!" Leuna sent her voice ahead as she led Sati a few steps into the forest. Thankfully, Jartz had left a few indistinct signs for her to follow or they'd have had to stand out in the road calling for them.

"Hello!" Jartz took it for granted that she'd made sure of her surroundings before giving them away like that. "And what took you so long?"

Sati surprised them all by laughing merrily. "You must be hungry. My papa always gets gruff when he's hungry." She held up the bundle of food she was carrying. "I'll have supper set out in a moment." She hummed as she worked, glad to be away from the chaos of Gertuk.

Jartz reddened slightly at her innocent chastisement.

"It did take a little longer than we expected," Leuna observed tactfully. "However, I think you'll be pleased with the results."

"Just so long as the boat we're booked on is watertight," Jartz mumbled.

"*Morning Song* is a beauty," Sati answered. "At first, she looked like every other boat to me. Then, while Leuna was bargaining for our passage, I kept seeing little personal touches."

"*Morning Song?*" Jartz looked narrowly at Leuna. "Only fools and fishermen give their boats such fancy names." To Jartz, it would make as much sense to start naming his traps.

"Well, I wouldn't know about that." Leuna knelt beside Sati and helped uncover dishes of steaming rice, beans, and a thick blue sauce. They cut the hot buns open and slathered them with butter. Was it her imagination, or was Jartz drooling? "I do, however, strongly suspect we'll be more comfortable on this fishing boat than we would be cooped up on one of those dreadful cargo haulers."

"Were there no transport ships available?" Neba queried. He'd succeeded in reshaping the spoiled section of staff and was now busy rechecking the length of it for rough spots.

Sati wrinkled her nose. "Not according to the," she swallowed the insult, "shipping agents we spoke to first."

Leuna bit her lip to keep from smiling. "We leave at sunup tomorrow," she announced.

Neba and Jartz came over to join them while the food was hot and silence reigned while they all savored their first meal prepared by someone else in days.

"I'll sleep well after this meal." Jartz leaned back and patted his stomach.

"I think we all will." Sati smiled dreamily. That was one good thing about dragons. They made excellent guard animals.

Leuna was too stuffed to move, so she curled up right where she was.

"I'm still surprised it took so long to book passage and find supper."

Leuna opened one eye to look at Neba, who'd spoken. "My fault," she murmured. "I wanted to get supper from a particular eatery and it was clear across Gertuk." She shifted a little and her other eye opened as she remembered something. "It wasn't easy finding my way, either. It's been quite a while since my last visit, so things have naturally changed. What made it worse, though, was that several shops were closed, and I missed a turn so we had to go back."

"Closed?" Neba looked up from the staff with a frown.

"Mhmm. There were big signs in the windows about orders from city officials. And warnings about what would happen to anyone caught trespassing while the signs were up." She paused briefly, unsure as to whether or not she should share the most important part. "The warnings were in Lurrakian and Marroi."

Neba set his knife down and scrubbed his hand over his face. "You think I'm involved somehow?"

"How could you be?"

"I won't know that until after we find the mind manipulator," he retorted grimly. "Did the signs say why the shops were closed?"

"Yes, they all said the same thing. That they were complicit in illegal trafficking of goods."

"Dragon goods," he corrected gently. "That was it, wasn't it?"

She nodded slowly. "They're illegal on both sides of the river now, except by special permit."

He blew out a breath. "I guess we had the right idea this morning, splitting up so that some of us could keep an eye on the dragons."

Leuna shivered. She hadn't thought of that. Whether the dragons were spotted by soldiers or poachers, it added up to danger for them all. Was that what had prompted the attack a few days ago? Doubtful. Surely poachers wouldn't be so stupid as to rush an unknown camp and get themselves killed…would they? Which brought up the original question about the surprise attack on four travelers—why had they attacked at all? She'd turned that question inside-out hunting for an answer and didn't like her conclusions even a little. It was possible they were just so desperate that they'd jumped them on the blind hope there would be something valuable amongst their things. Or they'd been watching for someone specific. Like Neba.

"We probably should do the same thing tomorrow." She looked over at where Presa and Sparks were sleeping, side by side. "Sati and I can go ahead to the *Morning Song* and meet you and Jartz upriver a mile or so." Better to keep Neba out of sight for as long as possible, just in case she was right.

"All the while hoping that we haven't run into a patrol of some sort." Neba grunted and shook his head. "Jartz had better go with you tonight. I can handle the dragons and he can help handle your gear. Maybe help you handle the boat captain, too, just in case he doesn't like the idea of making an unscheduled stop."

"I don't think Ginte will give us any trouble once we explain," she began to object.

"Explain?" Neba grimaced. Putting on his most harmless expression, he said, "Excuse me, Captain, but would you mind anchoring near the shoreline and picking up our friend? He's traveling with two, well, sort of wild dragons that we didn't want the soldiers to know about."

"When you put it that way…" Leuna frowned. "You're sure they weren't seen today?"

"They stayed pretty close." Neba half-laughed. "I think they were as happy for a day off the trail as we were."

"We didn't hear anything about forest patrols," Leuna frowned thoughtfully, "but I wouldn't count them out."

"We'll be careful. Just keep an eye out for two dragons sunning themselves on this side of the river." Neba got to his feet.

"You're leaving now?" Leuna hadn't expected that.

"No, I'd never get them up and on the trail without a huge fuss. I'm just going to sleep over there so I'm sure to wake up when they do." He placed the staff beside her on the grass. "Here."

"Thank you." She didn't know what else to say, but her fingers curled around the cool wood.

"I'll see you tomorrow. Upriver." He didn't sleep well that night, and not because Presa kept 'accidentally' slapping him with her tail. The solution to that was to roll up under Sparks' wing—and the good fellow hardly stirred.

Neba's mind simply wouldn't stop spinning. Patrols were his biggest concern. While he might be able to explain his own presence in the forest to a patrol's satisfaction, they were still too far inside Lurrak for domesticated dragons to be common. With the present uproar about illegal dragon goods, they'd probably feel justified in assuming the worst. And now that Sparks was more or less full-grown, he couldn't exactly hide behind a tree; nor would Presa even countenance such an idea.

Rubbing his face, he shifted positions. Leuna'd

mentioned something about Marroi dignitaries and dragon stables in Ibilia, which he sincerely hoped Presa would tolerate.

All in all, their best chance seemed to be to head straight for the river once the dragons were up. A short stretch of their wings—a precarious ride on Sparks' unpadded back for himself—and they'd be a mile or two upriver before the others were even awake. Unless he fell off and floated downriver a mile or two. Just how big was this river, anyway? Jartz called it the Ubide River earlier.

He must've drifted off after that, because the next thing he knew was when Sparks rose and stretched. Presa's scales rattled as she shook herself vigorously.

"Shhh, now." Neba rolled smoothly to his feet and out of their way. "Let's not wake the others, alright?" Reaching out, he stroked Sparks' muzzle. "Are you up for a short adventure?"

To his complete surprise, Presa shouldered Sparks aside and stood before him, wings half-extended in an aggressive posture. She crabbed a few steps to her left, then a few to her right, coming incrementally closer to him. He hardly dared breathe as the formerly prickly dragon deigned to lower her muzzle.

She shivered under his hand, as though she wasn't sure whether or not she liked having a non-dragon touch her. Abruptly, she shuffled back out of his reach, shook her head, fluffed her wings, and put Sparks between them. Not wanting to risk startling the now-skittish Presa, Neba picked up his gear and headed for the road, whistling softly for Sparks to follow.

"Hey, fella." Neba wrapped a spare bit of rope around his pack and knotted it in front in case he actually did fall off. "I need you to let me ride you again, if you don't mind." If he did mind, things were going to get a lot more difficult.

Sparks allowed Neba to run his hand down the column of iridescent blue scales that formed his neck before sidestepping. Ducking his head, he blew softly on Neba's hair, mussing it thoroughly.

"Oh, you're so funny." Neba raked his fingers through his hair, smiling. At least Sparks was in a good mood. "How about that ride, hmm?" Again he ran his hand down Sparks' warm neck. "We'll go to the river and you can fish. How does that sound?" Sparks' ears had definitely twitched at the word *fish*. "We haven't had fresh fish for days."

Sparks whined and pranced a bit, but permitted Neba to find a toehold on one of his scales, swing a leg over his shoulders, and cautiously seat himself. Neba's fingers had barely closed over the protruding edges of two neck scales when Sparks began bounding down the road. His wings spread, pumped, and they were up, soaring over the treetops. Presa was only an instant behind in taking off and flew at Sparks' wingtip.

"I hate to say this, but we're too low." Neba thumped twice with his heels, which elicited a disgruntled growl from Presa, and leaned closer to Sparks' neck.

Reacting as if he'd understood Neba's words, Sparks drove them higher and higher into the skies. He hadn't had his breakfast yet, but flying was a reward unto itself. He'd spent the first nine months of his life alone, an orphan.   After huddling in shadows and stealing food to survive, he basked in his dominance of the air.

Neba rode close, eyes searching the terrain below. The pink light from Argia, the third moon, was waning, but Lehen had risen in her full strength. Together, the pink and yellow moonlight turned the clouds above a creamy orange.   The river beneath him, when he spotted it, was a liquid lavender.

Sparks banked, plowing through a layer of clouds that chased along Neba's bare arms and made him shiver.   Then they were above the clouds, flying where the starlight rivaled the moonlight in its brilliance.

The air sparkled with dust from those stars.   A few warm grains landed on his outstretched fingers, made strange crackling noises and vanished.   He rubbed his fingers together, but there was nothing left of the dust...had he absorbed it?   The dust grew thicker as they climbed higher, covering his exposed skin and entering his lungs when he breathed.   They had reached the itxi, the lowest level of weakened stars—and flown inside one.

Neba looked left and right at Sparks' wings.   Had they stopped moving?   Were they about to fall to the ground far below?   The sound of blood rushing in his ears grew until it crowded out everything else…   A shadow of movement from ahead jerked his attention forward.   Squinting through the brilliant haze of stardust, he saw the outline of a handsome man on a magnificent scarlet dragon.

Except what he saw wasn't really there.   Like the other snatches of memory he'd relived, this completely displaced what he knew was going on around him.

"I control my mind." He whispered the mantra Leuna had taught him. "No one else." The man and the dragon stayed where they were. And this time, there was no pain.

It's alright, Son. The man smiled. *I know the star expanse is enormous and a little frightening, but there's nothing to fear. The wild dragons come here to play in the stardust. I brought you here because I wanted you to see it, to know it's here.*

'Here' was the night sky, miles above Jatorri. Wherever Neba looked, stars of every hue and shape filled his view in a breathtaking display. At first glance, it looked as though the stars had chaotically popped into existence. With time and study, however, a pattern could be found, one that allowed each kind of star its proper size and number in a never-ending, ever-cycling sequence.

"Doesn't everyone know it's here?" Neba heard himself voice the question he knew he'd asked when this actually happened.

No. I wish they did. The man—his father?—looked terribly sad. *Most people know very little beyond what they have seen for themselves. They think and plan and do according to their needs or the needs of those they know and love. You and I can't be like that. We are Marroi,* Neba felt himself sit a little taller, *but cannot live only for our own people.*

"Why not?"

The man didn't answer the question right away. The scarlet dragon shook its head, playfully sucked in a huge gulp of stardust, and expelled it as an awesome red fireball that streaked across the night sky. The man chuckled and patted its neck. Dropping his hand to his thigh, he sighed.

Because that would be like this star only sharing its light with a handful of the people on Jatorri instead of shining to benefit them all. The health, sickness, prosperity, and poverty of our neighbors all affect the choices we have to make, Son. And we must keep our honor as bright as these stars.

Neba felt his eyes trying to close and realized that he was inhaling in short bursts through his nose and mouth. He was going to sneeze! No! Not now! He stared at the man, trying to memorize everything about him. The confident set of his shoulders. The expensive tailored clothing. Neba's eyes were starting to water, yet he knew he needed to see with his mind's eye—if he could just…hold…on!

His sneezes startled both Sparks and Presa, sending them apart and then down in a steep dive. Down. Down. He'd stopped sneezing, but now he couldn't breathe. The air rushed at him and past him too quickly for him to inhale it. Holding on for dear life, he squeezed his watering eyes shut.

Sparks and Presa spread their wings at almost exactly the same instant, breaking their power dives and gliding close enough to the river's surface that they could snatch up unsuspecting fish. All was well until the non-dragon on Sparks' back rocked limply from one side to the other, then fell heavily into the river. Chagrined, Sparks watched with Presa as the ripples expanded further and further, sending the fish fleeing for shelter.

With something akin to a sigh, Sparks reached out with his tail, plucked the non-dragon out of the river, and dropped him on the bank. Then, still ravenous, he joined Presa at a shallow spot where dozens of fish foolishly thought they could hide.

On the bank, Neba rolled over and coughed up most of the river water he'd been shocked into inhaling.

"Thanks." He coughed to clear the gravelly sound out of his throat and tried again. "For the rescue, I mean." Grinning because neither dragon looked up, he drew his knees up and took off his boots to pour the water out of them, too. A short, barefoot scouting trip convinced him that they were alone for the moment, though on which side of the river he couldn't tell. Upriver? Downriver? That remained to be seen. Once the sun came up, that was.

In the meantime, he could at least be more comfortable. He changed into semi-dry clothing from his pack and arranged his wetter gear to dry on some fairly convenient branches and bushes. The feathers on his arrows were soaked, so he did his best to address the damage done to the fletching, then flung himself down on a fairly twig-free patch of bank to rest.

He was still wide awake when the sun's rays began stretching across the sky like working men and women preparing for a new day. After adding a sketch of the man from his memory to the now-dry journal, he started hunting for a nice, tall tree.

Brittle blue leaves shook loose from the branches of the urdin tree he chose to climb, but he supposed that was all to the good. If it had been earlier in the year, the fresh, new leaves would've obscured his view at the top. As it was, he couldn't actually see the town, just the smoke curling up and spreading out from dozens of chimneys. Some of the tension eased from his shoulders as he confirmed that he was, in fact, upriver from Gertuk.

Chapter 6

"If I'd known ye was smugglers, I…"

Leuna cut off Captain Ginte, as he'd asked to be called, with an impatient gesture. He'd been making the same basic statement ever since they'd told him Neba would be waiting on the bank upriver. It was giving her a headache.

"If we were smugglers, making a *daylight* run," her tone stressed the stupidity of that idea, "we'd simply have stolen one of the other vessels. The wharf where fishing boats dock is essentially deserted and nobody would've noticed."

"At least," Jartz interjected with a grin, "not before we'd had time to sneak the boat back into its slip." He was enjoying himself. There had been no need for physical persuasion, despite Neba's concerns on the subject, and he rather suspected Ginte was having the time of his life. After all, what did a fisherman like better than a good story? And this would undoubtedly be the story of the year by the time Ginte got done telling it over the table back at Gertuk, whether or not they turned out to be smugglers. Once they found Neba and the dragons, Ginte wouldn't even have to embellish it. Though he probably would anyway.

Ginte glared at both of them, then hollered at his grandson, who was in the bow keeping watch with Sati. "Keep yer eyes peeled, Bilo."

"Yes, sir!" Bilo, who was tall and thin for his nine years, scanned the bank ahead eagerly. He'd never seen a live dragon, and despite his grandpa's insistence that these folks hadn't either, he couldn't help hoping that they weren't lying, thieving smugglers.

Sati had her own opinion of things, which she discreetly kept to herself. Ginte might not be a 'rocking chair pirate,' but he was certainly an opportunist. For example, he'd apparently also agreed to deliver the box of shoes she was perched on—and no doubt was collecting a separate fee for said box. Shaking her head at the world in general, she passed the time by watching the other bank.

A movement along the bank caught her eye and she opened her mouth to call for the others. Hesitated. Ginte and Bilo had both scoffed at the idea that Neba might turn up on the bank she was watching. The idea of anyone crossing their great Ubide River without a conveyance of some sort had actually elicited snickers from Ginte. Of course, he was discounting the dragons, so...she watched silently for a few more seconds. And when she was absolutely positive it was a yellow dragon wing glinting in the sun, she cleared her throat.

"Bilo, is this going to be your first overnight stay on a boat?" He shook his head but didn't look her way. "It will be mine." Still nothing. She bit her lip. The *Morning Song* was a trim little sailor and travelling fast 'before the wind,' as Ginte called it. She made one last try. "Actually, I've never even been on a boat before."

Bilo's head whipped around so that he was looking at her, eyes wide in shock. It was almost more than his young mind could fathom, that someone as old as she must be had never been on a boat. In her entire life! He didn't know what to think or say, so he began turning back to the other bank. Then, he saw it.

"GRANDPA!" Bilo pointed wildly, nearly jumping up and down in his excitement. "I see them, I see them!"

"Them who?" Ginte bellowed crossly. "River Patrol?" He shot Leuna a look that said they were all about to get what was coming to them.

"THE DRAGONS!"

"Boy, don't you…" Ginte's jaw went slack as he looked around to see two dragons wading into the river ahead of them. A dark-skinned stranger rode on the shoulders of the blue dragon.

Jartz' sudden coughing fit snapped Ginte out of it. Scowling, the old man began shouting orders. In short order, the *Morning Song* had slowed and was nosing in toward where the dragons waited, semi-patiently.

"Don't worry, Sparks." Glancing at Presa, Neba grimaced. Her wings were rising confrontationally, her tail was lashing from side to side, and her lower jaw was working as though preparing to fire on the strange floating beast. In short, she was making Sparks nervous. If his hands had been free, he'd have used the deia, or dragon whistle, he'd carved while working with Sparks. Instead, he whistled a soft, soothing trill.

"They're no danger to you, either," he told Presa when she finally looked at him. He held her gaze, keeping his posture relaxed and trilled again. Her neck reached forward, her chin dipped down, and she blinked. "Good girl."

By the time the boat was close enough for him to swing aboard, Presa and Sparks had both calmed to the point of simple curiosity.

"Oh!" Leuna staggered when Sparks bumped the hull with his shoulder. "Nice to know he's in a good mood." From her position aft, she was able to lean over the railing as they passed and touch Sparks' head briefly. "Good boy."

"I hate to mention it," Jartz turned to Ginte, who was gaping at the dragons just like Bilo, "but if we go any slower, we're going to be travelling the wrong direction."

Ginte didn't even bother to look at him, just hauled on the line that raised the sail he'd lowered in order to slow down. His hands were still moving automatically when he made the line fast to a belaying pin. That done, he joined his grandson at the aft rail, watching the dragons as they frolicked in the water.

Jartz, who'd been keeping an eye on Ginte in case he decided to do anything drastic to the 'smugglers', stepped over to the wheel and unlashed it. The river was, as yet, devoid of other traffic, and he figured he could handle things for a minute or two. Long enough for Ginte to get over his astonishment, anyway.

Leuna quietly drew Neba amidships, ostensibly to show him where he could drop his pack alongside theirs.

"Are you alright?" she asked, one hand lightly on his arm. "Did something happen?"

"What do you mean?" Neba snugged his pack up against the others, then retied the restraining line.

Wordlessly, Leuna reached out and plucked something from his hair. She had to cup her hands together for him to see it glowing in the much-brighter sunlight, but he knew instantly what it was.

"Oh. That." Neba chuckled and leaned back against the rail. "I tried to fly Sparks upriver. He had other ideas."

"Such as?" Leuna had a feeling there was lot more to it than he was trying to make it appear.

"He and Presa wanted to play, so they took me up to the lowest level of the stars." He gestured toward her still-cupped hands. "That was stardust."

"Was?" Opening her hands, she gasped in surprise. "What happened? Where did it go?"

"It's alright." He took her gently by the wrists and turned her hands so that her empty palms were facing upwards. "Your skin absorbed it."

"It did?"

His eyes softened in response to the innocence of her question and he nodded. "I don't know how much I absorbed last night," he smiled. "That just happened to get trapped in my hair instead of washing away with the rest of it."

"Washing away?" she echoed, reluctantly taking her hands back.

"Yes, I," he shrugged, chagrined, "startled the dragons."

"And you fell from all the way up in the…"

"No." He held up a hand to stop her. "No, I managed to stay on Sparks until we reached the river. That's when I fell off." He laughed a little, trying to make light of it.

She took a deep breath and shook her head to clear it. The idea of Neba hurtling through the air toward certain death persisted, despite his standing before her, whole and hearty, and she shook her head again.

Cluing in to her distress, he looked up at the sky. "You can't see the stars now, of course, but last night, well…" He ran his fingers through his hair, dislodging one or two more specks of stardust, which his skin quickly absorbed. "So beautiful."

Intrigued, Leuna leaned her shoulder against his and waited. "And?" she prompted when he pretended not to notice. "You can't stop there!"

He surrendered with a laugh. The *Morning Song* continued sailing upriver at a fair clip while they talked and ate, napped and talked some more. True to his word, the good captain had them at Auzo by suppertime on the third day. Sati said a fond farewell to Bilo, who giggled when Sparks' blew on him, mussing his hair.

"Here." Neba handed Bilo the last of Sparks' baby teeth, which had fallen out that morning. "Something to remember us by."

"Thank you again, Captain Abizenak." Leuna smiled, slipped him the rest of his fee, and joined the others on the dock.

"This time," Jartz adjusted his pack, "I'll get the rail coach tickets."

"Excellent." Leuna was quick to agree. Auzo was a much more sedate port town, given more to receiving and sending persons than freight, and she remembered it well. "We'll go straight to the Bonny Breeze and secure rooms for the night."

"I better stay with the dragons," Neba pointed out.

"Oh, they'll be fine," Leuna assured him. "There aren't dragon stables here, but I remember hearing about a man who rents out a riverside meadow to Marroi travelers."

"Those travelers are riding well-trained, domesticated dragons who are used to strangers. And even then, I doubt their riders leave them completely alone." He looked over to where a crowd was gathering around Sparks and Presa. The cockier ones were already reaching out to try to pet them, which prompted vehement warning hisses from Presa.

Leuna and Sati exchanged disappointed looks. Presa was just being herself, but Neba was right. Dozens of things could go wrong if Presa was left to her own devices, up to and including the destruction of the entire town.

"You're right," Sati agreed, despite the protests of her aching body. "Let's go."

Neba blinked. "What?"

"Come on." Leuna pointed with her chin. "I think he's over this way."

"Save a soft spot for me," Jartz laughed. Waving, he headed off.

When Neba saw Leuna and Sati roll their eyes, his chagrin deepened. He hadn't expected his own reluctance to sleep under a roof to ruin the plans of the others. He missed most of the bargaining with the landowner while he tried to think of a way to rectify his mistake.

"Wait," he said as Leuna reached into her money pouch. "I'll pay." It was the least he could do, though he groaned a little as he handed over his last six arranos. His journey was far from over. He abhorred the fact that he'd allowed Leuna to fund his passage thus far, yet he'd seen no alternative. And now in a single act, he'd wiped out his entire purse. How could he proceed coinless?

Some tiny part of him querulously asserted that they should've been allowed to sleep there in exchange for not burning down every building on the place. Ashamed of himself for the thought, he took a deep, cleansing breath. He was angry with himself, not the landowner.

"You two don't have to sleep out here just because I am," he told the women as they all walked toward the meadow. "Actually," he caught them each by an arm, "I'd rather you didn't. We've been travelling for eight days. You're both looking forward to a hot bath and sleeping in a soft bed."

"You're not?" Leuna lifted an eyebrow in disbelief.

"Not as much as I'm looking forward to a few more nights under the stars," he answered honestly.

"So, you really don't mind if we…"

"Absolutely not," Neba interrupted before Sati could finish. "Go." He released their arms as if he'd been restraining them. "Have fun. I'll be here in the morning."

"We'll send you some food," offered Sati, who still felt a wee bit guilty for leaving him there alone.

"Actually, we'll tell the landowner that there's just one for supper and breakfast," Leuna corrected. Wisely, she'd included meals in her bargaining, but apparently neither of the others had been paying attention. "Sleep well."

"What about Jartz?" Sati asked abruptly as they turned away.

"The ticket office is between here and the inn. If we don't encounter Jartz on the way, I'm certain Neba will tell him when he sees him." Leuna kept her tone cheerful as she gently tugged Sati along with her. It needed only a moment to advise the landowner of their change in plans—and finagle a small refund in consideration of the fact that they wouldn't be eating there after all—and then they were off!

Leuna looked wistfully at the stars, sighed and said something to fill the silence.

"Just think. Two more days and we'll be in Ibilia."

Sati's stomach dropped to her toes. "Actually, I was trying *not* to think about that."

"Still nervous?" Leuna squeezed her arm. "I'll make a kava steep to help you sleep."

"Why didn't I think of that?" Sati questioned, her tone full of disgust. "I would've prescribed that to Scholar Jakin in an instant!" Herrixka's town scholar prided himself on staying as up-to-date on world affairs as he reasonably could with month-old newssheets. As a result, he was often a nervous wreck. Belatedly, she realized that a kava steep would've done Leuna a world of good as well. By silent agreement, none of them had mentioned Leuna's nightmares, but while on the *Morning Song* Sati had been jolted awake more than once.

"Doctors make the worst patients!" Leuna laughed aloud. "We are always busy doing and thinking, usually about others, so that it's easy to overlook the obvious. It takes practice to tend ourselves. Honestly," she confessed, "that's the one drawback of being the only doctor in Herrixka. Suppose I should need a second opinion?" Leuna made a face.

Sati, caught off-guard by the levity, burst out

laughing. Her stomach returned to its rightful place anterior and to the side of the sixth descending backbone.

"And what're you two doing here?" Jartz chuckled inwardly when they jumped, but outwardly maintained a stern expression. The answer tumbled out of Sati almost faster than he could catch it! "Alright, alright." He held up his hand to stop the flood of words. "You're sleeping at the inn. Got it."

"*We*'re sleeping at the inn?!" Leuna had to pause after that. Was that a question or a statement? "I mean…aren't all three of us sleeping at the inn?"

"Nah." Jartz shook his head. "I *will* eat with you," his stomach growled its agreement and he turned toward the inn, "but I agree with Neba. There's no roof as can match the sky on a fine night."

"How about the tickets?" Leuna wanted to know.

"Four tickets for the coach leaving at eight in the morning," Jartz answered promptly. "This time tomorrow, we'll be in Ibilia." His pronouncement and the sight of the inn lifted everyone's spirits.

The Bonny Breeze lived up to its name from the ground all the way up to its third floor, boasting colorful wind spinners on the velvety front lawn, chimes on the porch, and boat flags strung across the railing of each balcony. Perched on the peak of the roof, a jaunty brass sailor perpetually stared through his spy glass in whatever direction the wind was blowing. Right now the wind was carrying the scent of supper to their noses and they fairly flew down the street to claim a table.

"Leuna!" The innkeeper's wife, Afaria, left what she was doing and rushed over to embrace her.

"Afaria!" Leuna hugged her back. It was impossible to forget the dark-haired, petite woman who had the boundless energy of an excited five-year-old child "How are you?"

"Never better!" Afaria beamed. Her smile seemed to take in Leuna, her friends, and everyone in the general vicinity. "But you've been travelling and I know you're hungry. Come, sit down, and I will bring you a feast!"

Leuna was still laughing when the whirlwind of a woman dashed off to the kitchen. Out of habit, she went to the table where she'd always sat with her father and took the chair facing the room. From there, she had a good view of the front door, the stairs leading up to the sleeping areas, and the kitchen. She'd learned a lot from her father, including the subtle art of people-watching.

"I hope she meant what she said." Jartz eyed the fancy wooden contraption in the middle of the round table that held cloth napkins. "I'm hungry enough to eat my own cookin'!" Ginte had fed them, he didn't mean that. It was just that a man's stomach could only take so many meals of ship's biscuit and salt fish before something had to change.

"You must be desperate," Leuna winked. More and more during the course of their journey, he'd let Neba take over that chore. Neba was not only willing, he was a genius at turning the plain fare they'd packed along into tasty dishes.

"We'll start you off with some brown bread, fresh from the oven." Afaria slid two loaves onto the table and plunked a saucer of rich butter beside it. While the waiter who'd come along behind her served them frosty mugs, she continued, "Hot auroch steaks, mashed gurin potatoes, and a green salad will be right out."

Jartz tore off a piece of the brown bread, smeared it with butter, and stuffed it into his mouth. His stomach growled again anyway, louder than before!

Afaria, delighted to know her food would be going to someone who would appreciate it, smiled and bustled off to tend her other customers.

"How much is this going to cost?" Sati whispered.

"Don't worry about it." Leuna patted her hand and began slicing the other loaf of bread. "I have an account here."

"A what?"

"An account," Leuna reiterated. "As you know, I don't come through Auzo often." She buttered a piece of bread for herself and took a bite. "So, instead of trying to carry enough coin to take care of my stays at the Bonny Breeze, Afaria and her husband simply send a bill to the bank in town. The bank here is sort of like a little brother to the bank in Ibilia and has an account in my name."

"Oh, yes…" Sati paused, trying to sort it all out. Leuna had explained banks before, that they were buildings where people could store their money if they needed or wanted to. When people did that, it was called 'opening an account.' "You mean you have enough money in the bank here that the innkeeper is willing to go there to get his due?"

"Something you might as well learn now as later," Jartz kept his tone casual, "is not to talk much about money amongst large groups of strangers." A man at a nearby table—who reminded Jartz of a kastore with his long nose and too-close-together eyes—had definitely perked up at the mention of Leuna's bank account. "There are folks what figure to relieve others of any extra money they might or might not be carrying."

"You mean robbers?" Sati gasped. Flushing, she lowered her voice, never mind that it was too late. "You mean robbers?"

Leuna nodded, both to Sati and to Jartz. He'd been subtly watching their neighbor, moving only his eyes, and she thought he was probably right. A public eatery would be the perfect place for a robber to pick a target. Weary travelers such as themselves dropping (and slyly gathering) valuable clues like how much they could afford to eat. All her years of people-watching and she'd never made the connection between an eatery and a waterhole in terms of predators lying in wait for prey. It nearly gave her the shivers!

Instead, she straightened in her chair. "Here come the steaks!" She watched in amusement as Jartz reached for his fork and knife. It had taken Afaria ages to learn not to be offended that her guests automatically assumed her steaks required a knife.

"Look at this!" Sati held up the piece that came away when she inserted her fork.

"It's melt-in-your-mouth tender!" Jartz agreed enthusiastically. Scraping up a forkful of mashed potatoes, he stabbed a second piece of steak and twisted. The meat separated easily and he raised it to his mouth. "Should've ordered two!"

Leuna didn't laugh because that was usually how she felt after a long absence from the Bonny Breeze.

She'd even wheedled a cooking lesson out of Afaria and hadn't managed to master cooking an auroch steak. Hers were passable, but not spectacular.

Deliberately, Leuna spread her focus around, savoring the green salad with its tangy dressing between bites of the delectable steak and potatoes. As tempting as the idea of ordering a second steak was, while at university she'd learned the hard way that watching her figure meant more than observing the food approach her mouth.

Jartz had no such reservations. Years of hard work and 'eating his own cooking' left him uniquely prepared to consume a second and yes, even a third steak!

Rather than staying to watch him relish the food she couldn't have, Leuna waved Afaria over and spoke to her quietly.

"I thought you'd be wanting to spend the night." Afaria favored them with one of her dazzling smiles and handed a key to each of the women. In a discreetly lowered tone she went on, "I started the kitchen lad filling your baths as soon as you sat down to eat. If you're ready to head up, I'll send along the hot water."

"Afaria, you're amazing." Leuna kissed the woman's cheek and rose, barely spotting the woman's signal to her kitchen lad. He started up the stairs almost immediately, carrying a steaming bucket in each hand. "You read my mind."

"Mine, too," Sati agreed, rising as well. The effects of a full stomach caught up with her and she had to put her hand on the back of the chair to steady herself. It was all she could do to stifle a yawn. "I don't think I've ever had a meal like that in my life." Afaria's answering smile was somehow both satisfied and humble at the same time.

"Sleep well," Jartz encouraged, wiping his mouth on a napkin.

"You, too." Leuna chuckled.

"Come along." Afaria ushered them over to the stairs. "Go. Relax and enjoy. I'll be up in a while to show you how to drain the tubs."

"I'll show her how to do that," Leuna promised. She paused, her foot on the first step. "And would you please send kava steep up to Sati's room?"

"Oh, that's alright." Sati's cheeks pinked slightly. "I don't think I'll need it after all."

Not a stair creaked as they made their way up to the first floor and stepped into a long, open hall. In keeping with the inn's sailing theme, each door was marked with a palm-sized boat carving just above the doorknob.

"How cute!" Sati showed Leuna the small engraving on the head of the key she'd been given. "My key matches my door!" Turning the key over, she laughed at discovering a number on the other side. "So clever!"

The kitchen lad came out of Leuna's room just then, gave them a polite half-bow, and hurried off.

"If you think that is clever," Leuna motioned for her to open the door, "wait until you see their plumbing system."

While Sati wasn't usually interested in plumbing, she had to admit that most everything about the Bonny Breeze fascinated her, from the steps that didn't squeak to the tall bed in the corner. Was that a footstool she saw peeking at her from under the bed skirt?

In truth, the Bonny Breeze was simply but sturdily built. The second and third floor housed guests and the architect had wisely designed for maximum economy, including shared chimneys and pipes for the rooms that also shared walls. In this case, the copper pipe that protruded from the shared wall was overlaid with a wooden casing for camouflage. The attached faucet hovered over the tub and could be used to fill it partway with room temperature water.

"Here." Leuna tapped a copper lever located on one end of the tub. "When you're ready to drain the tub, pull this down until you hear a click."

"Then what?" Sati was curious despite herself.

"Then that circle down there," Leuna pointed at the bottom of the tub, "will rotate out of the way and the water will drain out."

"So simple," Sati shook her head and yawned at the same time. "And yet so terribly clever."

"Bolt the door behind me," Leuna admonished after showing Sati where the soap and towels were. She waited in the hall until she heard the metal bar click into place, then stepped into her own room, securing the door behind her. She'd never heard of trouble at the Bonny Breeze, but attributed at least some of that to the intelligent use of the safeguards the innkeeper had provided.

Choosing a straight-backed wooden chair, she sat down and unlaced her boots, sighing in relief as she toed them off. Ordinarily she would've added a pinch of lavender to the bath water to aid in falling sleep, but tonight she settled for the rose-scented shampoo. It wasn't very much later that she sank into the soft bed and a wonderfully dreamless sleep.

The stately city of Ibilia stretched for a full mile in all thirty points of the compass. Its straight roads and perfectly circular shape were a point of extreme pride with the students of architecture. More than the capital city of Lurrak, Ibilia was the center of learning and knowledge for all of Jatorri. Scholars flowed to and from the city in a never-ending cycle. Some privileged few actually lived there.

One such man was Xelebre Izan, who was presently out for a late afternoon stroll. He took a walk every day, considering it vitally beneficial to his health, but today he'd been delayed by one meeting after another. The wonder of it was that he was already retired. His handsome face twisted in a wry smile. Truth be told, he'd had more time to himself while he was working full-time. Good thing he'd retired while he was still relatively young and spry!

From the shadows cast by the halls of learning and local supporting businesses emerged a silent, ragamuffin band of street orphans, following him. Xelebre noticed and smiled at them. He'd never given much thought to the street children until his granddaughter, Leuna, had arranged for the adoption of one Muti, an agile little scamp she found freezing to death outside the medical research buildings. That was several years ago by now, and, according to her letters, Muti was flourishing in a loving home in Herrixka.

After expending months of time and energy trying to convince Ibilia's appointed officials to set up a school for the street children, since they had no homes of their own in which to be educated, he'd taken matters into his own hands. Petty crime had dropped off thirty-two percent since then, a potential result he hadn't even considered when presenting his persuasive arguments. Sadly, the same officials who'd refused him assistance were too busy congratulating themselves on whatever it was they thought they'd done to bring it about to make the connection. At the end of the street, where the tall buildings gave way to a patch of grass and supremely uncomfortable metal benches, Xelebre seated himself and addressed them.

"Good morning, everyone. Are we ready for today's tests?" Out of capacious pockets came half-a-dozen apples. "Ume, how many apples am I holding?" He pretended not to notice the new little waif on the edge of the group. Judging by the way the lad was staring at the apples, he hadn't eaten in a while.

Ume, another young boy who possessed perhaps as many years as Xelebre had apples, counted slowly. He always struggled at math. The other children remained silent, having learned long ago that taunting and cruelty were the only sure ways to be banished from this strange man's presence.

"Six?" Ume ventured at last.

"Very good!" Xelebre handed him an apple as a reward. "And now I have five. Ikasi." He smiled at the willowy girl and made a mental note to find a safe place of employment for her before bruma, the cold time. She was getting prettier every day and would soon attract the attention of the scum that even an enlightened city such as Ibilia feigned ignorance of. "Seven of you haven't had any apple at all this morning. How can I share the remaining apples equally with all of you?"

Doing her best to ignore the tempting sounds of Ume crunching away at his whole apple, Ikasi took a deep breath and set to figuring. With a little effort, she came to the conclusion that thirty-five was the smallest number that could be evenly divided by both seven and five.

"We would need seven equal pieces, Jaurle Izan." She bobbed a curtsy, not the least bit bothered by the ragged state of her clothes or the dirt on her face. He'd never required them to use his title when addressing him, but he'd never objected, either. Anyway, she liked the way it rolled off her tongue.

"Well done, my dear." He handed her an entire purple apple, knowing that was her favorite. Producing two more apples, he handed the rest to the largest boy in the group. "Pass these out please, Itzel." He smiled fondly at the lad as he obeyed. A few short months ago, Itzel had been a bully, a tormentor of the others. More and more, however, as Xelebre put him in the position of proxy benefactor to the littler ones, Itzel was changing. Growing. Why, if things kept on as they were, Xelebre looked forward to recommending him as an errand boy for the city guard, who very often promoted from within.

"Thank you," whispered the new boy.

"Thank you," chorused the others, including Itzel.

"You're most welcome. Now." Xelebre pulled out the small pocket watch he always carried and checked the time. There was still a little while before the food carts were due to start making their evening rounds of the city. He'd once seen a supper cart out before dusk, but that was several years ago during the now-legendary rivalry between two different bakeries. "Shall we try some basic geography?"

Cheerfully, he assigned each child the name of a city and had them form up in a loose representation of their various locations. To keep things simple for their newest arrival, Xelebre dubbed him Ibilia. The others measured their distance from him, assuming that the direction he was facing was deko, where the sun rose each morning. Counting a step, heel-toe, per day's travel between cities, they managed a haphazard model at best. Of course, that was to be expected, given the different sizes of their small feet.

It was chaos and good fun. When they were all positioned, Xelebre called on them and asked what the city they represented was known for.

"Agriculture!" shouted one.

"Fashion," called another.

"And you, lad." Xelebre had saved the new boy for last and now he smiled at him. "How are you called?"

"I…Slip, sir."

Xelebre had to strain to hear him, but he continued smiling. "Slip, eh? Well, Slip, can you tell us what Ibilia is famous for?" He smiled while he waited.

The boy's eyes grew wide. His breathing became shallow and rapid and beads of sweat popped out on his forehead, all in a matter of seconds.

"Don't know?" Xelebre asked hastily, truly concerned for the lad. "Well, how about the rest of you? Does anybody remember what Ibilia is famous for?" He opened the question to the others.

"Learning!" They shouted as one. Giggling, they broke from their geography positions and ran to the public water fountain.

Itzel hung back and made eye contact with the boy. "Come on," he invited gruffly. "We have to wash our faces and hands before the food cart gets here." Once they were close enough for him to lower his voice, Itzel added, "Ya don't have to be afraid of him, kid. He won't hurt ya."

After they'd finished scrubbing, Itzel examined the fingernails and faces of the younger boys while Ikasi checked those of the girls. The sound of cheerily jingling bells prompted them to finish quickly and take their places at the end of the lines.

"Meat pies today." Xelebre rubbed his hands together as the food cart came into view. There was no mistaking the bold signs on the side of the cart, even though his aging eyes struggled to make out the lettering at this distance. "Excellent!" Putting his hand lightly on Itzel's shoulder, Xelebre asked, "What kinds of meat pies do you think he'll have tonight?"

"Hard to say, sir." Itzel's smooth young face wrinkled in thought. "The drovers brought in a mixed flock of goats and sheep earlier this week. But I also saw fresh antzara feathers being delivered to the millinery shop this morning."

"Superb fact gathering and deduction, young man." Xelebre praised Itzel and noted the pleased flush on his face. "I happen to know that permits were granted just two days ago for a herd of auroch to use the corrals on the hego side of the city." The seasonal winds should ensure that most of the...barnyard odors would be swept out of the city.

"Auroch pie." Ikasi cocked her head to the side. "That sounds expensive."

"What makes you say that?" Xelebre had to clasp his hands behind his back to hide his eagerness for her response. To think that her bright, eager mind had been in danger of going completely to waste on the streets. Or worse, being warped and twisted by crime.

"The butchers will make sure that as much of the meat as possible will go to expensive cuts, such as steaks and roasts." Ikasi spoke with all the assuredness of one who'd spent six lunars living in a large, broken wooden crate on butchers' alley. "What's left after that will be sold for stews, soups, and hashes. There won't be much left over for the bakers and they'll pay what's asked because they know they can sell it at a profit."

"Sure, I getcha." Itzel nodded enthusiastically. "That's why the carts come this way to sell their wares." He gestured at the buildings surrounding the small park. "Big business, big pockets. And late hours."

Xelebre, sobered by their assessment, looked over at the bank where he used to work. How many times had he dashed out of that door in a mad rush to catch a passing food cart? *The stack of work was waist high*, he'd tell his wife when he finally dragged himself home. *And that was after I set it on the floor so I'd have room to work!* How long had it taken him to realize his third-floor office was nothing more than a prison cell with a view?

"Here we are." He flagged down the cart driver. "Two meat pies apiece, if you please."

"Two?" Itzel blurted. He'd been drooling at the thought of one! "I mean," he turned crimson, "thank you, sir."

"You're most welcome." Xelebre winked at him. "I think you also mean you'd like to know what makes tonight a two-meat-pie-night."

"Yes, please, sir." Itzel uttered the courteous words in complete earnestness.

"While you and Ikasi were explaining the economics of the meat pie industry," he held up a gold arrano and handed it to the cart driver, waving away any change, "you demonstrated a wisdom far beyond your years." All of the children had stopped to listen and their foreheads were unanimously furrowed in puzzlement. "In short, you two know something that it took me years to learn. So please. Enjoy your meat pies."

Xelebre selected a single antzara pie for himself. Again, he waved away the change. Most of the cart drivers were married men with families to support. Besides, Xelebre liked the way he smiled at the children as they clamored over which pies they wanted. Patience should be encouraged. He bit into the perfectly browned crust. The pie wasn't bad, either.

"Dragons!" A city guardsman came pounding down the street toward them, eyes wild with fright. "Dragons!"

"You!" Xelebre stepped in the man's way, prepared to forcibly detain him if necessary. From the corner of his eye, he saw Itzel move into a supporting position, knees bent and clearly ready to do battle on his behalf. "Halt!"

"Get out of my way," bellowed the guardsman, barely managing to stop himself in time to keep from crashing into him or the cart. "I'm on official business!"

"Then I, Jaurle Izan, officially demand that you control yourself," Xelebre snapped. As soon as he saw his words taking root in the man's mind, he continued sharply, "You're making a fool of yourself, scurrying through town, shouting about dragons as though you'd never seen one in your life."

"But sir!" The guardsman dared to interrupt. "They're wild dragons! No riders!"

"No riders," Xelebre repeated, allowing frustration to creep into his tone. How was he supposed to convince Itzel to join the guard after witnessing this blockhead's performance? "So they haven't attacked the city. Or raided the stockyards." He pointed at the man, too late remembering the half-eaten pie in his hand. "Did you even stay to see them land?"

"Stay?" the man squeaked. "My sergeant ordered me to run to the barracks for reinforcements!"

Xelebre debated briefly with himself. He technically had the authority to countermand the city guard, at least up to the rank of captain. However, on the off chance that these were truly wild dragons and a threat to the city, there was no time to waste.

"Did he also instruct you to scream your fears at the top of your lungs, creating chaos and panic among the citizens?"

The man blinked several times. "N-n-n-no, sir," he stuttered.

"Then save your breath and run as fast as you can to the barracks instead." He jerked his head in the direction of the barracks, dismissing the guardsman. As the man ran off, his light armor jingling and clanking with his movements, Xelebre comforted himself that it would soon be in the hands of Commandant Borrok, a highly intelligent man who'd served the city well for nearly fifteen years.

"Good you caught him here, sir," Itzel observed, his eyes still following the guardsman. "Might've scared folks near to death otherwise."

"I think you're right," Xelebre smiled. He'd been thinking the whole time and now arrived at a conclusion. "I'm going to go see these dragons for myself." He held up his hand as the children began to protest. "Let us consider. That guardsman is not a very fast runner. The nearest post in that direction," he pointed at where the man had come from, "is at the railway station, over a quarter of a mile away. If the dragons were truly dangerous, we could see the smoke by now."

"I'll go with you, sir." Itzel squared his shoulders.

"Me, too," Slip announced around a mouthful of meat pie.

"As you wish." He'd only meant to convince them there was nothing to worry about, not persuade them to accompany him. He couldn't help the tiny shiver of fear as they all trooped along beside him, heading toward the dragons.

The cart driver hesitated, then turned his cart around and followed them. He rationalized giving in to his curiosity by thinking about the crowds that were guaranteed to be at the railway at this time of day.

The last rail coach of the day, full of hungry passengers, should have arrived by now. Not to mention the gawkers who would be drawn like magnets to the commotion.

They didn't have to go far before they began to hear raised voices. At least one of them was angry.

"This is your last warning! Stand aside!" roared a man's voice. "We will fire!"

"This is *your* last warning!" a woman answered, sounding serene somehow despite the volume at which she was projecting her voice. "You're agitating the dragons, and if you aren't afraid of *their* fire, you should be."

Xelebre impolitely elbowed his way through the gathering crowd until he reached its front lines. The city guard were arrayed in front of the railway station, weapons—such as they were—out and at the ready. Across the small field from them were two gorgeous young dragons and four tired-looking travelers. One woman stood in front of the group of travelers, chin up and shoulders squared.

"Sergeant!" Xelebre strode into the center of the field. "Do you know who I am?"

Bewildered, the sergeant stared at him. It was possible that one or more of the guardsmen under his command muttered questions regarding the older man's mental state, but the sergeant knew better. Oh yes, this was just what he needed. First, his simple assignment of checking the papers and baggage of the arriving passengers got fouled up by a private investigator who claimed to have captured a would-be coach robber during the railway ride over from Auzo. Well, he didn't mind that, not really.

Made things more interesting. But two wild dragons plus a jaurle was going to tax his patience something fierce.

"Jaurle Izan." The sergeant identified him at last.

"Quite right." Discovering that the children had all followed him into the field, Xelebre took a deep breath. "Leuna?" he called over his shoulder to his granddaughter.

"Yes?" Wisely, she refrained from revealing their familial connection. The sergeant looked ready to spit nails and she didn't want to antagonize him with what might be misinterpreted as nepotism.

"Are those dragons a threat or not?" Xelebre asked bluntly.

"So long as they feel threatened," a strange man's voice answered, "they are and will remain a threat."

The crowd was instantly abuzz with shocked conversation.

"I see." That was definitely not the answer he'd been hoping for. "Why do they feel threatened?"

"They're really not used to people." Leuna ran her hand down Presa's neck. The dragon tossed her head unhappily, but didn't try to pull away. "If everyone could go about their business, that would be a great help."

"Sergeant, disperse the crowd. As quietly as you can." Xelebre spun on his heel, narrowly avoided tripping over Slip, and strode a few feet closer to Leuna. The yellow dragon swung her head in his direction and he prudently stopped. "My dear girl," he spoke to his granddaughter. "What have you gotten yourself into?"

Leuna laughed softly. "It's a bit complicated. Let us get the dragons to the stables first and I'll explain everything over supper. Alright?"

"Yes, that would seem the best way to do things. I…" He broke off when the crowd, which had begun muttering at his orders to disperse them, abruptly went silent.

Commandant Borrok stepped down from his horse and handed the reins to his aide. "Take the horses back to the barracks. Stand the men down from high alert and return on foot."

"I'll handle this," Xelebre promised. To Ikasi he murmured, "I think this little crowd should disperse as well."

She looked disappointed but, in the silent communication of street children, summoned the others and led them off the field.

The commandant approached slowly. He'd learned enough about dragons during his time in Ibilia to treat even the 'tame' ones with extreme caution.

"Jaurle Izan." Borrok bowed at the waist in acknowledgement of his civilian peer. "I was summoned here by a frantic guardsman," he pursed his lips slightly. "Well, a recruit, really.
He was babbling about wild dragons." Stepping up beside the jaurle, Borrok noted that the dragons were barely being kept under control. A man and a woman stood with each of the two dragons, speaking to them softly. "I came to see for myself, of course."

"Of course," Xelebre agreed pleasantly. He'd expected nothing less.

"And how is it that you happened to be here?" Borrok was mostly curious. Unlike the elected officials, he paid attention to everything going on in his city, including the time and energy one wealthy gentleman was spending with the street children. He only wished there were a dozen more like him.

"I was out for my evening stroll and noticed the recruit," Xelebre used Borrok's preferred term gladly, "rushing toward the barracks."

"I see." He also saw one Antze Tzeko, a private investigator, arguing with the sergeant. Turning to the group with the dragons Borrok solicitously informed them, "I will have the streets cleared for you between here and the stables." With a bow and a final look at the lovely woman by the yellow dragon, he executed a perfect about-face and marched over to see what the new trouble was.

Xelebre started to turn back to his granddaughter when he observed Slip from the corner of his eye. While the stranger who had

been arguing with the sergeant handed the commandant something to examine, he kept one hand on the arm of the rough looking fellow beside him— who had his hands cuffed behind his back. Slip only had eyes for the prisoner.

"Slip!" Xelebre called his name sharply. Their eyes met and Slip flinched. The prisoner appeared to grunt or do something to regain Slip's attention, but the lad had lost his nerve. Xelebre exhaled slowly as the boy darted in amongst the crowd, vanishing from sight.

"Grandpa?" Leuna tucked her hand through the bend of his elbow. "Is something wrong?"

The prisoner scowled at him, but even though some distance separated them, Xelebre saw beyond the hatred deforming the man's features. Indeed. He saw enough of Slip in the man's face to know they were related.

"Yes, child." He patted her hand gently. "Very, very wrong."

"Can I help?"

"Perhaps." He smiled and kissed her cheek. She'd always been a sweet, loving girl. "But for now, let's get your dragons somewhere safe."

"Well, they're not exactly my dragons," she laughed.

At the commandant's signal, they moved out from the railway station. Leuna waved goodbye to the investigator who'd thwarted the attempted coach robbery and followed the others. It took almost the entire walk to the stables for her to recount the tale of her finding Neba, who found Sparks, and so on.

"Gracious, what a story!" Xelebre shook his head. "And I thought that the stories your grandmother has been reading were adventures!"

"Wait." Leuna wrinkled her nose at him in disbelief as she removed her pack. "*Grandma* is reading adventure stories?"

"Oh yes." Xelebre took the pack from her. They'd reached the stables and the dragons were sniffing and prancing and exhibiting all sorts of nervous signs, so he imagined she'd be needed. "More on that later, eh?" With a wink, he made his way over to the young woman he assumed was Leuna's apprentice Sati. He was all sorts of curious about the young woman he'd agreed to take into his home.

Leuna laughed when he winked at her, kissed his cheek, and approached Presa with both hands extended.

"Sweet girl," Leuna crooned. "I don't suppose you're used to this many strange dragons, are you?" She hummed softly as Presa lowered her head and blew into her hands.

"You're right about that," Neba acknowledged. "Most dragon kabi's don't overlap unless something's gone extremely wrong."

"How d'we get them inside, then?" Jartz growled.

"We show them it's safe," Leuna suggested.

Neba nodded. "Jartz, stand right beside the doors, please." He glanced at Leuna. "They've both taken a shine to you, so let's try backing in together, alright?"

One of the stable's grooms appeared and handed them each a pail of what looked like palm-sized pressed cakes of...something. Leuna noticed that he immediately ducked back and out of sight, too.

"I don't know what these are," Neba pulled the pail back before Sparks could shove his snout in it, "but I think it's a great idea!"

Leuna nodded. Even Presa was focused on the cakes.

"Here, sweetheart." The greasy cakes slipped out from between her fingers and she had to bite back a noise of disgust. When she finally got a few in her hand, she offered them to Presa and took a slow step backward. "They're yours if you want them." It took a combination of humming, coaxing, and downright bribery with the cakes, but they got both dragons inside.

Leuna snuck a look around her while Presa daintily lifted a third cake from her palm. The outside of the tall building was plain wood, but inside was a different matter entirely. As large as the field they'd rented the night before, the inside walls were made of granite. Coarse, dull, ugly granite.

Sparks threw back his head and roared. Several heads poked out of holes in the walls that Leuna hadn't even noticed and she caught her breath. *Now what?*

"Sparks," Neba admonished. "Take it easy." Waving a cake in front of him, Neba tossed it into the air, making a game of it in the hopes of distracting him.

"I think we'd both better sleep here tonight." Leuna nearly jumped out of her skin when a hand touched her arm. Thankfully, it was just the groom from before.

"Against the rules to sleep here 'less you work here," he informed her, his grin making his white teeth stand out against his darker skin. He wasn't quite as dark as Neba, but clearly he had Marroi blood. From the cart beside him, he picked up a large fish. "I'm Ordez, nephew to Basa, Jatorri's greatest wild dragon wrangler." The twinkle in his eyes mitigated the boastfulness of his words. "Let's see if we can't get these two comfortable."

"No one but us has ever fed them before," Neba warned. He didn't attempt to interfere, however. Sparks had chosen to return after being set free. Presa had chosen to come with him and then traveled willingly with them over hundreds of miles. They would have to get used to other humans eventually.

Taking her cue from Neba, Leuna held still. The groom offered the fish to Presa first, sensing that she was the more difficult to convince. She promptly seated herself and wrapped her tail around her body, turning up her snout in icy indifference.

"Right then," Ordez chuckled. "How about you, big fella?" He waved the fish from side to side briefly, then flipped it in Sparks' direction. At the last second, Sparks' appetite overcame his dignity and he snapped the fish out of the air. "Good."

Chapter 8

Neba caught Leuna gently by the arm and walked her a few steps away from where Ordez was working with the dragons. He still felt a strong need to remain with them, but had to admit, the stables were *very* impressive. The 'roof' was a loosely-'woven' metal meshwork with an opening large enough for a single dragon and rider to enter or leave. Natural lighting and fresh air flooded the place and combined with the realistic-looking stone 'caves' to make it seem almost like a wild kabi's habitat. All of that aside, this was the closest to alone he and Leuna had been for the last nine days.

"Leuna." She looked up when he said her name and he swallowed hard. "We never got to talk about what happened. During the attack." He stopped himself there, leaving it to her to choose how the conversation went.

She dropped her gaze to his chin and took a deep breath. Nightmares had woken her from her sleep while aboard the *Morning Song*, but she hadn't realized anyone else noticed. At least, she'd hoped they hadn't.

"I always carry a little silver nitrate in my medical case," she said quietly. "It's useful for cauterization, which is a worst case scenario, but..." She was rambling. Exhaling slowly, she brought her mind back to the more difficult topic. "I think the sound of his screams will haunt me for the rest of my life."

Neba pulled her into his arms at the first sign of tears glistening in her eyes. Her hair came loose from its efficient bun and spilled down over his hand as he cupped it protectively over the back of her neck. As tightly as he was holding her, he could still feel her body shaking with silent sobs.

"Mourn the pain you caused him," he murmured in her ear. "But be grateful you were able to defend yourself."

Ordez hadn't heard a word, and he was more than happy to have the dragons to himself for a minute. A handful of other dragons in the field were calling to them, so he was watching carefully for warning signs. Putting several dragons together was the unpredictable part, for each individual dragon had its own temperament. As his Aunt Basa always said, wild dragons were just as dangerous as tame dragons.

Jartz cleared his throat discreetly. "You're doin' right well with those dragons, son."

Neba almost laughed at Jartz' self-appointed chaperoning. "We should probably go," he whispered to Leuna. "Are you ready?" He wiped a tear off her face with his fingertips and smoothed her hair back behind her ears. Thankfully his shirt was dark and wouldn't show the evidence of her tears for long.

"Will they be alright?" she asked, looking over at Presa and Sparks.

"I think so." Some of the other dragons had left off feeding from the artificial stream that ran through the field and were starting to play. "There's plenty of food and space here, so barring a badly-tempered dragon, there shouldn't be any trouble."

"And you're sure there aren't any dragons like that here?"

"Bad-tempered dragons aren't much use, m'lady," Ordez announced, pouring one half-empty pail of dragon treats into the other. "They cause all sorts of trouble. Everything from damaging equipment to starting fights, burning buildings down."

He shook his head. "Most dragon owners turn that sort loose as quick as they can. The ethical ones, anyhow." Leading the way into the field, Ordez shook his head. "Some owners are worse than the dragons, sell them to fighting rings or have them killed for whatever they can collect on the black market."

"That's awful." The instant she said it, the inadequacy of the words struck her.

"Awful inconvenient," Ordez snorted. "Waste of life aside, we get a lot of extra interference at the stables thanks to that sort of thing."

"How do you mean?" Neba asked, frowning.

Ordez shrugged. "I don't blame 'em, not really. The city guard has to look somewhere when they get tipped off contraband is coming into Lurrak."

"Ah, I see." Neba nodded unhappily. Then, to Leuna, he expounded, "Because it makes sense that illegal dragon goods could be easily hidden at the only dragon stable in all of Ibilia, that's the first place the authorities will look."

"Got that right." Ordez managed a rueful chuckle. "I'll be mighty glad when they shut down the poachers. Then they can knock off with the 'surprise' inspections and too-casual conversations at the local tavern. Things can get back to normal."

Jartz interrupted by clearing his throat again. "Your grandpa was mentioning something about not keeping supper waiting," he prompted Leuna.

"I didn't realize how much I'd miss them," she admitted as they left the stables.

"And I didn't realize how glad I'd be that Presa decided to string along," smiled Neba. "She knows more about being a dragon than he does, but he knows more about humans than she does. Should balance each other out pretty well, I'd say."

"There you are." Xelebre hugged his granddaughter fondly. "I sent one of my lads ahead to let your grandmother know how many to expect for supper." He tucked her hand into the crook of his elbow and gallantly offered his other arm to Sati. "Nevertheless, I recommend that we walk slowly. She'll have a job of placating Dari, for one thing."

"Hmm, that's one way to handle it," Leuna agreed. "If it were me on such short notice, I'd send out to a restaurant." For a modest additional fee, the better restaurants in Ibilia would pack up entire meals and transport them to dining halls or homes.

Xelebre snapped his fingers. "You're brilliant, my girl." Flagging down a bicycle carriage, he squeezed them all into it. Giving his address to the driver, he settled back against the cushions and laughed at the simplicity of her solution. Continued laughing until they had all succumbed to his contagious humor.

"What a day," he gasped, wiping a tear from his eye. "Four officer's meetings in the morning, dull as dishwater and one right after the other. Then dragons and granddaughters and restaurants this evening." They laughed their way clear into Xelebre's home, a relatively modest residence with only three floors and five guest rooms.

"Ah, Itzel." Finding the boy still waiting in the foyer of the home, Xelebre clapped him on the shoulder. "Have you delivered your message yet?"

"No, sir." Itzel stared at him, round-eyed. "I only just got here!"

"Astounding." Xelebre made a show of checking his pocket watch. "You came that distance in record time." What sort of record was anybody's guess, since Xelebre had no real interest in athletics. The point was… "Here. A reward for being so fleet of foot." He popped two small coins into the lad's hand and ushered him toward the door. He rarely gave money to the orphans, it just made them targets for the ne'er-do-wells that watched him suspiciously. "I daresay the city guard would admire to have a lad as fast as you. What do you think of that?"

"The guard?" Itzel gasped.

"Absolutely. You could run errands as fast as the wind." Here, Xelebre paused. "I could speak to them about it for you. But only if that's what you want."

Itzel thought hard for a moment and was still speechless.

"Would you like to sleep on it?" Xelebre suggested gently. He hadn't meant to rush either his own plans or the lad, the idea just sort of slipped out.

"Thank you sir," Itzel nodded. "I would."

"That is very wise." Setting his large hand gently on the boy's shoulder, Xelebre looked him in the eye. "Come around for breakfast tomorrow and we'll discuss it then, alright?" He was just opening the door when a thought struck him. "Itzel. How well do you know Slip?"

"Never saw 'im before today, sir."

"I see." Xelebre had a brief wrestle with himself before saying, "Find out what you can about him, please. I have a hunch he's in trouble."

Itzel nodded gravely.

The door had barely shut behind the lad when the lady of the house, Merezi, appeared at the top of the stairs. A lovely woman, confident in herself and in her husband's love, her graying hair was swept up in a loose chignon. The puffed sleeves of her soft green tunic tapered to her slim wrists and somehow made her narrow waist look even slimmer. The front of her tunic split at the waist, an embroidered black waist sash serving as an eye-catching accent above where the tunic tails draped over the top of her dark red slacks.

"Leuna!" Merezi's hand skimmed the railing as she raced down the stairs toward her granddaughter, her heart in her eyes.

Leuna allowed herself to be enveloped in the loving embrace, wrapped and warmed by the scents of honeysuckle and old books.

Neba looked away, a lump in his throat the size of a musker pit. *This* was how Leuna lived while in the city? These were her grandparents? Her grandfather was a jaurle, which was clearly some sort of city official. And her grandmother was presumably responsible for the appointment of this delightful home.

The house stretched out before him, no matter which way he looked. Carpeted stairs rose to the second level. On his left was a room full of books and comfortable-looking chairs. The hall ahead of him had elegant wooden paneling, all in a single color. In the room on his right he could see a table that would seat eight persons easily, perhaps ten in a pinch. There were no gold candlesticks or expensive tapestries or other excessive displays of wealth, yet the word that he would've used to describe what he saw was 'lush.' Followed immediately by 'cozy.'

"You must be Sati." Merezi didn't hesitate to hug the timid young woman. The hopeful light in Sati's eyes told her a great deal about her new houseguest. "Thank you so much for agreeing to stay with us." She made a mental note to keep an eye on Sati. Her slim form and trusting air could potentially attract all sorts of, um, suitors.

"Thank you for having me," Sati returned quickly.

"It's our pleasure, my dear." Xelebre came to stand beside his wife, slipping his arm about her waist out of habit. "You'll have a room to yourself and as many candles as you need."

"But," Merezi interrupted, "you must promise not to study yourself to sickness." She patted Sati's hand lightly, then released her. "And don't be surprised if we ask you to attend the occasional event with us."

Leuna smiled at Sati, catching her eye. "You'll find a quiet evening recital or garden stroll very refreshing."

"No need to make us sound dull," objected Xelebre, his eyes laughing at her.

"And who are these gentlemen?" Merezi turned her winning smile to the men still standing awkwardly in her entryway. "Why…you must be Jartz." She reached out to the tall, weather-beaten man with tiny white scars on his huge hands.

"Yes, ma'am." Jartz found his own hand folded within both of hers. He couldn't look away from her penetrating violet eyes.

"My daughter wrote to us about you." Merezi held onto his hand. "She was very grateful that her husband found such a good friend."

Jartz cleared his throat and still couldn't speak. Nodding, he shook her hand again and took a half-step back, as though that would somehow give him the space he needed.

"Grandmother," Leuna stepped forward. "This is our friend called Neba."

"Neba?" Merezi, master of a dozen languages, had been the one to teach Leuna the old tongue. "You have a most interesting name, young man."

Neba took her hand and bowed over it. "My name as yet is unknown. Your granddaughter most graciously calls me her brother."

Despite herself, Merezi's head tilted slightly to the side.

"Very mysterious, isn't it?" Leuna tried to laugh. It was just like her insightful grandmother to see right through them.

"I propose they tell us all about it over supper." Xelebre took his wife by the elbow and looked around at his guests. "My dear, I must apologize for bringing so many for supper unannounced. However, Leuna has made a most marvelous suggestion."

"And I heartily second it," Merezi interrupted breezily. "If everyone will follow me upstairs, I'll show you to your rooms. There should be ample time for you to freshen up before the food arrives from the restaurant."

Jartz and Neba exchanged startled looks, but Xelebre only smiled.

"She's been reading my mind for years," he teased

in a low voice.

"I recommend ordering from Txerri, dear," Merezi had already started up the stairs, the girls on her heels.

"Perfection, my dear." Xelebre nodded to the fellows and patted his stomach. "I'll send a runner right away."

Leuna waited until they were at the top of the stairs to whisper to her grandmother, "I thought he promised to have a transmitter and receiver installed?" Physics had never been her science of choice, but she found the new—or at least, new ten years ago—skipwave discovery fascinating. To be able to talk to someone miles away just by speaking into a sound transducer and have them respond? Utterly incredible! She secretly would have *loved* to order their supper from a local restaurant via a skipwave set.

"He did," Merezi chuckled. "But they've made so many 'improvements' to it since it first came out that it simply hasn't been practical to follow through. So many new discoveries, so little time." Turning to her left, she opened two doors. The revealed rooms shared a wall, complete with fireplaces. Comfortable beds occupied the walls furthest from the fireplaces, and the rooms were decorated in subtle tones of browns and greens.

"Neba. Jartz." She smiled at them. "I hope these rooms will be comfortable."

Neba stepped inside the room to the right and lowered his pack to the floor so that it leaned against the wall just inside the door. Cheery yellow accents seemed to pop out from amongst the soothing forest colors, lightening his mood considerably.

"It probably won't be cold enough for a fire tonight," Merezi thought aloud, "but I'll have the valet check your wood boxes when he comes to attend you. Of course, if you wish to open the windows, please do so." The valet would also show them the bathing facilities. She'd smelled considerably worse in her years of hosting her husband's far-travelling guests, but it never hurt to offer to let them wash off the journey.

"The window boxes have jasmine and lemongrass in them," Leuna blurted, drawing Neba's eyes to her face. "They do a pretty good job of hiding the city smells."

"That's true." Merezi's interest in Neba climbed a notch, given her granddaughter's obvious interest in him. "We also had creosote bushes planted along the sides of the house. The evening breezes stir the leaves and send up the most refreshing scent of rain."

"I am forever in your debt." Neba was bowing before he knew he planned to and almost sighed as he straightened. He was *really* looking forward to finding out who he was and why he did what he did.

Merezi smiled pleasantly though taken quite by surprise. She knew more than a few Marroi professors, their spouses, and even an ambassador or two. None of them were given to quite such flowery turns of phrase.

Jartz watched the women turn toward the other end of the hall, then quirked an eyebrow at Neba.

"Can't wait to hear what you think you'll owe *me* at the end of this." Unable to resist the opportunity to tease Neba for his peculiar behavior just now, Jartz punched him lightly in the shoulder, then stepped into his own room.

Neba laughed at himself as he shut his own door. It felt good to step out of his boots. Padding across the hardwood floor in stockinged feet, he began exploring. Inside the tall greenwood armoire, he found a handful of suits. Most of them were either too short or too narrow in the shoulders, but the last one looked likely.

Stripping off his shirt, he turned toward the ceramic washbasin by the window. Soap waited patiently on a small shelf that jutted out from the wall above the washbasin. However, there didn't seem to be any towels. Sliding open the door to the right of the washbasin, he sucked in a breath of surprise.

A white porcelain tub, long enough for even his tall frame, gleamed from stem to stern as he opened the second folding door. It rested belly-down on a layer of absorbent sandstone, with a stonework floor peeking out around the edges. A porcelain lever above a faucet invited him to try it and though the water was tepid, it was all the encouragement he needed. Plugging the hole in the tub's floor with the stopper, he began filling it. There were firestones set in the wall around the top of the tub and by their light he discovered an entire shelf of luxurious-looking towels waiting on one end of the bathing closet.

Glass bottles of various shapes and colors winked at him while he waited for the tub to fill and he reached for one. The tiniest whiff of its contents, a heady combination of amber and spices, sent him reeling. It was so…familiar.

He sat heavily on the end of the bed, the bottle still in his hands, and let the memory wash over him.

Don't let those idiots bother you.

The speaker sounded young. As always, Neba couldn't change the memory. Couldn't look around to try to determine where he was. Fortunately, his past self had looked around before addressing the speaker. A young man, square-jawed and with shoulders just beginning to show the full promise of power in their width, looked back at him. A mop of thick black hair was plastered to his head by sweat and bruises were beginning to show on his arms and torso. The sounds of water splashing and boyish voices raised in fun could be heard through the curtains that surrounded them, but they were essentially alone.

You should have let me face them alone, Neba's past self objected bitterly. *They'll never respect me so long as I'm hiding behind someone else.*

Do you hear yourself? The other boy stepped closer, his intense gold eyes, so like Neba's, boring into Neba's heart. *When one of them scrounges up the guts to face you alone, I'll be happy to stay out of your way while you thrash them. Until then,* his hand closed in a vicelike grip on Neba's shoulder, *they'll have to face me as well as you.*

Neba almost dropped the bottle as he reached out to hug his memory. It was like having his heart ripped from his chest to come back to the present, where someone was knocking on the door.

"Sartzen!" he barked, coming to his feet.

The valet, who luckily spoke a smattering of Marroi, entered as directed.

"Good evening, sir. My name is Eldris. Madam asked me to make sure you have everything you need." Impressed that the guest had gotten as far as he had without assistance, Eldris walked briskly over to the half-full tub and turned off the water with his free hand. The man was clearly more civilized than his current bare-chested, wild-eyed appearance made him seem. "Is the temperature to your liking, sir?" He didn't even glance at the wood box or fireplace. Keeping the house prepared for unexpected guests was part of his job and he took that quite seriously.

"It will serve." Too late, it occurred to Neba that his bewildered frown at his own behavior could be misinterpreted by the servant.

Eldris nodded. "I see you found the suits." Crossing the room to the armoire, he held up the largest and shook his head. "I believe we have one downstairs that will fit you better. With your permission, I'll fetch it right up, then take your travelling clothes to be washed and mended."

Neba simultaneously thanked and dismissed the man with a single gesture. It was so reflexive that it was surreal. Staring at his face in the mirror as the door closed behind the valet, he wondered for the thousandth time who and what he was!

Chapter 9

"Come in," Leuna answered the light tap on her door. "Oh, good, I was hoping it was you," she smiled at her grandmother. Lowering her right shoulder so she could look over it, she asked, "Could you help me with this?"

Merezi smothered a chuckle and came in, closing the door behind her. "How did it happen this time?" she asked as she came over to work Leuna's long hair free of the zipper on the back of her dress. Women's fashions had changed considerably in Ibilia since they'd commissioned the gown, but the simple lines and gorgeous colors were timeless. Especially when paired with her granddaughter's healthy glow and laughing, hazel-green eyes.

"The same way it always does," Leuna laughed and almost shook her head. "I forgot to pull my hair clear first."

"You must have a lot on your mind," Merezi observed. Looking up, she met her granddaughter's gaze in the full-length mirror. "Toward the end of your stay with us, this sort of thing only happened when you had an important examination coming up." Lifting the freed hair over Leuna's shoulder, Merezi finished zipping the dress. And frowned. "You've lost weight." She was about to offer to have her maid take it in for Leuna when she remembered that the dress would soon be returned to the armoire, where it would remain until Leuna's next visit.

"I've only lost a little," Leuna countered quickly. It wasn't as though the dress hung off her or anything. "Village doctors do a lot of hands-on work, gathering their own medicinal supplies, making their own salves, and so on." Actually, the sleeves were a bit snug now that she thought about it. Moving over to the small white dressing table, she picked up the brush and sat down.

Merezi smiled and took the brush from her. "I've missed this," she admitted as she ran the brush through Leuna's luxurious, cocoa brown hair. She'd found, first with her daughter, Leuna's mother, and then with Leuna herself, that shared time at the dressing table often meant meaningful conversations. Even shared secrets.

"Mmm." Leuna sighed contentedly. "I think this is the luxury I've missed the most while in Herrixka."

"You and Sati don't brush each other's hair?" Merezi asked, surprised.

"No." Leuna started to shake her head, then changed her mind. "I keep my apprentice busy with other things," she smiled.

"A pity." Merezi parted Leuna's hair and ran the brush through it, admiring the way the hair bounced back into its natural wavy lines. "I always wished you had a sister."

Leuna reached back and took Merezi's hand, squeezing it gently. It was nobody's fault that her mother—Merezi's only child—had died at such a young age. Not even her father's, though he'd spent the first year or two after her death mourning and blaming himself. Leuna remembered her mother complaining of pain in her back and arms. Then she'd had to cancel a harvesting trip because she was nauseous and dizzy, unable to catch her breath. The next morning, she simply hadn't woken up.

"I suppose you could say I had a dozen sisters," Leuna countered lightly. "I feel as if the entire population of Herrixka is family."

"But not Sati?"

Leuna sighed. "It was my responsibility to make sure Sati was ready to pass her entrance examinations. She has younger siblings and," she lowered her eyes, a little embarrassed, "I didn't want to usurp her time with them."

"It isn't selfish to have human needs," Merezi said softly. "Friendship. Sisterhood. You wouldn't have been doing Sati an injustice by socializing with her as well as mentoring her."

"Perhaps not." Leuna didn't really want to talk about it. Before her father's death, she'd been content with her relationships with the other women in the village. It hurt a little to be left out when the other girls her age began pairing off with the local boys, none of whom had ever interested her much. But that actually made it easier for her to go off to university, so she'd accepted it and moved on. Returning to Herrixka to find them all completely involved with their husbands and children—exactly as they should be—she'd withdrawn into her roles as her father's daughter and second choice as the village doctor.

"I see we timed our arrival just right." She was still amazed that Neba's needs coincided so perfectly with her plans to bring Sati to Ibilia. Entrance examinations were held at the end of each lunar, symbolic of the accepted students moving from their dim understanding to the blazing light of their promised education and training. "Sati can take her examinations in the morning and there will be plenty of time for us to tour the city afterward.”

“If I were Sati,” Merezi declared, reaching over to pick through the assortment of hair decorations, “I would want to do things the other way around! After days of travel, I’d be too worn to think straight.”

“Sati’s the opposite. The longer she has to wait to take the examinations, the more anxious she will become to be done with it.”

“Well.” Merezi decided on a dark hair comb and set it aside. “You know her better than I do.” There was a subtle change in her tone. “Now you must tell me all about what you’ve been doing in Herrixka.”

Leuna watched her grandmother in the mirror for a moment. “You want to know about Neba, don’t you?” She winked at her grandmother’s reflection.

“If he’s what’s on your mind, then yes.” The reflection winked back, not at all abashed.

Laughing, Leuna relaxed against the chair. “It’s…complicated.”

“How did you two meet?” Merezi asked encouragingly. Might as well start at the beginning.

“He saved my life.” Leuna smoothed her skirt. “I was out in the forest and got surprised by a narrasti that was at least as long as three of me. It slithered toward me and he shot it before it could get within striking range.” Now she smoothed down the bumps that had risen on her arms at the unpleasant recollection.

“Shot it?” Merezi couldn’t help frowning a little. “With an arrow?” There were no narrasti’s in or around Ibilia, a fact for which she was ceaselessly thankful, yet she knew how hard their scales were.

"An arrow with a steel point."

"Ah." Merezi set the brush down and deftly twisted Leuna's hair into twin loose ropes that she fastened at the nape of Leuna's neck. "And now he's returning home from his adventure?"

"It's not that simple." Leuna finished the story of his manipulated memories with, "Tomorrow I'm going to check with the curator of records and locate the logura who did this to him."

"I admire your confidence." Merezi positioned a dark wooden comb in Leuna's hair, making sure to keep the orange spinel gems, which formed tiny birds, clear of stray hairs, and stepped back with a sigh. As Leuna rose, she hugged her shoulders gently, careful not to crush her skirt. "I hope it goes smoothly for you tomorrow."

Leuna bit her lip. "You know how I feel about him."

"Yes, of course. As well as how he feels about you." Merezi patted Leuna's cheek softly. "And I'm terribly proud of you both for not giving in to infatuation."

Just as Leuna opened her mouth to ask exactly how her grandmother knew that, her grandfather called from the hallway.

"Everyone who is planning to eat supper should join me downstairs in the next five minutes!"

Merezi and Leuna laughed, though for different reasons. Leuna had been gone a long time, but she could picture how her grandfather had stood and the amused quirk of his lips as he broke the 'house rules' by 'raising' his voice. Merezi, bless her, wasn't the type to be mortified by her husband's outlandish behavior. Rather, she fully intended to tease him about it at the first, and indeed, *every* private opportunity.

"Your grandfather." She raised her hands, palms up, in a gesture of surrender. "When he's hungry, there's simply no containing him." She paused just outside the door, all but staring at Neba. He looked startlingly different in formal attire. Noble, almost. Familiar, as if she'd seen him somewhere before. But surely not. It was only that she'd seen the suit before, so many times and on very different guests.

Leuna was still laughing merrily when she followed Merezi into the hall, where she saw Neba. His thick black hair was swept mercilessly to one side and the knot of his necktie was so precisely snugged up against his throat she couldn't understand how he could breathe. The soot-black suit coat he wore was embellished with gold and fire-red stitching wherever two sides met in a corner. His liquid gold eyes, always a vivid contrast to his dark skin, were impossible to ignore and she stared into them helplessly.

He stared back, though not just at her eyes. Her glossy chesnut brown hair softly framed her face, and the gems in the decorative comb twinkled like stars. This was the first time he'd seen her in a dress. The filmy material flowed around her like a pale yellow cloud, with the deeper layers of the skirt shot through with rays of red and orange as if from the setting sun. Sensible square-toed slippers poked out from under the hem of her skirt, making him smile for the first time since his memory.

"Now that we're all here," Merezi linked arms with Sati and Leuna, smiling at the men in turn. "I do believe we had better hurry down. My husband never jokes about food."

Jartz gave Neba a dirty look. The man had no business looking so at ease in his borrowed suit. Jartz slid two fingers between his shirt collar and his throat. Accustomed to comfortable, collarless shirts with no starch at all, he felt stiff and awkward in his button-down shirt. He'd had the good sense to leave the suit coat on the hanger in the armoire.

"I like a man who takes food seriously," Neba announced, and fell in behind the others.

Jartz sighed. Defeated, he also headed down the stairs. How was he supposed to eat when he could hardly swallow?

Xelebre noticed Jartz' downcast expression as soon as the man walked into the dining room. While seating Sati and complimenting her choice of the dove gray dress with elegant white piping, he made eye contact with his wife and drew her attention to Jartz. A slight shake of her head told him she didn't know what was wrong.

"Baimentzen dit?" Neba bowed to Merezi, indicating the chair she had stopped beside. Before she could answer, he swayed slightly.

Leuna looked around sharply from where her grandfather was assisting her. Taking a wild chance, she spoke to Neba in Marroi.

"Zure adimena kontrolatzen duzu." *You control your mind.* She held her breath, waiting for…whatever was going to happen next. She hoped he wouldn't have a mind fever.

He looked over at her, but his eyes were those of a stranger. Then he blinked and looked around the room, as though remembering where he was and with whom.

"Mighty kind of you to take us in like this," Jartz offered in Lurrakian, his collar forgotten. Dragging out his chair noisily, he sat and made a show of scooting close enough to the table. "Travelling always makes me hungry." In his experience, basic needs like hunger could ground a wandering mind. He'd never known anyone with mind fevers before, but he had encountered a few aging folk that suffered mental lapses.

As he responded to Jartz, Xelebre kept one eye on Neba. The fellow, upon finding his hand on the back of Merezi's chair, was seating her—with considerably less noise and spectacle than that with which Jartz had managed to comfit himself. "I know exactly what you mean," Xelebre assured Jartz, taking his own chair. "I find I'm invariably ravenous after a business trip."

Neba, still feeling a little befuddled, sat down opposite Leuna and surveyed the table. Dishes of white and brown rice were flanked by deeper dishes of thick green and brown sauces. An assortment of cooked vegetables filled a wooden tray as wide as his hand and as long as his arm. Plates piled high with cylinders of thin, fried dough were positioned strategically about the table. Two tall pitchers of pure-white milk sat within easy reach of those seated centrally or at the ends of the table.

A maid entered as he was about to look to Leuna for guidance. She was pushing a silver cart that had an upside down cone that appeared to be made of clay and a large, covered wooden dish. She served Merezi first, offering her a tender piece of flat bread from under the cone, then a ladleful of steaming spiced meat chunks from the wooden dish.

In the quiet murmuring of the next several minutes, dishes of food were passed to those who desired them, polite comments were made on how good everything looked, smelled, etc., and nobody mentioned Neba's moment. Finished with her serving, the maid parked the cart near the idle fireplace, curtsied, and departed as silently as she'd come.

"If you'll pardon my saying so, sir," Xelebre cast a glance at Neba, "your dilemma is most interesting."

Neba tore off a piece of the flat bread with unnecessary force and tried to smile. "You're pardoned." It was the least he could do for his host.

"Yes, well, what I meant was that I thought we might be able to help each other." Xelebre used his fork to load meat and sauce-soaked rice onto a piece of bread. "I'm currently conducting experiments on the inherent physical abilities of different nationalities."

"You are?" Surprised, Leuna spoke without thinking. Her grandmother's foot came to rest gently on hers and she stilled instantly.

Xelebre continued as if she hadn't spoken. "If you could spare me an hour or two tomorrow…in the morning, perhaps? To date my participants have all found additional motivation in, as they perceive it, their national pride. You would be the first to demonstrate what you can do simply because you are." He poured himself a glass of milk and casually added, "I would compensate you for your time, of course."

Neba's hand stopped halfway to his mouth. He was vaguely aware of the sauce dripping down onto the plate from the bread held precariously between his fingers. He wasn't sure if he was appalled at being offered money by Leuna's grandfather or grateful that he had a chance to accumulate funds for his trip.

"We're aware of the pressing nature of the endeavor that has brought you here, and have no wish to delay you, but I do wish you would accommodate him," Merezi said earnestly. "It would add a great deal to the value of his findings."

Merezi approved of all of her husband's benevolent endeavors, yet she had an especially soft spot for his method of aiding the underfunded university students. His usual technique was to invite them to his home a little before mealtime, 'test' them on something, and persuade them to join him for lunch or supper as well as 'compensating them for their time.' In consequence, she always had Cook prepare enough for guests—though tonight definitely would've been a stretch—and usually took over once she'd been introduced to the students. Possessed of a large, warm heart, Merezi adored mothering the neglected souls her husband brought home. And while Neba was evidently intent upon leaving as soon as he knew where he was going next, travelling was an expensive prospect.

Jartz cleared his throat. "Have you tested anyone from Herrixka yet?" he inquired cheekily. The tension eased noticeably and everyone else smiled. Even Neba.

"I haven't." Xelebre liked this man more every time he opened his mouth. "I absolutely should, however. Takes a rare sort of person to live so far from a large city for so long. Indeed." He looked back and forth between them. "I might even ask my friend, Professor Kide, to join us. He has a profound interest in the medical sciences." Privately, he was wondering if he'd stumbled onto a study idea that was actually worth pursuing.

"Professor Kide?" Leuna looked at Sati. "That is one professor I heartily recommend cultivating. He is widely renowned for his studies of the human body, knows every fact ever discovered, half of which have already been forgotten by everyone else. He'll make his entire medical library available to you if he likes you." She smiled at fond remembrances of rainy afternoons in the professor's study. The crackle of the fire, the smell of ink and old books, and an affectionate old kaleko curled up in her lap. "I suppose Betiko has died," she murmured absently.

"Yes, poor dear." Merezi shook her head sadly, knowing how many times the kaleko had comforted Leuna. "But you'll never guess what happened because of it."

Leuna waited, the corners of her lips creeping up in anticipation of a smile.

"After a handful of his acquaintances offered to replace Betiko," Merezi shrugged as if to say, 'Because you can just supplant a dear, old friend with a new one,' "he opened his back yard to kaleko's from all over the city!"

"No!" Leuna clapped her hands, excited as a child.

"I can vouch for his having done it," Xelebre inserted. "The last time I was at his home, there were a dozen milk bowls and two shallow water troughs in his backyard. And I understand that twice a week he invites his neighbors to set out meat as they choose."

Jartz frowned. "It's one thing to look after a few stray kalekos," he muttered. "But that sounds like a recipe for disaster to me. Trashcan robbers must swarm the place."

"Not in Ibilia," Merezi chuckled. "The kalekos keep guard at night and during the day, there are always at least a few students or families that spend time playing with the animals."

"Quite a few happy children have found a pet to take home there," Xelebre agreed.

Neba wondered why Leuna had never mentioned this professor to him. They'd once spoken of her working in the kitchen garden during her time at university, and how that soothed her nerves. That was when it struck him that they'd had precious little time to talk about anything. That he knew next to nothing about her. He certainly never would've guessed she came from such a well-to-do family.

"I thank you for your offer, sir," Neba said abruptly. "And I'd like to accept."

"Excellent." Xelebre glanced at the mechanical clock on the fireplace mantle. "I'll send a runner to the professor's home tonight, since it isn't late."

That led to a conversation about the transmitter and receiver set he'd never had installed, without much input from the guests at the table. Sati was mostly interested in mastering this new eating style, which consisted mainly of carrying food to the mouth with a minimum of utensils. She hated risking a stain to the dress, and that slowed her progress considerably.

Eventually, the conversation turned to more general topics that everyone was able to discuss. It was a merry company that ate until their appetites were sated, then retired to the conservatory so the servants could clear the table.

"Miss Doctor." A weary Sati touched Leuna's elbow, stopping her in the hallway outside the conservatory. "May I be excused, please?"

"Why, you darling." Merezi appeared beside them. "You can hardly keep your eyes open." Slipping an arm about Sati's waist, Merezi nodded at Leuna. City dwellers kept much later hours than their country counterparts, something she'd known but forgotten. "We sleep at all hours in this house, so let's go upstairs and get you comfortable for the night."

Sati couldn't quite be embarrassed in the face of Merezi's sympathetic smile. She did wonder, as she snuggled under her covers, what she might be missing out on. However, short of the house catching fire, she had no intention of leaving her bed until the sun came up!

Chapter 10

The next morning, Leuna rolled over in bed and looked out the window. The room was still dark, but there was just enough light coming in from outside to tell her it was time to get up. She felt deliciously young and light-hearted as she moved about her old room, getting ready for the day. Everything was as she'd left it and she was confident that this was as close as she'd ever come to revisiting her past.

Standing in front of the armoire, she reflected that it was a real pleasure after the long hike to have more than two sets of clothes to choose from. Since she wore britches daily in Herrixka, today she opted for a dress as green as the grass in the meadows. It had a lace-up back, so she would be able to disguise that she'd lost weight since it was last fitted to her. Though certain elements of the dress' design might be out of style, such as the puffed sleeves, it was modest and she loved the full skirt. It swirled out when she twirled and she was laughing as she left her bedroom to check on Sati.

"Good morning." Leuna smiled at her grandmother's maid, who answered her knock on the door to Sati's room. They'd met briefly the night before when Leuna asked her to help Sati dress in the morning. "Is Sati awake?"

"Awake and ready." Smiling, the woman stepped aside to reveal Sati. A very grown-up looking Sati!

Leuna stared, speechless. Sati's usual tight braid had been abandoned in favor of a loose chignon, so that her light brown hair, with its sun-bleached streaks, softly framed her face. The sky blue, button-down shirt she had chosen made her eyes seem even bluer than usual. Sati was pleasingly plump and the slacks she was wearing accentuated that.

"Do I look alright?" Sati's tan hands smoothed the charcoal gray slacks she had chosen and she smiled shyly. Unlike Leuna, she wore a dress nearly every day in Herrixka and was excited to try the new, city styles.

"You look…stunning." Leuna suddenly understood some of the concerns Sati's father had over sending his daughter to Ibilia. Granted, Sati would have the exact same astute advice and discreet chaperones that Leuna had been graced with. Still. Leuna couldn't help wondering if she'd ever been as naïve and adorable as Sati was right now. "You'll have to use my staff to keep the men at bay." Especially if she continued to choose slacks.

Sati darted a nervous glance at her mentor. Her parents had warned her strenuously against city men. Would she really need to defend herself?

"That's a joke." Leuna reacted instantly to the distress in Sati's eyes. "Thank you," Leuna dismissed the maid with a smile. "Come here," she directed Sati, holding out her hands.

Sati timidly put her hands in Leuna's.

"The men in Ibilia are no better or worse than you'll find anywhere on Jatorri," Leuna told her seriously. "I only have two pieces of advice on the subject. First, listen to my grandparents. They have lived in Ibilia for a very long time and know far more than either of us." When Sati nodded, Leuna took a deep breath. This next bit she'd learned by not taking her first bit of advice. "Second, be wary of men that are experts with women. If flattery rolls off their tongue with ease, it is usually because they've had a lot of practice."

Sati's gut twisted. "They sound dangerous."

"As a sweet poison," Leuna confirmed soberly. Then, because she wasn't trying to make Sati paranoid, she clarified. "A man truly interested in courting will naturally wish to spend time with you and say pleasant things. But he will also respect you enough to court you openly. He will protect both your virtue and your reputation with his own life."

Sati nodded slowly and some of the tension drained out of her. She hadn't come to Ibilia to find a husband, after all. Yet—she didn't want to still be single when she was Miss Doctor's age.

"Now." Grinning, Leuna gripped Sati's hands fiercely. "On to more important matters. Are you hungry?"

Sati laughed aloud and nodded. Giggling like children—like sisters—they darted down the stairs and into the kitchen. Dari, the cook, had a large pot of delicious germade simmering on the stove. Scrambled eggs were being stirred by her assistant while a covered metal tray sang with the spits and pops of the fat from the meat inside. Little puffs of steam escaped the meat tray through small slits on either end and the accompanying smells were enough to make their stomachs grumble about their empty state.

"Dari!" Leuna hugged the tall, thin woman who presided over the kitchen. "It's so good to see you!"

"Bless you, Miss." Dari held Leuna out for inspection and frowned. "You've lost weight!"

Leuna laughed. "Of course I have! I cook for myself most days." She tactfully omitted that some days she settled for cheese and bread rather than bothering with a full meal. "Dari, I want you to meet my apprentice, Sati. She's come to Ibilia for the medical examinations."

"Welcome, Miss Sati." Dari looked at the young woman a little enviously. No matter how hard Dari tried to put meat on her own tall frame, it simply refused to happen.

"Now, you're the best cook in all of Lurrak," Leuna looked Dari in the eyes, "but keep in mind that I can't gain all that weight back in a single meal. It wouldn't be at all healthy!"

Dari bustled about and scolded them and fed them until they were both at serious risk of popping.

"Hear that?" Leuna nudged Sati's elbow as the bell tower two streets over rang the morning in. "By now half of the city is well awake and hard at work. But because the other half wants to sleep in, they don't ring the bells until the sun's shadow strikes the sundial in the main square."

"How odd." Sati automatically scraped her plates and piled her dishes together. "In Herrixka, everyone's been up for hours."

"Welcome to Ibilia, Miss." Dari reiterated. Deftly, she intercepted Sati on her way to the sink and relieved her of the stack of dishes. She'd no wish to spoil the girl, only to help her realize that things were done differently here.

"Thank you for breakfast, Dari." Leuna's conscience nagged at her for leaving her own dirty dishes on the table as she rose. However, like Dari, she knew Sati had quite a bit of adjusting to do and wanted to set an example of what was considered 'normal' in Ibilia. "Please tell my grandmother we've gone to the university." The open examinations would be going on all day, but it would be far simpler to get started before the flood of mid-morning apprentices.

"Of course." Dari nodded, her assistants curtsied, and Leuna led Sati out through the kitchen door.

"This is where I used to come when I longed for a bit of home," Leuna confessed, walking slowly as she inhaled the scents of mint, cumin, and other herbs grown in the tiny kitchen garden so they could be gathered fresh as needed. "I'd sit in that chair," she couldn't believe it was still there, "and study or just watch the clouds float by."

Sati smiled. "I will remember."

"I'm glad." Leuna linked her arm through Sati's. "And you must write to tell me about your favorite places."

She was finding it difficult to not overlay her own experiences onto Sati. During the rest of their walk, she pointed out landmarks, told silly stories, and generally tried to keep Sati from stressing over the examinations. It wasn't until they reached the steps of the brick building where she would take them that Sati paused. A short line of apprentices and their older—sometimes much older—mentors had already formed.

"Part of the examinations will be oral." Sati ascended the first step. "Other parts written." Leuna listened quietly, nodded a few times, and let Sati recite what she knew about the examinations. By the time they reached the top of the stairs, where a small flat area was crammed with registration tables, the line had dwindled and they were able to walk right up to a table labelled in large letters MEDICINE.

"Leuna Oneko, Master of medicines and physician to Herrixka, sponsoring Sati Neska for the medical examinations." Leuna signed her name in the appropriate column, added the date beside it, and picked a bright white ribbon from amidst the other colors. Turning, she tied it around Sati's upper arm. "This ribbon lets people know you're here for the medical school," she said conversationally. "If you need directions or any help at all, just look for someone else wearing a ribbon like yours, alright?"

Sati gripped the hand Leuna offered her. "I know you can't come in with me," she tried to laugh, "so I'll say goodbye here."

"Not goodbye." Leuna put her free hand on Sati's cheek and ignored the pain radiating from the hand trapped in Sati's vicelike grip. "I'm going right over there," she nodded at a squat, gray building not far from where they stood. "I'll speak with the curator and come right back here, where I'll wait to walk back with you."

Doctors were required to keep their credentials and records up to date. The credentials were usually a simple matter of completing and returning a test packet, or publishing a useful paper once or twice a year. Only if a doctor relocated did they have to send in a notice with their new town of residence.

Sati swallowed hard, nodded once, and walked away, head held high. Leuna watched in case she turned around, but she didn't.

"Tough lettin' them go, isn't it?" queried a gruff voice from beside her.

Turning to look, Leuna found herself face to face with one of her favorite people. "Professor Belar!" Without thinking, she went up on her toes to kiss his cheek as she used to. Only it wasn't as far up as she remembered. And the muscles on one side of his face drooped a little. Silently she assessed and diagnosed her old friend as the victim of a brain attack.

"Older than you remember, eh?" He smiled, choosing to ignore the dismay he saw on her face.

"More dashing is more like it." Resting her hands lightly on his stooped shoulders, she wished she could trundle him off to Herrixka for a nice long rest. "I've always been attracted to men with silver hair."

He barked a laugh and swatted her leg lightly with his cane. "Silly child." Taking her hand in his, he tugged her along with him as he headed for the stairs. "Got an apprentice, I see."

"Yes." Leuna took the steps at his speed. "Her name is Sati."

"She's a looker," Belar grumbled. "Always hated it when I had a looker in class, 'cause that's all the fellows would do. Look at her! Instead of paying attention to what I was trying to teach them."

Leuna's lips twitched. "Sati doesn't have a lot of experience with men," she admitted. "She's staying with my grandparents, so I'm sure she'll be alright."

"Wouldn't hurt to have another set of eyes watching out for her, though, would it?" He grinned and squeezed her hand. "Glad to do it." He pointed at the hall of records with his cane and started in that direction. "That's where you're going, eh? Going to hunt up some old classmates?"

"Not exactly." Leuna tucked a stray hair behind her ear. "I'm looking for a logura."

Belar stopped abruptly. "A what?" He continued as if he hadn't asked the question. "Whatever for?" Like most doctors of his generation, he was highly suspicious of the entire field of mind manipulators.

"Why, for a patient."

"Oh." Belar blinked, his shaggy eyebrows bobbing. "Thought for a moment you might be thinking of switching disciplines."

"No, not at all." Leuna laughed, relieved to find such a simple explanation for his odd behavior. For an instant, she'd had the horrible thought that there were others like Neba, their memories taken from them and left to wander.

"Well, you're in luck. There's a reputable logura not far from here. I can take you there myself, if you like."

"I..." Leuna hesitated. She'd told most of Neba's story to her grandparents, including the mind fevers, but had purposefully not mentioned their suspected cause. It didn't feel right to give even Professor Belar full details of Neba's condition, either. "I'm looking for a specific logura. It's important that I find the right one."

"Hmm." He resumed his shambling walk toward the hall of records. "Comes highly recommended, I suppose."

"No one's recommendation could be higher than yours," she soothed his ruffled feathers. "My patient has already gone to her once," a slight variation on the accepted truth, as Neba refused to believe he'd done this voluntarily, "and I need to consult her before proceeding with any treatment."

"Long way to come for a consult," Belar grunted. With some difficulty, he opened the door for her and allowed her to precede him into the hall of records.

"It's a delicate case," she assured him.

Firestones gave off a warm light as they walked past them to the curator's office. She wasn't in, so they spoke to a junior curator, who directed them to the basement, where the older records were kept. The basement, as it turned out, was a single room filled with rows of metal filing cabinets as tall as they were. The rows stretched back and back as far as she could see! Leuna took a deep, steadying breath and sneezed because of the dust, which stirred up more dust.

"Here." Belar gave her his handkerchief. "Put that over your nose and mouth for a minute until these microscopic bits of matter settle back to where they were."

Amused at his description, she did as she was told, breathing through his handkerchief while they squinted at row labels.

"Here." Belar set his cane on top of the first filing cabinet marked 'Logura' and opened the top drawer. "What's her name?"

"I…don't know." The handkerchief muffled her voice, but did nothing to disguise her chagrin.

"You don't know her name?" Belar's eyebrows rose until they looked like a terribly unruly part of his hairline. "And she's the one you have to consult?" She nodded. "No one else will do?" She shook her head. Belar sighed. "Take a seat, then." Hauling out the top drawer, he plunked it down on the corner of the nearest table. "Going to take a while."

"How many women logura's can there be?" A sense of dread came over her as she watched him pull a second drawer from the cabinet.

"At least fifty," he snorted. "Weren't many at first," he pulled out a third drawer. "We're gettin' more of them, though."

"And how many do you suppose are still practicing?" She sank into the chair, heedless of dust streaks on her dress.

"That'll be on their paperwork." He put the fourth drawer on the table and took a seat as well. "Mind you put it all back as you find it," he warned. "The curator is not a person to rile."

"Right." Standing back up, Leuna drew the basket of firestones closer and arranged a few around the files so she could see without squinting.

"What do you know about this logura?" Belar asked, already a few files into his drawer.

"Very little." Leuna sat and pulled her drawer closer to her. "She's petite."

"And?" he prompted when she hesitated.

"And she likes bracelets?" She couldn't blame him for snorting at her. It had seemed like such an important clue at the time that Neba drew a sketch of the logura scene. That was right after a mind fever, so she hadn't pushed him for more detail when she'd seen how hard he was struggling to draw the logura. Medically, she still agreed with her decision not to push him. Practically speaking, however, it was beginning to look as though they'd never find the logura with such scant information.

The curator's filing system, at least, was straightforward. Women's files were in folders of one color and men's in another, simplifying their search substantially. That was where the good news ended, however. Each orange file had to be individually opened and reviewed.

"Deceased," Professor Belar announced, slipping a file back into place. "And the first file I've come across with a black dot after the name."

"Excellent observation." Leuna scanned her drawer hopefully, but none of the orange files had black dots. A quick peek into the third drawer showed two black dots and…something else. An orange file with three gray *x*'s after the name. It was the only one like it. "Professor," she lifted the file out. "Look at this."

He took it from her, read the name. "Jabea Burua." Frowning, he tapped the file against the table. "That name gives me a bad feeling." Opening the file, he skimmed the contents of the top sheet and nodded slowly. "I remember now. She was expelled for performing unsanctioned experiments." He looked up when Leuna shivered. "I was on the board that questioned her and made the decision," he admitted sadly. That had been his first experience with expulsion.

"Then you can tell me about it." Leuna was aware that a transcript of the board's interview and the summary of their decision was publically available—there was probably a copy in the file he was holding—but it would be so much faster to get the information from a live source. She remembered nothing of the story, perhaps because it happened well before her time at university and perhaps because she'd never been one to enjoy another's downfall. "To start, why was she expelled?"

"Because she would not be persuaded that the governing board had any right to govern her." Belar's shrug expressed his continuing confusion over that fact. "She claimed her experiments were providing useful information and asserted that was more important than the mental health of her volunteers."

Leuna nearly gasped. This was terrifying new information. And yet it was eerily reminiscent of Neba's angry question: *What kind of doctor would do this to someone?*

Chapter 11

"But she can't be the logura you're looking for." Belar frowned. "She wouldn't dare practice without the license of the medical authority."

"Why not?" Leuna asked weakly. "She had the audacity as a student to perform unsanctioned experiments. What could be simpler upon expulsion than to go somewhere remote and set herself up as a reputable logura?"

Belar's frown turned into a scowl. "You say your patient has been to her once before?"

"I…" Leuna blinked. "I'm not sure."

"Burua, Jabea," Belar read from her file. "Measured at five feet, two inches. Weight at the beginning of her last year at the university was a mere two-hundred and twenty scale stones."

"Petite," Leuna summed up quietly.

"And, if I remember correctly," Belar handed her the file, "she wore bracelets throughout her official interview. She defended herself passionately, with quite a bit of arm movement, and her bracelets made the most distracting racket." The aggravating sounds had driven him to the edge of his patience, a difficult thing to forget.

Leuna opened the file, flipped past the expulsion documents, which were right in front as she'd speculated they would be, and hunted for her original registration papers.

"Apprentice to Zentz Uduna, of the city of Nahiko."

"She wouldn't have gone home." Belar shook his head. "We sent notification of her expulsion to her mentor by special messenger."

Leuna set the file down and put her hands over her face. "I suppose that at least eliminates one of the places she could be practicing. Out of thousands."

"She's clearly not been in Herrixka, either," the professor teased. He chuckled when she glared at him through her fingers. "Let us consider." He stroked his chin. "A logura with some training and few, if any, scruples."

"It would have to be someplace where no one had ever heard of her, so probably somewhere that the newssheets aren't distributed." In Ibilia, the scandal of an expelled logura student would have been front page news. "That gives me an idea."

Belar was already nodding. "Come." He held out his hand for the file. "I think I know who can help us."

Leuna rose and picked up a drawer. "I'd like to ask the curator for a copy of this file." She slid the drawer home and reached for the next one. "Whether she declines or not, she can put the file back herself." Leuna did her best to brush off the worst of the unavoidable dust streaks on their way to the curator's office, where thankfully, she was in.

The curator did not decline, thanks mostly to Professor Belar's persuasion. After securing her promise to have the copy delivered to the home of Leuna's grandparents, Leuna and the professor hurried out to catch a bicycle carriage. The cyclist, a young, rakishly handsome man, delivered them to the front door of Ibilia's most prestigious newssheet building. Leuna paid him, including a handsome tip, and asked him to wait, which he gladly agreed to do.

"*The Record* has printed the best newssheet in Ibilia for the last two generations," Professor Belar announced as he held open the door for her. "Kaze Tari covered the interview personally." He pointed to a door marked with that name.

Noticing that he was struggling for breath and showing other signs of fatigue, Leuna led him gently but firmly over to the nearest bench.

"You'll need me to help you convince him to talk," Belar insisted as she loosened his tie and unfastened his top button.

"You're probably right," she agreed soothingly. "But we don't want him to see you like this, do we?" She also, intensely, wanted to avoid giving the professor another brain attack. "You can see right into his office from here," she pointed out. "I'll try talking to him first, and if he absolutely refuses to budge, I'll signal to you."

Belar, loathe to admit how tired he was, nodded grudgingly. "I'll come right in and pry the answers out of him if I have to."

"My hero." She smoothed a stray silver hair or two, pressed a light kiss to his forehead, and straightened. "Here goes nothing."

Kaze Tari waved her in at her first knock, though he didn't look up from the paper he was apparently proofing, judging by the red ink marks in the print. A forlorn looking kava plant in the corner was nearly hidden behind a stack of books.

"Who are you and what do you want?" he asked bluntly.

"I'm an admirer of the great Kaze Tari."

He looked up from his work, looked down, then

blinked and looked up again. Setting down his quill, he leaned back in his chair and assessed her brazenly. In an instant he took note of the out-of-date style of her green dress, which, aside from the slight dust marks, looked as if she'd only just had it made. It was an odd combination topped with hazel-green eyes and cocoa brown hair in an appealing face.

"And he's an admirer of yours, pretty lady." He pushed his work an inch or two to the side.

"Then perhaps he wouldn't mind answering a few questions about one of his more infamous stories," Leuna suggested hopefully.

He smirked and gestured to the one empty chair in his small office. "Interviewing the interviewer. I like your approach."

Leuna smiled and seated herself. "What do you remember about the expulsion of Jabea Burua?"

"The crazy logura? I remember everything about her." He sounded almost wistful. "Hasn't been a story like it since." Covering that story had done more than cement his position in the ranks of the greats. It had taken distribution of *The Record* to new heights. While that meant nothing to him at the time, in his current position he was painfully aware of circulation numbers and so forth.

His eyes suddenly narrowed and he leaned forward. "Why? Something new going on with her?"

Leuna did her best not to squirm under the intensity of his gaze. If she didn't know better, she would swear his flaring nostrils were from his scenting a new, scandalous story.

"With Burua?" She batted her lashes and tried to look puzzled. "How could that be? She's all but faded from memory."

He relaxed marginally. "That's true enough. Haven't heard her name in a score." Leaning back again, he asked casually, "So why your interest in this has-been?"

Leuna couldn't tell him that. It was too big a risk that a sketch of Neba would end up on the front page of every newssheet in Lurrak. She bit her lip. How could she possibly coax this man into telling her what he knew about Burua without betraying her true intent?

"As I said, I'm a fan of yours. Her story was fascinating…"

"Sensational!" he corrected.

She nodded and continued, "And while I was in town, I wanted to talk to you, the one and only Kaze Tari." She hoped she wasn't overdoing the adoration. "What was it like, listening to her rant?"

His eyes narrowed briefly. Odd that she'd ask about something he'd written about in great detail. Then, reminding himself that she was the prettiest thing to cross his threshold in weeks, he decided to humor her. "Gave me nightmares. Hearing her defend what she was doing, scrambling the memories of those poor souls and claiming it was all for the good." Satisfied with Leuna's answering shudder, he went on to tell about how the bracelets Burua wore had driven them all to the brink, clanking and rattling whenever she gestured, which was every time her mouth opened.

"Such a horrifying tale." Leuna's discomfort wasn't affected. The idea that anyone could be so twisted…she shuddered again. "Perhaps the most shocking part is that she was *able* to fade into obscurity."

"Too right." Kaze pointed at her. "I followed her for a solid month after she left town, then tracked her down again a few years back, hunting for a story."

Leuna's eyes widened in genuine surprise. "I never knew that!"

"Ah, well, what I found wasn't worth writing." Kaze shrugged. "She was a shipping clerk in Ilun, a tiny town just downriver from Gertuk." He stopped when she gasped. "You've heard of it?"

Leuna scrambled wildly for control. "Gertuk? Yes, of course. I've got a friend there, a fisherman."

"You're friends with a fisherman." Kaze restated her words and watched her nod. He reconsidered her clothes and admitted they were a very old-fashioned style. Still. He was tempted to question her further, but decided he might actually get more out of her by playing along.

"Anyway." He smiled as if nothing struck him as odd. "She was too boring for me to even bother interviewing again."

"How strange." Leuna smiled back. "For her to go from such destructive behavior to such normalcy." Her eyebrow quirked as a thought struck her. "Did she ever marry?"

"Nah." Kaze dismissed the idea out of hand. "Townsfolk seemed to like her alright, though." His brow creased slightly. "One thing I never could figure out," he muttered, not liking to admit it. "Her house."

"Her house?" Leuna repeated. "Was there something unusual about it?" she prompted.

"The opposite. It was a nice place. Flower beds out front, little piece of ground out back. Place even had a spare bedroom." He watched her face as she tried to figure out why all that would be worthy of note.

"You said she was a shipping clerk?" Leuna watched him nod and got the funny feeling he was enjoying the riddle more than she was. It gave her great satisfaction to watch his face fall when she observed, "The average shipping clerk in Gertuk lives on company property. No flower beds or frills."

"Exactly," he returned tersely. He hadn't expected her to catch the discrepancy so quickly, if at all. "So how can she afford to set herself up like that?"

"No one in town knew?" she asked curiously.

"I didn't say that."

"Then you know." She was disappointed. He knew what Burua was doing to earn extra money and hadn't written a story about it. Therefore, it was most likely not criminal or questionable. Must be something boring, like investing in the company or running her own goods on the side.

"I didn't say that, either." Kaze leaned forward, drawing her in for the final bit. "Nobody in town would tell."

Leuna sat up straight. *Nobody in town would tell.* Jartz had said something similar after his visit to Gertuk to see if he could learn anything about Neba. Except that the reason he'd given was that the people were all nervous because of recent actions by the city guard. Cracking down on contraband, smuggling to avoid taxes, and basically anything remotely illegal. What were the people in Ilun afraid of?

"Thank you for your time, sir." Leuna stood, smiled, and left so quickly that he didn't have a chance to protest. She was so busy collecting and updating the professor that she completely missed the arch to Kaze's eyebrows and speculative twist of his lips as he watched them leave.

"He actually knows where she is?" Belar asked as Leuna helped him into the waiting bicycle carriage.

"He knows where she was quite recently," she corrected. The sound of chimes told her what time it was and she stopped to consider. If Sati failed at her first or second examination, then Leuna had completely misjudged her readiness. On the other hand, and more importantly, in that event Sati would need her mentor badly. She instructed the cyclist accordingly and sat back to think.

"I can see the wheels turning in your mind," Professor Belar remarked. "What're you going to do now?"

"I don't know," she sighed. "I'm not the only one concerned here. I have to think of my apprentice as well as my patient."

"If I know anything about patients," Belar snorted, "it's that they're usually *im*patient."

She laughed with him at the old joke, then they both sobered.

"If she's practicing," Belar said in a low tone, one eye on the cyclist, "we need to know it."

"Yes, of course." Leuna almost sighed again. That made one more thing to consider. Which did she hope for? That Burua was the logura who'd hidden Neba's memories and could be reported for punishment? Or that the same Burua, who'd found some measure of peace in a tiny town, would be innocent and…they'd have to start hunting for the right logura all over again.

She stepped down reluctantly at the university. This was all giving her a headache.

Back at her grandparents, unbeknownst to her, her grandfather was nursing a headache of his own. He'd made the mistake of explaining his tactics to the illustrious Professor Kide, lifetime student of physiology. Kide had congratulated him so enthusiastically on his cleverness that he'd nearly tipped off Jartz and Neba as they came in from the kitchen. Thankfully, their arrival had suitably distracted the professor, who'd gone on to take several measurements, including their height and so forth.

After two straight hours, Professor Kide showed no signs of slowing down. Neba, on the other hand, was starting to sweat. Jartz noticed it first and caught Xelebre's eye.

"Professor, I hate to interrupt," Xelebre made a show of checking his pocket watch. "Unfortunately, my guests have a very important errand to run."

"Errand?" Professor Kide's wispy white hair lifted briefly off his head due to the energy of his scoff. "Nonsense. This is important research!" He was completely serious, too. This young Marroi man was a fascinating specimen.

"It's an important errand." Jartz dropped his pencil beside the mostly blank map of Jatorri and got to his feet. "Got a couple of half-wild dragons to check on."

Neba caught the balls he'd been juggling and handed them to Professor Kide. "It's been a pleasure to meet you, sir."

Hastily, he followed Jartz out the door. Once outside, the door closed firmly behind him, he took several deep breaths.

"Good idea," Jartz agreed and followed suit. "Nothin' like bein' cooped up inside to make a man's head feel like it's gonna explode." Clapping Neba on the back, Jartz struck out for the stables. He might not know all two hundred or more of Jatorri's major geographical points, but he knew how to find where he'd been. Even if it was only once.

"Feels good to stretch my legs," Neba said after they'd been walking a while.

"Yeah, well, you'll have to forgive me if I don't go inside the stables once we get there." Jartz grimaced. "I ain't real comfortable with Sparks and Presa, so thinkin' about all those other dragons together just gives me the jitters."

"I understand." Neba meant it, too. His first night at Jartz' cabin had been spent trying not to notice all of the partially disassembled trapping implements scattered across most of the raised, flat surfaces.

They paused for a dipper of water from a fancy fountain, crossed a few more streets at peril of their lives, and stopped in front of the stables.

"Y'know. Maybe I won't mind waiting for you." Jartz ran a hand over his recently shaved chin and eyed the women selling fruit from nearby carts. He was still jealous of the fact that Neba never seemed to grow facial hair, though he hadn't mentioned it.

"You're hungry already?" Neba asked, following his glance and stifling a surprised laugh. He'd never thought of Jartz as a flirt. Of course, that probably had something to do with the fact that every woman close to Jartz' age in Herrixka was happily married.

"Not particularly." Jartz grinned. "But haggling gives a man a good idea of what a woman's made of."

"Don't get lost," Neba warned, bumping Jartz' shoulder.

The main stable doors were closed, presumably to keep out some of the street noise. A much smaller, single door was located nearby and he let himself in through that. It was early in the day still and most of the younger dragons were gathered around the artificial stream, fishing and calling and wrestling. A handful of older dragons were making use of the meat troughs positioned closer to their 'caves.'

Neba chuckled as one particularly pudgy dragon, orange scales faded with age, nearly knocked over his neighbors when he tried to back away. Sensing the dragon's need, he picked up a clean bucket, filled it with water from another trough, and carried it over.

"Hello," he greeted the dragon when they were close enough to each other. "Thirsty?"

The dragon hardly bothered to look at him. It was thirsty and there was water in the bucket. Nothing else seemed to matter. Neba put out a tentative hand to stroke the dragon's neck. The dragon continued slurping down the water greedily, paying him no mind. Disappointment flooded Neba, as though he'd found the dragon was somehow a giant wind-up mechanical toy. It was more than just an extremely mild temperament. The dragon seemed to have lost its personality altogether.

"I see you found Tristea." Ordez stepped out from where he'd been watching. "He's a dull old boy, isn't he?" Fondly, Ordez reached up and scratched the dragon's shoulder.

"Dull?" Neba looked sadly at the dragon. "Is that the word for it?" It seemed much worse to him. It seemed that the dragon, nearing the end of its years of servitude to its owner, had, over time, been deprived of that unique something that made each dragon its own being.

Ordez shook his head. "No, not really. This is one of the worst parts of the job." Indicating the large, enclosed field, he said, "Most of the time, people prefer to have younger mounts. They're faster, have more endurance." A cloud outside shifted position and the sun's rays struck a handful of the dragon's spot on, its touch turning their scales into a brilliant display of color. "They're even flashier."

"Every so often, though." Ordez patted Tristea regretfully on the shoulder and lowered his hand. "We get dragons like this one. Had the life sucked out of them until they're barely more than beasts of burden."

"Who does Tristea belong to?"

"Why?" Ordez managed a saucy grin. "You goin' to buy him and give him his freedom?" His grin faded as he looked at Neba's eyes. "Listen." He took the nearly-empty bucket from Neba and began coaxing Tristea over to the actual water trough. "Tristea's got a dry place to sleep and plenty of food to eat. When it's time for his final breath, he won't die lonely." His voice rose marginally, his poorly hidden frustration with what had happened to Tristea winning out as he tried to defend the practices that were responsible.

Before Neba could respond, he heard Sparks' glad cry of greeting and knew he'd been spotted. His throat tightened painfully as Sparks and Presa left the others to gallop over to him. Perhaps there was a fate worse than death at the hands of poachers. Or at any rate, just as bad.

Chapter 12

A series of sharp raps on the front door brought Xelebre's head around from the newssheet he'd been perusing. Waving away the footman, Xelebre opened his own door. Cautiously. It might easily be Professor Kide, hoping that Neba and Jartz were back. Xelebre certainly hoped those two hadn't gotten lost.

"File for Doctor Oneko," announced a young fellow, holding out an unmarked tan envelope. He'd rather be doing almost anything else besides acting as a campus runner, but he needed the service hours. As he surrendered the file to the rather old-looking servant, he added, "And can you tell Jaurle Izan that Doctor Oneko would like to speak to him at the university, please?" He had his doubts, initially, as to whether the illustrious jaurle would bother with an ordinary medical doctor, but if she was receiving deliveries at his house that put an entirely different complexion on things.

"Consider him told." Xelebre was enormously amused by the shocked expression on the fellow's face. "Anything else?"

"N-n-no, sir." Belatedly, he noticed the small lapel pin the man was wearing, the closest thing to a uniform that jaurles wore.

"Wait a moment." Xelebre spoke as the runner started to turn away. "You might as well ride along, assuming you're headed back to the university." Clapping a hat on his head, he stepped out the door.

The student meekly followed him to the street where, to his further surprise, the jaurle placed two fingers between his lips and let out a piercing whistle that summoned a bicycle carriage promptly.

"University," Xelebre directed as he climbed in. "As close to the examination building as you can." He sat, brooding on the events of the morning, until he spotted Leuna. Her green dress stood out against the gray of the examination building. The older man sitting next to her was talking animatedly, using both hands, a marked improvement in physical ability since his brain attack.

"Here!" Xelebre barked to the cyclist. They skidded to a stop and he hopped spryly out. As was his custom, he overpaid and waved away the change.

When he was safely out of earshot, the cyclist remarked, "Strange fellow."

The student-runner, who'd leapt out of the carriage to follow the jaurle before remembering that he had no reason to do so, stuffed his hands in his pockets. "Tell me about it," he muttered. What kind of a jaurle answered his own door?!

"Grandpa!" Leuna rose in the middle of Professor Belar's sentence and hugged her grandfather. "You remember Professor Belar?"

"Ah, yes." Xelebre's polite smile widened into a real one as the name and face clicked in his brain. "Professor," he shook hands with him. "It's been too long." He made a mental note to tell his wife whom he'd seen out and about for the first time in months. They'd been quite worried ever since the professor had secluded himself to 'recover.'

"So." Xelebre seated himself on the bench right next to where they were sitting. Fortunately, the benches were at a ninety-degree angle, allowing him to comfortably see them both at the same time. "What's the emergency?"

Leuna ducked her head. "I'm sorry, Grandpa. It isn't a real emergency. I just needed to talk to you away from where we might be overheard."

Xelebre quickly deduced that she wasn't referring to the professor sitting beside her. "You've learned something about Neba," he reasoned aloud.

"We think we have, yes," she agreed. "I can't tell you the details of his situation," she felt a wave of relief wash over her when her grandfather nodded his understanding, "but at the same time, I need your advice."

"Let's start with what you can tell me," he prompted kindly.

Professor Belar cleared his throat. "Perhaps I can help." He knew Jaurle Izan personally as well as professionally and trusted him implicitly. At Izan's 'go ahead' gesture, he took a deep breath. "Many years ago, a student of logura studies was investigated after she was charged with abusing her skill. Sadly, the accusations were proven to be true and Jabea Burua was expelled."

"I may remember the case," Xelebre interrupted. "If I do, she claimed her unscrupulous experiments should be permitted to continue." He cocked his head to the side, scrounging through a faded old memory. "Something about her belief that they would benefit logura patients in the long run?"

"Never mind that she was creating patients in the process," growled Belar. He patted Leuna's knee reassuringly when he saw that she'd gone pale. "It took the best we had, but all of her victims were restored to complete mental health."

"Shall I assume the worst?" Xelebre leaned forward, his face hardening. "Has she resumed her vile work?" The only reason she'd escaped criminal charges by city authorities was that she'd been permanently banned from furthering her education or doing any kind of work even vaguely reminiscent of logura.

"We're not sure." Leuna tried to smile despite the way her stomach was knotting and twisting.

Xelebre held her gaze for a few seconds, then exhaled slowly. She hadn't broken her vow as a doctor not to disclose details of her patient's condition unnecessarily. It was simply the only thing that fit. Neba had no memories. Now Leuna was telling him about someone convicted years ago of tampering with minds.

"Do you know where she is?"

"Probably," Leuna hedged.

"You probably know where she is. And she might—or might not—be doing something illegal." Xelebre frowned. "How can I help?"

She laughed softly and twisted her hands in her skirt. "Tell me what to do."

"Look into it." He watched her blink, clearly surprised at his prompt answer. "Without an official allegation, my hands are tied. Likewise, the university's." He indicated the professor. "So if you know something, *anything* that makes you suspicious, what choice do you have but to pursue it?"

Professor Belar put his hand on hers. "With extreme caution."

"I can assign a city guardsman to accompany you," Xelebre offered after a moment's thought. As her grandfather, he wanted to keep her safe, which meant he'd like to assign an entire squad of elite soldiers just in case. As he'd expected, however, she shook her head.

"No." She looked at her hands, squeezed the professor's fingers. He'd been in the process of telling her everything he remembered about Burua when her grandfather arrived. "Thank you for your concern. But if she is active again, she'll be more cunning about it this time. Brute strength was never her first choice." She stared out across the street, thinking so hard that she barely noticed when her stomach grumbled at her for neglecting it.

Xelebre's lips twitched. Grateful for the diversion, he looked around at the food carts swarming the area. He'd walked right through them without noticing just minutes before. The apprentices stood out from the crowd, even the Lurrakians, each of whom wore clothing styles that were similar but unique to their origin cities and gawking at everything. Apprentices from other countries dressed in their colorful native costumes stood back a little from the food carts, seeming to want to watch someone else order before trying it for themselves. Several professors and volunteers, all wearing the colored arm ribbons of their discipline, had come out for a meal break as well.

"Is that Sati?" Xelebre asked. She looked different today, and it wasn't just the borrowed clothing. He tapped his coin pocket absent-mindedly, remembering how he'd fretted every time a young man came to the house for Leuna. He strongly suspected he would be just as protective of her young, lovely apprentice.

Leuna got to her feet for a better look and smiled. "Yes. And she looks positively radiant."

"That might have something to do with the chap she's standing next to," mused Belar sagely.

"Oh dear." Leuna's smile disappeared. She hadn't even noticed the man beside Sati, who was now handing her something from the hatz cart…and paying for it.

"You needn't worry, my girl," chuckled Belar. "He's a decent sort. Know him from my botany classes. Good student, good lad."

Leuna relaxed a little on that subject, only to have concern for Neba flood through her again. It was as though she were standing on a precipice, unable to see clearly how far she would fall if she took that next step. She could guess. But there were so many variables! *IF* they found Burua. *IF* she was the logura they sought. *IF* she could be persuaded to reverse what she'd done. Her heart leapt and twisted at the same time. *IF* Neba was available…

"I think we could all do with some food," Xelebre suggested, rising and taking her arm. Not that he particularly enjoyed hatz. In his experience, the thin bread used to wrap the combination of rice, vegetables, and meats always got soaked and gave way, sending food tumbling down his shirtfront. While Merezi never scolded him for eating at the food carts, he knew she—and the servants—preferred not to have worry about grease stains in his clothing.

"None for me, thanks." Belar looked a little wistfully at the carts. He'd been put on a strict diet after his attack. It ranged from bitter to tasteless, yet he couldn't argue with the results. "My man will be along shortly to take me home."

"I'm so glad you came out today, Professor. I couldn't have done this without you." Leuna dropped back to the bench beside him and kissed his drooping cheek.

"Stuff and nonsense." He gruffly waved her away, his face a pleased pink despite himself. "You got us started, y'know." He stamped his cane against the sidewalk for emphasis and was fairly certain he hadn't changed her mind on the matter.

Leuna kissed him again, then rose to rejoin her grandfather.

Xelebre extended his hand to the professor. "Good to see you again, Belar. Don't be surprised if my wife sends round an invitation to supper one night soon." He'd done a little research into brain attacks after Belar's and knew they'd have to adjust the menu. A small concession to make in exchange for the professors company, of course.

"I'd be pleased to accept." Belar shook his hand and then wrapped his fingers around the head of his cane, looking away so they couldn't see the tear they'd brought to his eye. He was old and grumpy and he knew it. At the moment, though, he was just glad to have friends who put up with him.

"Well now." Xelebre discreetly led Leuna away to give the professor a chance to collect himself before his servant arrived. "Shall we interrupt your apprentice?" he teased.

"Only for a moment." Leuna shrugged when he looked down at her, eyebrows raised in surprise. "I need to know how she's feeling."

"Pretty good, I'd say." Xelebre eyed the lanky young man beside Sati, who was laughing with her at something one of them had said. It was impossible to guess where he would be at in his studies, since students came to Ibilia when they were ready. He had a kind air about him, though. Xelebre liked the way he kept his hand lightly on Sati's elbow and watched the crowd to keep her clear of the jostling.

"I won't intrude," Leuna promised. Slipping through the crowd, she made her way over to Sati and put her hand on her arm. To her astonishment, Sati immediately threw her arms around her.

"Thank you!" Sati whisper-exclaimed. Pulling back, she kissed Leuna's cheek. "If I ever, *ever* complained about having to copy over those journal entries, I would like to formally apologize!"

Understanding tickled Leuna's funny bone and she laughed aloud. "I take it the examinations are going well?"

"Yes, so far." Sati showed her Herrixkan upbringing by deftly avoiding a definitive answer that might break her luck. She flicked a glance at her new friend and giggled.

Leuna rested her cheek lightly against Sati's. She wanted to advise Sati to go somewhere quiet to collect herself. To do something normal for her, for their life in Herrixka. However, she knew how important friends would be to Sati in the strange new city and didn't want to discourage her.

"We have an hour for lunch," Sati said, knowing that something was bothering her teacher. "We were going to walk around the campus a little, but if you think I should…"

"You were?" Leuna went with her first instinct. The rest of the campus more or less shut down for the day during entrance examinations and would be a lot more peaceful than hanging around the food carts. "Wonderful!" She beamed at the young man, who'd taken a polite step back to give them a modicum of privacy when she arrived. "Be sure you're back in good time for the rest of the testing, though."

"I'll have her back at least ten minutes early," he promised unabashedly, his tone and eyes quite serious.

Satisfied, Leuna nodded, kissed Sati's cheek, and shooed them along. She'd never felt so old in her life as she did watching them walk away, exchanging shy glances and munching on their hatz.

"Everything alright?" Xelebre asked, coming up beside her.

"Better than alright." Leuna smiled. "She thanked me for some of her study exercises."

"Excellent." Xelebre arched an eyebrow. "Now that she's taken care of, what are we in the mood for today?" He motioned towards the carts.

Leuna felt as overwhelmed as several of the wide-eyed apprentices looked. And yet her mouth watered at the memory of a particular kind of food.

"Do you see a skewer cart?" she asked.

"Hmm." Xelebre saw several that were offering fresh-cooked food, their open flames dancing on top of their metal-shielded carts. Others were devoted to raw fruit or delectable baked goods. Then... "Over there."

He pointed to a cart that was a little wider than the others. A group of students were walking away from it holding skewers lined with delicious-looking roasted meat and vegetables.

"I've tried and tried to recreate these," Leuna inhaled deeply as they got closer to the cart. "There's always something missing."

"Nothing missing at this cart!" grinned the vendor. "We have some of everything." He winked and leaned in as if to share some secret. "Provided you get here early enough!"

Leuna laughed, appreciating his sales technique.

"What can I get for you?" He'd leaned back already and now his voice boomed out, attracting the attention of others, precisely as he'd intended. He'd learned a long time ago that happy customers attracted other customers. Tapping the pots with a fresh skewer, he startled to rattle off his list of options. "Today we have fresh whitefish, rockfish, and pinkgill. There are four kinds of peppers, crisp apples, and…"

"I know what I want," Leuna interrupted. "Auroch meat, pinkgill, apple, potato, the lavender pepper, and more of the same."

"A lass that knows her own mind," grinned the vendor, skewering chunks of the desired items.

"I do believe she's been dreaming about this moment since the day she left Ibilia," Xelebre teased. "Make one of those for me, too, please."

The vendor gladly obliged, setting the completed skewers above the flames to cook. "And you, there?"

Leuna waited semi-patiently while he helped the next few customers, pleased to see him rotating their skewers as needed.

"And here they are," he announced to everyone in

earshot. "Careful now," as he handed over their skewers, "they're piping hot!"

Chuckling, Xelebre dropped a coin in the man's box and they walked away, blowing on their food to cool it.

"Quite a character, that."

"The vendors have to be." Now that she had her skewer, Leuna was desperately missing the quiet of Herrixka. "Plenty of customers let their minds be made up for them."

"And your mind?" Xelebre walked his granddaughter to the corner of a nearby building. Once they stepped around it, much of the cacophony of noise from the vendors and students was blocked out. "Is it made up?"

Leuna nibbled silently on her hot food, savoring the different flavors.

"Yes," she said at last. "I'll go with them to Ilun."

Xelebre tucked the town name away in his mind in case he should need it later. "Go with Neba and Jartz?" He nodded and tried a bite of his food. It was still too hot and he covered his partly open lips while he inhaled and exhaled through his mouth to cool it further. "They'll take good care of you."

"Do you like Neba, Grandpa?"

He coughed to hide a smile, then took another bite. "This is delicious."

"Grandpa?"

"Yes, my darling, of course we like him." He automatically included his wife in the declaration. They'd naturally discussed Leuna's unusual patient before retiring the night before. "Were you worried that we wouldn't?"

"I don't know." She leaned against him when he wrapped his arm about her shoulders. "I knew falling in love would be complicated. I guess I just never…" She held her skewer carefully so that it wouldn't stain his clothes and wished she could stay in the safety of his arms a while longer. A year, perhaps two.

He squeezed her when her words ran out. "I think we all know," he rested his cheek against her forehead, "your grandmother, myself, and yes, even you, that you're strong enough to keep making the right choices."

"Thank you, Grandpa." Leuna straightened away reluctantly and resumed nibbling on her skewer. "How did this morning go?" she asked slyly. "Were Neba and Jartz able to help with your studies?"

"Oh, it was enormously successful." He followed her lead when she headed back around the corner. "Professor Kide was terribly impressed with their dexterity and mental acuity."

"As demonstrated by?" she challenged, wondering how he would answer. Her grandmother had explained his scheme in a whispered exchange during supper and Leuna was highly amused.

"By," Xelebre hunted quickly for a suitably vague answer, "the tests." He beamed at her, highly pleased with himself for escaping the conversation without revealing his philanthropic ulterior motives, and she laughed, accepting her defeat gracefully. She could've pushed further, but one of the vendors pulled out an instrument and began playing a merry tune that set her toes to tapping. A few of the apprentices sang out for a reel and soon they were holding an impromptu dance right there. Those that didn't know the steps clapped along instead, laughing as if they had already passed their examinations.

Chapter 13

Neba pulled the door to the stables firmly shut behind him and tried to shrug off the cheerless feeling that came from watching Tristea struggle into his ground level 'cave.' Presa and Sparks had crowded around him briefly, but overall were in fine fettle. They'd danced about and teased him, showed him the stream, then taken off for a short, low-level flight that landed them amongst several other dragons roughly their age. He was grateful that Presa was young enough to adapt so easily.

Shoving his hands in his pockets, Neba's fist bumped into the silver coin Xelebre had pressed upon him before the tests started that morning. He hadn't wanted to take it without earning it, but Xelebre insisted that it was his standard practice to give partial payment at the beginning. Something about not wanting to adversely affect the outcome of the tests and paying for his time, not perceived success or failure.

Neba took the coin out and flipped it into the air. It spun several times before he caught in his palm and looked for Jartz, who had an identical coin. Which was no doubt what he was using to buy food with, assuming he'd ever gotten around to that. Neba finally spotted him on the other side of the street, engaged in conversation with a pretty redhead. They were both smiling, so Neba didn't hurry over.

He crossed the street, careful of the traffic, and wandered over to a cart that still had some cheese and fruit on it. It would be time for a real meal soon, but he wasn't ready to go back to the house just yet.

"G'day, sir," smiled the vendor, wiping his hands on a clean cloth for show. "What'll you have?"

Neba studied the cheeses, waiting for a hint from his subconscious. When he cooked, he did so instinctively. This herb or that ingredient—he almost never stopped to think about how adding them to what he was making would affect the dish. But now, nothing happened.

"Do you allow samples?" he asked, making eye contact with the vendor for the first time. The man's already ruddy face darkened and he folded his arms across his chest.

"No spongers here," the man declared. "I got to pay fer these to sell 'em, so you can pay to eat 'em."

"Spongers?" Neba repeated, grinning easily. "You'll have to forgive me. I'm new to this city and don't know what that means." That wasn't completely true. While the man's voice had been fairly calm, his body language screamed his disapproval of the idea of asking for food one didn't intend to pay for. Casually, Neba flipped his coin into the air again to let the vendor know he had money.

The vendor relaxed a little. "How big a sample?" he asked curtly. It'd been a long day in the sun and his temper might be a little short, but he needed the coin more than he needed to store the cheese in hopes of selling it tomorrow.

"The tiniest sliver," Neba assured him. "I can't decide between these two." He pointed at what was left of two cheese wheels—one white, one yellow— almost at random. When the vendor offered him the first sample on the edge of a sharp knife, Neba took it with the utmost care so as not to cut himself. Placing the paper-thin slice on his tongue, he let it sit there and dissolve. Then repeated the process with the second slice.

"How much for a wedge of that one?" he asked, pointing to the white cheese. By watching the vendor cut into the wheels, he'd been able to confirm that the yellow one was the harder of the two cheeses. The white cheese, on the other hand, had an open texture and a milder flavor that pleased him.

They haggled over the price, the vendor regaling Neba with the dramatically difficult process of making, aging, shipping, and so forth, of cheeses. To Neba's poor stomach, it seemed to be years before he was finally able to put his coin in the vendor's hand. In exchange, he received a generous wedge of cheese, plus a few even smaller coins in change. Still, he'd made eye contact with Jartz—who'd hastily turned back to the woman—and the cheese tasted good. Of course, it would taste even better with... Neba sauntered over to where a woman was starting to pack up her fruit stall. It took the rest of his coins and his best smile, but she surrendered two round, firm apples.

Content now to wait while Jartz sought his future amidst the female vendors, most of whom were also packing up for the afternoon, Neba strolled along the street, alternating bites of juicy apple and the soft, rich cheese. As he walked, his shadow went before him, the extra apple making a slight bulge in its hip pocket, too. It disappeared when he turned a corner to walk down a relatively empty side street and noticed the first closed shop he'd seen in Ibilia. Like those in Gertuk, it had a huge padlock and signs in each of its otherwise empty windows that warned in three languages of what would happen to trespassers, smugglers, etc.

He thought he saw movement from the corner of his eye and looked around. There was nobody there. Walking a few steps further in, he felt a curious sense of familiarity with his surroundings. Curious because he couldn't once remember having had that feeling, not like this. It was an ordinary street, lined with metal poles that supported head-sized firestones, whose glow only became visible as the sun went down. Except…they were glowing now. But he knew the sun was up, so how could that be? Confused, he looked up. There wasn't a cloud to be seen.

A wave of nausea swept over him and he dropped his half-eaten apple to clutch the firestone pole. When he reopened his eyes, everything had changed. It was as if all of the firestones were glowing, their light straining to reach the middle of the street as well as the buildings on the far side of the wide walkway. The only sound was that of his own breathing. Letting go of the pole, he wavered a little, then steadied himself and moved forward, hugging the side of the nearest building. He'd say he was having a mind fever, except that he knew he was wide awake. No, this was a memory!

What had he been thinking, stopping under a firestone like that? While the street was apparently deserted, he had the strangest feeling that the 'empty' buildings had eyes in every window. Bad business if he was caught there. Being spotted would probably result in his death.

Stealthily, he approached the warehouse at the end of the street, eyes and ears open for the faintest sound, the slightest movement in the shadows. Convinced he was alone, he crept closer and reached for the doorknob. But it wouldn't budge.

"Neba?" Jartz came to a corner and looked both ways before spotting his friend. "Neba, over here!" He shouted and waved, then, puzzled, headed in that direction. How could Neba not have heard him? What was Neba doing at that closed shop? On a street lined with closed shops?! Jartz started to jog, then broke into a run when Neba launched himself at the barred door.

This isn't right! Neba's mind insisted, urging him from rattling the doorknob to throwing his weight against it in a mere instant. *It should open. Must…get…inside!*

His shoulder bruised from violent contact with the door, Neba stepped back and aimed a powerful kick at the dull gray wood. Driven to a frenzy by his need to get in, Neba kicked the door again and again until the wood cracked around the lock and the door burst open.

Too late, Jartz realized his shouting was drawing attention from everyone but Neba. As the worst, most rotten of luck would have it, a duo of city guardsmen just happened to be patrolling in earshot and now came running to see what was going on. He stopped to try to ward them off while Neba shoved the mangled door out of his way and disappeared into the warehouse.

"Hey, fellas!" Jartz grinned at them, hands up and out to his side. "What's the rush?"

"You tell us," one of them challenged. His partner ran past them to deal with the trespasser. "You're the one who was shouting."

"Right."   Jartz was savvy enough not to try physically detaining them but he couldn't help grimacing as he watched the second guardsman enter the building behind Neba. "My friend there, the man you saw go inside? He's sick, ok? We've come to Ibilia with his doctor to get him some help."

"That's a new one," the guardsman snorted. "But, if your friend tells the same story when my partner brings him back, we'll make sure he gets all the help he needs."

Jartz did his best to ignore the faint sneer in the man's tone. "I doubt he'll be able to tell you anything," he muttered. "He didn't respond to me at all. He may not even be able to hear your partner!" Trying to think what to do, and wishing Leuna was there, Jartz raked his fingers through his hair and looked around. And made eye contact with a familiar looking street urchin.

"You!" Jartz pointed at the lad, who reflexively shrank back. "I don't remember your name, but maybe you remember seeing me last night at Xelebre's house?" The boy nodded warily. "Wonderful! I need his help." He pointed at the warehouse. "Tell him Neba and Jartz need his help. Hurry!"

"Eh, that lad's got wings on his feet." The guardsman grinned sardonically as the lad sprinted away. "Last we'll see of him." Grabbing Jartz by the shoulder, he spun him around and marched him towards the warehouse. It sounded like a wrecking crew was at work in there!

Itzel bounded around the corner, narrowly avoided a food cart and sprang onto the back of a moving bicycle carriage that was heading in the right direction. Thankfully, he didn't joggle it much when he landed and it kept on going. Stealing rides was dangerous and he knew the jaurle wouldn't approve, but he didn't see as how he had a choice. Barring a knot of traffic, he'd never be able to run as fast or as long as a carriage and he was in a hurry.

Inside the warehouse, the second guardsman was warily proceeding down an unlit stairwell towards the sound of pounding.

Neba, who'd found the hidden entrance to the stairwell as if there'd been an arrow pointing to it, was oblivious to the fact that anyone was present but himself. Weak firestones were embedded at intervals in the earthen walls, providing just enough illumination to see by. He backed away from piles of dragon hides that shone even in that dim light and knocked over a stack of boxes. The top box landed with a crash and split open, spilling dragon tusks and teeth out onto the floor. One unnaturally round and straight tooth rolled and rolled until it came to a stop at the base of a wall fitted with rows of shelves. He turned away before he could get a good look at what was in the bottles that lined those shelves.

The guardsman, who had followed Neba down, forgot what he was about and gaped in shock at the stacks of illicit goods. He'd helped search this warehouse immediately after shutting it down and had never thought to look for hidden doors or secret rooms.

Sick to his stomach, Neba turned to the darkest corner of the room. Images of dead and dying dragons flickered before his eyes, tormenting him further. Where had he seen those images? What had he been doing? Anger and bitter frustration welled up in him until they boiled over. Enraged, he slammed his fists against the wall. Over and over he struck the hard, packed earth, not caring when his knuckles split and began to bleed.

"Stop right there!" the guardsman cried, grabbing Neba's arm. "You're trespassing on officially barred property and…" He took a powerful right to the jaw and fell in a heap on the ground.

They've found me! Neba took a step back but there was nowhere to go. The guardsman lay still, the only other person in the room. Neba bit his lip and tasted blood. *This isn't right. This isn't how it happened!* The room spun about him and his ears filled with a roaring sound. *Happened?*

"You!" The first guardsman shoved Jartz further down the stairs and glared at Neba. "I'm taking you into custody for trespassing and assault against a city guardsman!"

Neba blinked at them, his vision still tainted by the overwhelming memory. **Another** overwhelming memory, much stronger than anything he'd experienced so far. He wobbled on his feet, and nearly fell.

"Neba!"

He heard Jartz nearly scream his name. Except it wasn't his name. His name was… He scrabbled for it in the confusion of his mind, but it was gone, vanished like a soap bubble. Sagging back against the wall, he was unable to hold back a bewildered sob.

The guardsman on the floor groaned, catching everyone's attention.

"Still alive, are you?" snapped his partner. "Then get up already and go for reinforcements."

"What?" The man rolled onto his side and lurched onto his knees. "Oh, my head!" What had the Marroi hit him with, anyway? He hadn't seen any weapons.

"I said on your feet!" bellowed his partner, making him flinch.

"What's going on here?" barked a new voice. A sergeant appeared at the head of the stairs and assessed the situation with a cold eye. He found the kneeling guardsman particularly interesting. "Ganged up on him, did you?" The guardsman by Jartz gulped and didn't dare contradict him. "Well. You'll just have to pay for that."

"Sergeant, d'you see all off this?" Jartz spoke up quickly. "My friend just found it for you—a whole smuggler's cache!"

"So." The sergeant's eyes narrowed. "You admit to being smugglers, too." He ordered one of the men behind him to call for a patrol wagon. "Good thing we were nearby."

The city's many clocks all struck the hour at the exact same moment, much to the pride of the university's engineering department. Those in the hidden room barely heard it, but halfway across town from the warehouse, Leuna and Xelebre emerged, laughing, from amongst a group of dancers. The apprentices had all filtered back inside by then, leaving several of the mentors to enjoy each other's' company and work off a little of their own nervous energy in the dance.

"Are you alright?" Leuna asked, looking around

for somewhere for them to sit.

"Probably." Xelebre really wasn't sure. His right ankle felt like he'd wrapped a burning branch around it. "That is definitely the last time I do the shuffle in these ridiculous dress shoes, however." The flat, smooth soles had helped him spin and pivot, but there was no ankle support whatsoever. He leaned on her shoulder, planning to hobble over to the bench she was pointing at. "It was fun, though."

"Jaurle!"

Xelebre's head whipped around so quickly that he almost fell over. "Itzel!" He stared at the boy, alarmed. Itzel's chest was heaving and his dirty, too-large shirt was stuck to his chest by sweat. "What's wrong? It is Ikasi? Or one of the others?"

"Easy." Leuna reached out and placed her hands on the boy's shoulders. "You're doing fine, just catch your breath." She didn't have to feel for his pulse. She could see it pounding in his neck vein. "Shall I summon a carriage?" she asked, a tingle of apprehension tickling the back of her mind. Itzel's blond head bobbed in an emphatic yes and she hurried off to do so.

"Itzel." Xelebre took his cue from Leuna, moderating his voice so that he at least sounded calm. "Are you better? Can you tell me now?"

"Your friends." Itzel wiped sweat and mucus off his upper lip with his sleeve. Why did running make his nose drip? "The men from your house," he gulped another breath. "The guard has 'em."

"The guard?" Xelebre repeated stupidly. His typically quick brain couldn't seem to process the information, the idea that Leuna's friends were picked up by the guard because… "Do you know why?" he asked, his ears pricking up at the sound of Leuna calling his name. Ignoring the pain in his ankle, he put his arm around Itzel's damp shoulders and walked towards the street where a bicycle carriage waited.

"No, sir." Itzel's lungs still burned, but his young heart was recuperating rapidly from his all-out run. He'd done fine until he'd been almost to the jaurle's house. He'd just abandoned his second stolen ride when he saw the jaurle and a skinny fellow getting into a bicycle carriage. They hadn't heard him yell, so he'd chased pell-mell after them, dodging and ducking all the traffic going the other way.

"Get in." Xelebre climbed in after Leuna and somehow tucked Itzel between himself and the door.

"Where to?" inquired the cyclist.

"Itzel?" Xelebre nodded at the boy when he hesitated.

"The Biltegi warehouse." Itzel was proud that he'd been able to read the warehouse's sign on his own.

"As fast as you can," ordered Xelebre.

They were travelling against the current of carriages flowing from the business districts to the residential areas of Ibilia, but the cyclist knew Xelebre's reputation for overpaying and threw himself into the job with a will. They had just paused at a cross street when Leuna gasped.

"Grandpa, look!"

Xelebre followed her finger and his grip on the carriage's door tightened. "Never mind the warehouse, driver. Take us straight to guard headquarters."

The driver swallowed a vile-tasting concoction of vinegar, water, and lemon juice, then did as he was told. His legs felt like lead by the time the headquarters came into view, but he wasn't disappointed. The jaurle didn't even ask after the fee, he just pressed two gold double arranos into the driver's palm and hurried off with the others.

"Sorry," the driver told a well-dressed woman advancing on his carriage. "I'm done for the day." Dismounting, he carefully stretched his legs and began wheeling his vehicle towards home.

Chapter 14

"Commandant!" The sergeant sprang to his feet as a small group walked through the door. "I was about to send for you."

"You were what?" Commandant Borrok's face was a picture of disbelief.

"We've seized a large cache of illegal goods," the sergeant explained hastily, reaching up to straighten his rumpled jacket. "And taken two prisoners that I thought you would want to interrogate personally."

"It's those prisoners that we're here about," announced Xelebre, attracting the sergeant's attention for the first time.

The sergeant frowned slightly, wondering if the jaurle was planning to interfere somehow. As for who the girl was, he had no idea. She carried herself like she was someone of import, yet he surely didn't recognize her. He darted a glance at the commandant before deciding to respond.

"One of them attacked my guardsman," he announced brusquely. "But they're both where they belong now. In the smuggler's cell."

"You put him *where*?" Commandant Borrok barked. The smugglers they'd captured so far were a rough, uneducated lot that professed to know nothing about anything, least of all smuggling. He'd become more inclined to believe their claims to ignorance the longer he had charge over them. For one thing, when bored they beat each other up for the 'fun' of it. More than a few of them had stayed overnight in the infirmary over the last few weeks.

"With the rest of the smugglers," the sergeant reiterated. "Sir," he added belatedly. The mere fact that the commandant was asking after his two newest prisoners should have given the man some idea that he'd fouled up badly, but he was still cockily waiting to be praised.

"GET HIM UP HERE NOW!" roared the commandant. He wasn't entirely convinced by Jaurle Izan, there were definitely questions to be asked. However, that could be accomplished much sooner if the prisoners were conscious!

"And Jartz," Leuna reminded timidly. She'd met Borrok socially a few times and this was a side of him she'd never seen before.

"They aren't there anymore," clarified the frightened sergeant. He *had* seen this side of Borrok and it only showed when things were about to get worse for the guardsman being roared at. One very distinct disadvantage to having an ex-military man for his commandant was that the sergeant had never succeeded in talking his way out of trouble.

"Where is he?" Borrok ground out.

"Infirmary," squeaked the sergeant. "There was an altercation in the cell and…"

Leuna didn't stay to hear anymore. Wheeling around, she nearly ran from the dingy little office that was the seat of the sergeant's erstwhile power. The doorway was only a few stairs above ground level, but everything was so drearily the same in the city guard complex that most of the buildings were marked with identifying signs. She spotted the sign for the infirmary almost immediately and hurried towards the squat, narrow building.

The infirmary windows and doors seemed oddly placed, shorter and lower to the ground than ordinary, as if the architects who designed it were from the much shorter Txiki race. Outside it was made from the same bland tan stone as every other building. When she went inside, it was open as far as she could see. A comforting antiseptic scent washed over her and she paused to let her eyes adjust to the somewhat dimmer interior lighting. Two rows of neatly made military cots were separated by an aisle wide enough to push a wheelbarrow down it.

Leuna's relief at spotting Jartz and Neba was quickly replaced by indignation.

"Stop!" she ordered, marching over to where an orderly was clumsily wrapping Neba's arm. "My apprentice could do a better job than that!"

"You can't be in here!" protested a guard.

"Tell that to the commandant," she retorted, closing the distance so rapidly that the orderly jumped out of her way. "He'll be along in a minute." She could hardly bring herself to look at Neba's badly battered face, so she concentrated on his arm. "What's wrong with this arm?" she snapped. "Do you even know?"

"It was like that when they brought him in," the orderly responded curtly. "Said he went crazy, started hitting a wall." He shoved his fingers through his hair. "I patched him up and sent him off, then they brought him back looking like this!" He gestured at Neba's face.

Leuna forced herself to look Neba in the eyes. Well. Eye. His left eye was swollen shut. A gash on his cheek was deep enough for the white cheekbone to peek out at her. They'd probably had to cut off his shirt, which was nowhere to be seen. Bruises of various shades and depths were still forming all over his exposed skin.

"I am Doctor Oneko," she told the orderly quietly. "If you'll take care of the other patient," she nodded at Jartz, who appeared to be in better physical condition than Neba, "I'll tend to this one."

"I don't think I've ever heard your family name before." Neba watched while she unwrapped what the orderly had done so far.

"Everyone in Herrixka already knows it," she shrugged. "Does this hurt?" He flinched at her touch and she lifted her finger from his forearm. "Move your fingers." He did so, slowly and with obvious difficulty. "You need more than a wrap for this arm."

"Do you know how to make a hezur potion?" She addressed the question to a nurse who was hovering nearby.

"Of course." The nurse nodded his head. "We see broken bones aplenty here."

"Please bring me a braceboard and a potion, then." Turning her attention to the rest of his injuries, she cleaned Neba's cuts and painted on a thin adhesive to glue the flap of skin back in place on his cheek. The lesser cuts she simply smeared with a healing salve.

Neba sat rigid under her fingers as she explored his ribs and injured right arm. Because of his many bruises, Leuna opted to wrap Neba's cracked ribs with a wide bandage instead of fitting him with a stiff vest. By the time she'd finished, the nurse was back.

"Thank you." Leuna took the braceboard. "Make sure he drinks all of that potion." She glanced over at Jartz and nodded her approval of the orderly's work. Then, she picked up another wide bandage. Setting Neba's right forearm on the cushioned braceboard, she made absolutely certain the forearm was correctly positioned before she wrapped it tightly.

"Wriggle your fingers," she instructed dispassionately. At some point, she'd slipped into professional mode, which was best for them both. She would be doing him a grave disservice if she became distracted by worries over adding to his pain. Given the sheer number of bruises he'd sustained, she couldn't have wrapped his ribs or arm without causing additional pain. In the long run, however, he would be much better off with properly healed bones.

Neba complied and complained at the same time. "This potion tastes like rotten musker fruit mixed with ground-up river rocks and swamp water." It made his loose teeth ache, too.

"Leave it to you to be able to describe it so perfectly," Leuna muttered under her breath. "If you wanted Dari's cooking, you should've stayed at the house," she parried aloud. "Now. You have a handful of broken bones and they can either take several weeks to heal or three days. It's your choice, but I recommend that you drink every potion that I prescribe for you." She fastened the bandage she'd finished wrapping around his forearm. "I'll have to immobilize your hand, too. You broke a few bones in it as well as your arm when you punched the wall." She made eye contact with the nurse, who quickly fetched an adjustable glove.

A little angry, Neba took a deep breath and downed the rest of the potion. Grimacing, he tossed the mug to the astonished nurse and waved him away. His stomach twisted this way and that, then seemed to accept the potion as an established fact.

"Leuna." It wasn't easy for him to speak with his swollen lips, but he had to. "I've been to Ibilia before." She didn't look up from where she was working on his hand. "It's a true memory. It led me straight to a smuggler's cache." Slowly, she lifted her head. "I mean it. I know I've been to that room before. I think I was attacked there."

She frowned thoughtfully. Ibilia and Herrixka were nine days apart, unless someone had hired a horse to take him out and dump Neba in the middle of nowhere. She couldn't begin to guess why anyone would do that. Anyway, there was a more important 'why' she needed the answer to.

"Is that why you wanted to hurt yourself?"

"I'm a poacher." Unable to bear seeing condemnation in her eyes, he looked away. "I don't deserve to live."

"Don't be ridiculous." Leuna eased the glove onto his hand and adjusted it. She made a mental note to check it again later after the swelling had gone down. "I've seen you with Sparks and Presa. I've seen you hunt and you take no pleasure in your kills. You're no more a poacher than I am."

He stared at her, wishing he had the use of both eyes. "But the evidence!" he objected.

"I've seen plenty of evidence." She used a swab to apply a little numbing salve to his lower lip, which stuck out from his face like a mountain ledge.

"You're kind and gentle and strong. You're not very interested in money, either. What's left that would motivate a poacher?"

Neba had no answer for that. He wasn't greedy, he'd proven that at Xelebre's that morning. Barbarism and sadism were abhorrent to him, as Leuna observed. It didn't make sense. None of it did.

"What am I then?" he mumbled. Irritated that he'd now lost all control over his lower lip, he went cross-eyed trying to glare at the painfully tumescent tissue.

"I'd say you're too smart to be a smuggler," Commandant Borrok remarked dryly. He'd entered the infirmary some time ago but nobody'd noticed. Xelebre, in fact, had already come and gone by the time Borrok reached the infirmary. They'd entered together with nobody seeming the wiser. Now Xelebre sat next to the other stranger, watching and listening, two things that made him such an unusual jaurle.

Borrok looked closely at the man Leuna was attending. "Have we met?"

Leuna stopped moving. Stopped breathing. Her eyes met Neba's and they stared at each other for a handful of heartbeats. Neither of them had expected that.

"It's possible," Neba hazarded at last. "I don't remember the last time I was in Ibilia, though."

"Hmm." Borrok had an excellent memory for names and faces. He had to, it was part of his job. "And I don't leave Ibilia often."

The men stared at each other, trying fervently to remember why or when they'd met, or even what they'd been doing at the time. Borrok couldn't imagine. He was no diplomat. He hardly had any contact with the Marroi, or any other foreigner for that matter, so long as they honored the laws of Lurrak. In the end, he was left to wonder what it was about the man that filled him with such urgency to act. It fairly consumed him, yet he had no clue what he was supposed to do.

Neba leaned back, dejected. He'd been sure that he'd finally found someone who knew him.

"Commandant." Leuna wasn't ready to give up yet. "Could we speak to you privately, please?"

With a gesture, Borrok dismissed all those under his command. When it was just the five of them, he took advantage of one of the empty cots to sit down so they would all be at the same eye level.

Leuna nodded to Neba, then went to wash her hands.

"I don't know who I am," Neba told the commandant. "In truth, I have no conscious memory of anything before about five weeks ago." He wasn't sure what else to say. How much he dared say. His and Leuna's desire to believe in his innocence didn't make it a fact. If he told the commandant how he turned up at Herrixka, wounded and alone, anything might happen.

"Extraordinary," murmured Borrok. "Why, it's been almost exactly that long since your government petitioned mine to help them stop the trafficking of dragon poacher's goods."

"Perhaps there's some connection." Xelebre frowned thoughtfully. It was a bit of a leap of logic, but not impossible. "I was present when the petition was made." As a city official, he'd not been consulted, but curiosity had compelled him to attend the meeting just the same. "This wasn't publically stated and, as a rule, I have a deep distrust of spectacular rumors…" He paused, fidgeted with the button on his cuff, then continued, "The whispers said that the Marroi were planning to use infiltrators."

"Of course." Borrok slapped his knee in delight. "There is some use in capturing all of the poached goods that we can, yet at that point the damage to the dragon population is already done. Nor can we hope to capture all of the goods." He spread his hands, palms up in a helpless motion. "There are far too many places to cross too many borders and, yes, too many buyers. So, the poachers will go right on with their vile slaughter—possibly redoubling their efforts—with the intent of overwhelming their enemies. And some of it always gets through."

"Fight harder, not smarter," smirked Jartz. "On the other hand," he started to lean forward, winced, and sat back. The smuggler who'd hit him in the side was small, but powerful. "If the poachers' camp is discovered, then they can be rounded up and maybe stopped altogether."

"Precisely." Borrok shared a hunter's grin with the man.

"The shame of it," Leuna rehung the towel she'd dried her hands on, "is that there's a market for these items." Coming back to sit by Neba, she shook her head. "A tooth or a claw or a hide here and there could easily be harvested from dragons that die of natural causes. In many cases it's the erroneous belief that these and other items possess some strange power that creates the demand." Spreading some items out on the bed by Neba's legs, she began preparing cold packs.

"You're right." Neba spoke without thinking and kept on doing so. "There are even hunting seasons for the velour and sapid dragons, who are desired for their soft skin and delectable meat. There is no reason for such wanton killing."

"Clearly," Borrok cocked an impressed eyebrow at Neba, "you were an infiltrator. I don't understand how you lost your memories, though."

More in response to the questioning look on her grandfather's face, Leuna half-explained, "During my first examination of him, I found evidence of a head wound."

"Ah." Borrok nodded gravely. "I'm sorry your memories haven't yet returned." Privately, he suspected they never would. He'd come to Ibilia from the Lurrakian military and had some idea of what a head wound could do to one's mind. "You said earlier that you went straight to the hidden cache. Do you remember anything else that might be useful?" If the answer satisfied him, he saw no reason to detain the jaurle's guests further.

Neba shook his head slowly. "So far all that I have remembered are specific events. It's as though I'm reliving them. I can change nothing from how it occurred, not even such a small thing as looking in a different direction." Leuna slipped her hand inside his then and he wondered why he hadn't shared all of his memories with her. Told her that he'd seen his father, then his friend or cousin or someone… He chuckled inwardly, admitting that the second memory was perhaps less useful than the first.

Leuna swallowed hard. He'd never discussed the subject so calmly, which only made her worry more about telling him what she'd discovered about Burua.

"I must thank you, Commandant," Xelebre spoke up, sensing that the time had come, "for your quick action on our behalf."

Borrok studied Neba a moment longer, then smiled. "I'm glad to have been of service. And embarrassed at what happened to your guests while they were in custody. You are, naturally, free to go." He looked at Jartz, then Neba. "You may be interested to know that the sergeant is in the process of removing his stripes and replacing them with corporal's chevrons." To Leuna he said, "Please, keep the braceboard and glove as long as you need. It's the least I can offer."

"Thank you." She smiled sincerely at him.

Bowing to Leuna and nodding to the others, the commandant took his leave. Scowling, he called a corporal over and assigned her to organize another search of all the seized buildings, with a special emphasis on hunting for hidden doors.

Leuna gasped in horror as she came face to face with a small clock on one of the counters.

"Sati!" Her hands flew to her mouth. "She'll be done by now and looking for me." She felt a hand on her arm and found her grandpa at her side. "I promised I'd be there, Grandpa. I told her she'd come out from her examinations and we'd walk back to the house together!"

"It's alright," Xelebre soothed, bending to pick up

the pair of scissors that she'd dropped. Thankfully, they hadn't landed on her foot. He had enough invalids to worry about as it was. "It's alright. I got here right behind you and heard what you said to the orderly about your apprentice." He lifted a jug of water and some small lehorra cloth sacks from the infirmary supplies to go with the blue bottle she hadn't dropped. "So I went straight out to where Itzel was waiting and sent him to tell Merezi. I'm perfectly confident that when Sati came out of her examinations, Merezi was waiting for her."

"That poor boy." Leuna's mind switched fears with dizzying speed. "I know Itzel's young and probably used to running, but Grandpa, I don't think it's good for him to…"

"I gave him carriage fare," Xelebre interrupted gently. "And Merezi probably sent him back to the kitchen to sample whatever Dari is preparing for our supper." He patted her shoulder with his free hand while she leaned against his chest, breathing deeply. "You've had quite a day, my dear. Let's mix up these cold packs for our friends and go home, shall we?"

Leuna nodded wearily. With a little help from Jartz and her grandfather, they mixed the water with the contents of the blue bottle and poured it into the waterproof lehorra bags. Xelebre helped Jartz arrange his against his side while Leuna tucked a few into Neba's bandages and gave him the last for his eye.

Chapter 15

"Thank you, Dari." Leuna smiled at the cook, who was pouring boiling water over the crushed loaren leaves in two insulated mugs.

"Is this to help them sleep?" asked Sati.

"Yes. And to reduce inflammation." Leuna smiled apologetically. "I'm so sorry this happened, Sati. This was your big day." Looking around the kitchen, where she'd finally been drug away and seated before a plate of leftovers, she sighed. "This isn't a very good way to celebrate your acceptance into the medical program."

Sati surprised her by laughing. "It's the perfect way!" Holding up the mugs, she tipped her head towards the door that led into the house. "I'm going to go help injured people. What else would I be doing?"

Leuna smiled wearily and leaned against the back of the chair while Sati cheerfully went upstairs. After passing her own examinations, Leuna had celebrated by going out with her father and grandparents for a sumptuous meal. A lighthearted week of collecting necessary medical supplies and attending fittings with her grandmother had followed.

"I like her," Xelebre observed from where he'd slipped into the kitchen unnoticed.

"Grandpa." Leuna's face lit up in her first real smile in hours. "When did you come in?" She touched his arm as he came over to sit beside her.

"Just a bit ago." Xelebre set down two more mugs—he'd signaled Dari for the leftover boiling water—and pushed one towards her. "It's your favorite."

Leuna took a sip of the sweetened gerezi steep and sighed.

"Delicious. Thank you, Grandpa."

He patted her hand and took a sip of his own, bitter steep. Ground arnasa root tasted like the dirt it had been dug up from, but it eased his breathing throughout the bruma. With the days and nights getting colder, he supposed he might as well get a head start.

"How's Neba doing?" he asked solicitously.

She lifted a shoulder. "Cautiously hopeful. He wants to believe that he's innocent of poaching." Her lips twisted in a rueful smile. "I think in a way, though, that he's afraid to."

"Afraid that it will be proven otherwise?" He watched her nod. "I find that hard to believe."

"So do I." Leuna twisted her mug this way and that. "Maybe he'd be more confident if he knew for certain that infiltrators had been used." She had to keep telling herself not to be irritated with him for struggling to believe in a rumor. If she was honest, her own desire to believe stemmed primarily from her feelings for Neba.

"I don't know anything about that, I'm afraid." Xelebre tapped his thumb against the handle of his mug before offering, "But I can tell you that the petition was presented by Prince Zain himself."

She cocked an eyebrow at him. "I don't remember as much about my Marroi studies as I should. Is that their crown prince?"

"Yes, for now." Xelebre chuckled at her confused expression. "He's the cousin of King Txoko." His eyes flicked down and to the right, an indication of sadness. "The king is currently in seclusion for the Marroi mourning period. His wife died less than a year ago."

"Oh, how terrible."

"He's expected to remarry, of course, and produce an heir."

"Ah." Leuna nodded in understanding. Prince Zain was simply next in the family line. Once the king had children, Zain would be supplanted as heir. "They must have needed our cooperation badly to send him."

"I believe they have petitioned all of their bordering neighbors," Xelebre offered as a slight correction to her thinking. "Marroi is the natural habitat of all of Jatorri dragons. While some few species have been successfully domesticated, or even more rarely, transplanted to other countries, Marroi takes her responsibility to the dragon family very seriously."

Leuna finished her steep and smiled. "I'm glad. Most of what I knew about dragons before I met Sparks and Presa was that they're dangerous."

"It is very often the case," Xelebre observed wisely, "that the more we learn about the unknown, the less frightening it becomes."

"Thank you, Grandpa." Rising, Leuna kissed him lightly on the cheek.

Before going upstairs, she washed out her mug and set it to dry on the rack. Her hand was on her doorknob when she hesitated. Even with the soothing steep, she would find it hard to sleep with all that was on her mind. The only solution for that was to talk with Neba, whom she hoped was already asleep. And, if he wasn't, telling him about Burua would only ensure that they both lay awake till dawn. Sighing, she opened her own door.

"Neba!" Shocked, she pulled back. The last thing she'd expected to find was him sitting by her window box. Thank goodness the sleeping fashions for men were roughly the same throughout Ibilia. The only real difference was that material of his sleep pants and shirt would be a little softer than his day clothes.

"Sorry. I didn't mean to startle you." Sheepishly, he set the small carving he'd been rolling through his fingers back on the windowsill where he found it. "I couldn't sleep."

She pinched the bridge of her nose between two fingers and massaged it lightly. "So you came here."

"To wait for you. I didn't realize how long you'd be."

"Why didn't you wait in your own room?" She folded her arms across her chest.

"I…didn't want to miss you."

"Mhmm. You were afraid you'd fall asleep."

"Maybe." He winked unrepentantly. "You learned something today. About the logura."

Looking over at the wall that separated her room from Sati's, Leuna shook her head. "We can't talk here. Come on." She held out her hand. "But if you fall asleep on the couch downstairs, I'm leaving you there until morning," she whisper-threatened as they moved out into the hall.

"Fair enough."

Leuna went ahead to clear the excess cushions off the couch and so she didn't have to watch Neba wincing his way down the stairs.

"Thanks." He eased himself down onto the couch, his face drawn and damp.

"Here." She removed his slippers and helped him lie down on his back.

"No, don't," he objected when she opened the back of her grandfather's easy chair and reached for one of the neatly folded covers that were stored there. "If I get too comfortable, I won't be able to stay awake."

"Night is for sleeping, silly." She relented and closed the chair again. Drawing a lighter chair over by the couch, she sat down and used a handkerchief from her dress pocket to blot his forehead. "I can't believe you're still awake, actually."

"I drank the whole potion." He held out his hands as if to ward off the suspicious look she was giving him. "And I feel much better."

"I'll have to make yours stronger tomorrow night," she decided.

"So, we'll still be here tomorrow?" he asked, dropping his hands to the couch.

"You're stubborn enough to make the trip as you are," she folded her hands in her lap to keep from smoothing an errant black lock of his hair, "but I really should stay and show Sati around town a little. Help her find the best deals for the materials she'll need for her classes."

"That's what your father did, isn't it?" His heart was beating erratically, but his breathing had slowed, so his ribs felt much better.

"Yes." She smiled fondly. "We had such fun."

"I'm glad that you have that memory."

"Yes., well" She ducked her head, feeling more than a little guilty for going on about her memories while Neba's were still hidden. "You were right. I did learn something about a logura," she held up her hands now as he tried to sit up, "who may have had something to do with your memories."

"*May* have had?" He lay back, fighting to control his breathing as additional pinches of pain attacked him.

"I know I told you that there wouldn't be many women in the field of logura." She bit her lip. "I hope you didn't bring any muskers along with you."

"What? Um, there are some at the stables. I guess they import them for the dragons, but I have no idea what that has to do with anything that we're discussing."

"I promised to eat a raw musker if there were more than three women practicing logura," she reminded him, making a face. Musker fruit had its uses, she couldn't deny it. Eating a raw musker, however, would most likely make her pucker for a week!

He laughed, then clutched at his ribs. "Don't make me laugh," he wheezed.

"Alright, alright." She mopped his face again, her touch feather-light on his bruises.

"How many of them do we have to track down?" he asked, closing his eyes.

"Oh." Leuna sat back and he inhaled deeply. That was odd, but she shrugged it off. "Well, we found one name that seemed very likely…"

"We?" he interrupted.

She nodded and continued, "So we stopped researching the others and focused on her."

"And the rest of that 'we' is…?"

"Professor Belar, an old friend of mine." She forced herself to stop speaking before she started explaining that he was truly an older man and just a friend.

He waited for her to go on, then cleared his throat. "You must've had a good reason for selecting this woman."

"Yessss." She was still reluctant to tell him the rest. "Luckily, we were able to track her to a nearby town as recently as two years ago. We'll have to go by way of Auzo, but since Ilun is downriver, we should reach it in just two days."

Neba absorbed the information. So close and yet so far. He also noted the way Leuna was twisting the handkerchief in her lap. Something deep within him admired how artfully she'd ignored his implied question.

"You should stay here, then," he suggested. "Jartz and I can…"

"No!" Leuna sat bolt upright, then sagged back against the chair. "I mean…"

"I heard what you said." He cocked an eyebrow at her. "Why so vehemently?"

She closed her eyes and took a deep breath. "Because the woman, Jabea Burua, was expelled from the university for unethical logura experiments."

His mind leapt back to the conversation she'd already referenced. Leuna had not only promised to eat a raw musker if she was wrong about the number of women practicing, she'd insisted that the doctor of logura who'd manipulated his mind must have had some plans to restore his memories. Because, by her own declaration, Leuna couldn't bear to believe otherwise.

Reaching out, he took her cold hand in his warm one and kissed it gently. "She's no doctor, Leuna. Your faith in others like yourself is well-founded." Her fingers tightened around his.

"Professor Belar and my grandfather both agree that I have a professional obligation to investigate her activities." She turned her free hand palm up. "And personally, I would feel better if you waited for me. It isn't enough to find her, you know. No matter what you tried—persuasion, coercion, bribery," she shook her head, "you could never trust what she said."

"She might agree to help, then turn on us." Neba blew out a breath. "I hadn't thought of that."

"Then you'll wait?" Their eyes met and she felt suddenly bashful, as though she'd asked him to accompany her to a social event and was waiting for his response.

"Of course." He smiled and considered the hand he was still holding. "I'd like you to be there when I get my memories back." He watched her turn an adorable shade of pink and knew she understood what he couldn't say. Yet.

"Excellent choice, young fellow," Xelebre said from where he'd been standing in the doorway, listening. "Now. It's quite late." He offered Neba his hand and pretended not to notice that Leuna had only just tugged hers free. "I suggest we all get to bed and try to sleep. Alright?"

Neba gripped Xelebre's hand firmly and did as much to pull himself into a seated position as Xelebre.

"Excellent," he paused to breathe, the pinching pains having started up again, "idea." Once he'd regained his feet, he offered them as much of a bow as he could manage, then started up the stairs without waiting for them to join him.

Leuna repositioned the chair she'd been sitting in and slipped her arm about her grandfather's waist. Given the rate Neba was hauling himself up the stairs, there was no hurry.

"I came off a horse when I was younger," Xelebre mused aloud, listening to the occasional creak in the stairs and tracking Neba's slow but steady progress. "Managed to roll out of the way of his hooves, but my friends said I bounced at least once when I hit the ground."

"Grandpa!" Leuna stared up at him, wide-eyed. "I never knew that!"

"It was many years ago," he chuckled. "I remember the bruised and cracked ribs as if it was yesterday, though."

Leuna saw the way his head was cocked, realized that he was counting Neba's steps, and went up on her toes to kiss his cheek.

"Leuna." Xelebre gently stopped her from going up the stairs, even though they could both hear Neba walking across the floor upstairs. "I meant what I told you earlier, that your grandma and I like him."

"But you're worried," she finished when he hesitated, "that I'll get hurt."

"I see you've already thought of that." Xelebre smoothed her hair and kissed her forehead. "Good girl."

Where Leuna hadn't expected to be able to sleep, it hardly seemed a moment after closing her eyes that someone was rapping politely on her door. Luckily for them, they'd brought breakfast. Sati joined her in time to help with her hair, and then they were off! The day was a whirlwind of shops and laughter with Sati, who'd been given a list of supplies to acquire for her classes.

"No, this one will last longer." and "I think they meant to get the raw materiel." Such conversations punctuated their day until, exhausted, they hired a carriage to transport the last of their acquisitions to the house.

"Could we walk to the restaurant?" Sati asked before Leuna could hail another carriage. "I mean, I know we've been walking all day, but…"

Leuna smiled, needing no further explanation. Linking her arm through Sati's, she set off at a stroll. The sun had already retreated behind the taller buildings and the carts were congregating around the firestone poles.

"Where do firestones come from?" Sati asked.

"Argia across the sea." Leuna dug into her memory of a history class. "A long time ago, they were plentiful and inexpensive. They found entire cave systems glowing with them and it was as simple as digging them out of the walls in their various sizes and shapes. Then they became harder to find."

"Is that why we don't have any in Herrixka?' Sati ventured.

"Yes, basically." Leuna turned a corner and paused to appreciate the row of stately buildings laid out before them. The view was gentled by the softer beams from the firestones. "Ibilia was built before my grandfather was born and firestones are in every building."

"They're so beautiful," Sati sighed.

Leuna slowed her pace to match Sati's. It was on the tip of her tongue to apologize again for planning to leave in the morning when she realized that was why Sati wanted to walk. She was prolonging their time together. They'd spent so much time together over the years, Leuna could understand that the prospect of it ending might be daunting.

"The other students say that the professors here are very stern. And some are supposed to be boring."

Leuna laughed. "Yes, there's always one or two that think their job is merely to stand at the front of the class and drone on."

"I'm glad you didn't do that."

Leuna patted Sati's arm. "I had a good mentor, too." The restaurant came into sight and Sati's steps faltered. "It'll be rough at first," Leuna said honestly. "New food, new faces, even a new bed and schedule. Hold onto why you're here. That will get you through the bad days."

Sati hugged her. "Thank you."

Chapter 16

The next morning, Neba took a deep breath—it felt so good to be able to do that again!—and gave himself the once-over in the mirror. When he first arrived in Herrixka, Leuna had graciously offered him some of the things originally purchased for her father. The practice was to have them tailored by a local seamstress, but there hadn't been a need after her father died, so the long sleeves were still long enough to reach Neba's wrists. Collarless and the color of yellow smoke, it was bland, which should help him blend in. The closer they got to the source of his troubles, the more likely that they would encounter trouble.

Neba bent to pick up his pack. Pinning it between his body and the wall, he waited for the pangs in his ribs to ease before swinging it into position on his back. He wouldn't have admitted it, but he was glad that the next two days would consist mostly of sitting in the railway car and riding on the boat to Ilun.

"Still mad about the potions?" Leuna laughingly teased from halfway down the stairs. "I'd have been fitting you with a vest instead of approving you for travel if you hadn't taken them."

"Don't go patting yourself on the back," Jartz snorted from the foot of the stairs. "You'll sprain something. Besides, it was Dari who brought them to us yesterday. Repeatedly."

"Ah, now I know why you took them so faithfully." Leuna grinned. Dari wasn't above using her food for manipulation. She could either tempt or threaten with it, so it was a doubly effective tactic. Leuna knew that first hand from her years in the house.

Merezi smiled at their nonsense and kissed Leuna's cheek. "I wish you could stay longer," she murmured. She'd hoped for at least a week with her granddaughter. Xelebre hadn't explained much, but Merezi at least understood that Leuna's early departure was unavoidable.

"I'll try to come again in uda," Leuna promised. "After the river thaws."

"We look forward to it." Xelebre hugged her as best as he could with her pack in the way.

"Thank you for your hospitality." Neba kissed Merezi's hand and shook Xelebre's.

"Yes, Ma'am." Jartz dipped his head. "You've got a comfortable home." Much to his surprise, she lit up at his praise.

"Jartz, I think that's the nicest thing anyone has ever said to me." Impulsively, Merezi kissed his cheek, too.

"Yes. I…um," Jartz floundered.

"We have to go." Leuna came to his rescue. "The railway won't wait for us." She'd said goodbye to Sati upstairs, so now she twirled her staff like an overgrown baton and they headed gaily off.

"You're sure we have to take the dragons with us?"

Leuna almost groaned at Jartz' question. They'd gone over it at supper the night before and again after getting back from the restaurant.

"Positive," Neba answered, his lips twitching slightly.

"Go ahead and laugh," growled Jartz. "I can't help wishing we didn't have them tagging along."

"But they're not tame," Leuna reminded him gently as she flagged down a larger carriage with two bicyclists. "They're just attached to us, even you." She winked to let him know she was teasing. "They wouldn't do well if we tried to leave them at the stables without us for that long."

"That's an understatement." Neba's smile turned into a frown as he climbed into the carriage behind Leuna. "This is an unusual situation. Typically, dragons are either raised as part of an established, domesticated kabi or thoroughly trained to the point that their wild instincts are dulled, making them dependent and cooperative. Sparks and Presa are somewhere in the middle. They still hunt for themselves and have barely received any training at all, but choose, so far, to remain with us."

"Perhaps you should train them," suggested Leuna, leaning back from giving directions to the cyclists. "At the moment, Jartz' description of them as 'tagging along' is quite apt. You know they could be useful."

"Yes." Neba closed his eyes and tried not to wince every time a carriage wheel hit an uneven edge in the street. "Anything like that, though… I'd rather wait until after this trip to start anything long-term."

Leuna opened her mouth to respond and a gasp came out instead.

"Leuna?" Jartz was suddenly on the edge of the back seat, his hand on her arm. "What's wrong?"

She passed a shaking hand over her eyes and whispered something.

"Speak up, girl," Jartz ordered, unable to hear her over the street noise.

Her eyes flew open and she turned so that her knee was touching Neba's.

"I thought I saw the man from the forest." She put her hand over her mouth now as guilt and relief began mixing with revulsion in her stomach.

"Easy," Neba soothed, taking her free hand in his. He waited for her to look at him, then asked, "What man from the forest?"

"The m-m-man," she stuttered, "who wanted to eat breakfast with us."

Jartz growled something that wasn't fit for polite company and twisted around to look behind him.

"How did you know it was him?" Neba asked, his eyes never leaving her wan face. He had to lean forward to catch her reply.

"I'll never forget his eyes." She closed hers again for a moment, then opened them to escape the sight of him. "He also had a semi-fresh acid burn on his face."

"Did he see you?" The wind from the front had blown enough of her words back to Jartz for him be absolutely certain she'd seen what she said. Between the rapid movement of the carriage and the erratic nature of the foot traffic, he hadn't seen anything useful.

"Yes." Seen her and *stared* at her.

Neba slid over and wrapped his arm about her shoulders, pulling her closer until there wasn't any space between them.

"We're leaving town," he reminded her. "This carriage could have come from any of a hundred places and be going a thousand others. You don't have to worry about him."

She rested her head against Neba's chest and tried not to think. She'd already set him out of her mind once using the logic that she'd never, *ever* see that brute again. How was she going to do it again? If he found them there, in Ibilia, a city of thousands, then mightn't he somehow find her in Herrixka?

Neba felt her trembling and almost pulled her into his lap so he could get his other arm around her.

"Should we wait?" offered one of the cyclists. They'd arrived at the dragon stables and been waiting patiently, but none of the passengers showed the least inclination towards leaving.

"Yeah, wait." Jartz eyed his two friends and clambered out of the back, leaving his pack on the seat. "I'll just be a minute."

The purse on his belt hung heavy with Xelebre's coin, a ridiculous amount given how little time they'd put into the tests, but neither he nor Neba had been able to dissuade him. He used some of it to settle with the stables, then rejoined the others.

"Here." Jartz plunked a bucket of smelly dragon treats onto the seat beside Neba. "Courtesy of Ordez."

The big doors rumbled open and Sparks leapt out, delighted to see Leuna again. Presa hung back, hissing at the passersby, who wisely moved to the other sidewalk as soon as they saw her.

"Presa." Leuna straightened a little, distracted from her fear by Presa's. "Come here, girl."

"The railway station," Neba told the cyclists. "I

don't care about the route so long as it's along the most deserted streets you know."

The cyclists consulted briefly, nodded, and stood on their pedals to get the carriage moving again.

"Presa. Sparks." Leuna wiped at a tear that had escaped and kept calling them. The growing distance as the carriage moved away, plus Sparks' coaxing, prompted Presa to exit the stables as well and begin following.

"Steady," Neba told the cyclists. "We're not in a hurry." Presa chose that moment to get distracted by a cart full of savory meats. Neba whistled and held up a dragon treat.

"I hope we have enough of these." Leuna tossed one to Sparks, who'd screeched jealously when Presa snapped hers out of the air.

"I hope your arms hold out," chortled Jartz, glad to see the color coming back into Leuna's face. He let them continue entertaining the dragons at the railway office while he bought their tickets.

"I suppose they'll still follow us?" Leuna asked, wanting reassurance.

"This is the only railway they've ever seen," Neba pointed out. "And there are fish at the other end of it."

They were still laughing when they piled onto the railway car, which was thankfully less than half full. Once they'd started, and were certain the dragons were following—more or less, since it was impossible to keep track of them as they darted and wheeled through the sky—Neba lay his chair out almost flat and fell asleep.

This trip was considerably quieter than their last.

None of the other passengers produced weapons and demanded their purses only to be foiled by an undercover railway agent. No, the other passengers talked quietly amongst themselves or slept, like Neba, until they reached the halfway point.

"Going to stretch your legs?" Jartz asked, eyeing the armed guards that kept the little outpost safe. He could've been worried by the fact that the military, which was notoriously stingy where civilian enterprise was concerned, had been prevailed upon to provide guards. Instead, he chose to take comfort that the guards he saw would be replacing the guards he hadn't seen so far. A cunning hunter himself, he knew that an ambush was only as good as one's hiding place.

"For a minute." Leuna knew the hostlers could change out the horses much more quickly than they did, but they understood that their passengers needed a break in the nearly day-long trip. Neba didn't even stir as she rose.

While exiting the car, she noted a few of the passengers collecting their things and wondered if the rumors were true, that a small town was being built a short distance from the outpost. Perhaps that was the real reason for the military presence at the outpost. To keep an eye on those headed towards the new town. Without watching directly, she saw that the soldiers had stopped a group of young men and were inspecting their luggage.

She cringed when everyone turned to look at her as Sparks and Presa landed near her with cries of welcome. The hostlers glared at her while they worked to settle the horses, just like on their last trip through.

So much for fading into obscurity, she thought as she passed out the last of the dragon treats and rubbed their necks in turn.

"Are those your dragons?" asked one boy, his eyes as large as saucers.

"Not exactly." She smiled at him. Maybe she hadn't been as compromised as she thought. During the forest attack, the dragons hadn't had time to respond. Becoming 'the woman with dragons' might actually help preserve her anonymity.

Sparks extended his neck towards the boy, sniffing curiously.

"I think he likes you," Leuna guessed. Sparks sneezed suddenly, which upset Presa, who squawked at them and rattled her scales. Leuna laughed and the boy tentatively laughed with her.

"She's not so bad," Leuna reassured him. "She just doesn't have a lot of experience with people."

"Are you a poker?"

Surprised, Leuna looked around to see whom the small, high-pitched voice belonged to.

"Not a poker," the boy corrected in a superior tone, looking down at the tousled blond head that was now peeking out from behind him. "A *poacher*. And she isn't."

"How'd ya know?" the little girl questioned, sticking her fingers in her mouth.

The boy sighed with all the long-suffering of a persecuted older sibling.

"Poachers kill dragons, dimwit. These are still alive."

The little girl kicked him with her bare foot but he didn't condescend to notice.

"Say." He turned back to Leuna. "How'd you get those dragons?"

"Why do you ask?" Leuna forced her stiff lips to smile. Where had these ragged but innocent-looking children heard of dragon poachers?

"Eh." The boy shrugged. "My grandpap promised to get me something if I was real good this trip."

"I don't know where you can buy dragons." Leuna hoped that would be the end of it. And it almost was.

"Got a hide already." The boy gave her a saucy grin, as if he fully expected her to approve. "Missing a few scales, but I don't care."

A bell rang. Once. Twice. The signal that the car was getting ready to leave. She suddenly hated the idea of letting either dragon out of her sight. Absolutely ignorant of how to kill a dragon, fear of their demise rose as a lump in her throat.

"Excuse me." She gave Sparks a final squeeze. "Be careful," she whispered. The dragons followed her to the car, crying a little when she climbed aboard.

Taking her seat, she gestured to the dragons, something she'd seen Neba do once. They screeched at each other briefly, then lifted off. She watched them, circling low, until the car began rolling forward. At that point, the dragons rose high into the sky and she lost them among the clouds.

An hour or two later, when Neba finally stirred and sat up, Leuna related her encounter with the children.

"Can't figure how a boy like that," Jartz had actually seen the two scamps, "got a hold of a dragon hide. One of the guards told me they're worth a small fortune. Supposed to make the wearer invisible or all powerful or something." He waved his hand vaguely.

"Not if they're damaged." Neba picked up a water skin and took a long pull. "It could have been buried or dumped in the woods anywhere along the route."

"That's a relief." Leuna opened the bag of nibbles Dari had packed for them. "I hated to think of those children being raised to such a brutal tradition."

"Tradition?" Neba repeated curiously.

She shrugged. "A child's first teacher is their parents. Whether the tradition they learn is to take their shoes off at the door or to twist the world to their advantage, the learning process is basically the same."

A somber silence settled over them. For the rest of the ride, they devoted their attention to eating and thinking, saying little.

"Do you think we'll have as much trouble booking passage in Auzo?" Neba asked as the car began to slow.

"It shouldn't be a problem." Leuna checked to make sure she wouldn't be leaving anything on the seats. "Afaria, from the Bonny Breeze, has four brothers and they all make their living on the water."

They went straight to the inn from the railway station, where they were able to book passage in a matter of minutes.

"Sit yourselves down," Afaria invited. "The *Wind Skimmer* won't be ready for another hour. Plenty of time for me to bring you hot stew and biscuits."

"Thank you." Leuna accepted before Neba could decline. When he frowned at her, she looked pointedly at his left hand, which held the ash stone he'd taken from his belt pouch. "Things are already moving too quickly," she told him quietly, letting Jartz lead off in following Afaria. "We will all benefit from a hot meal and a little normalcy." `

Jartz saw the dismay on Neba's face and hooted. His own, minor injuries were already healed, so he didn't have to take more potions and didn't mind reminding Neba of it.

"Don't worry." Jartz rapped the table with his knuckles since he couldn't slap Neba on the shoulder. "I'm sure the aftertaste won't linger throughout the *entire* meal."

Leuna rolled her eyes and asked Afaria for a clean mug and hot water. While she'd been out with Sati the day before, she'd discreetly ordered a few pre-made mixes from one of the apothecaries. It stung her pride a little to do it that way, but it was easier to carry and dispense the mixes than to try carting along the equipment she'd need to combine raw ingredients and so forth.

"Drink it." She set the prepared mug in front of Neba. "Then let this dissolve on your tongue." She handed him a thin, flat tablet.

"What's that?" Jartz asked, craning his neck to get a better look.

"That's geza extract mixed with pekt powder and allowed to dry. It will help cleanse the taste of the potion."

"Hmmmph." Jartz glared at her. "And where was that when I was taking your potions?" He abruptly sat up straighter and pointed an accusing finger at her. "Where was that when you made me take the birilak potion?"

Leuna stared at him in disbelief. "That was five winters ago during the rash outbreak!"

"And I can still taste it!" Jartz face contorted until it was barely recognizable.

"It saved your life," she countered indignantly.

"For which I'm grateful." He held up his hands, palms forward. "I just would have liked to have, oh, a dozen of those little tablets!"

Leuna threw up her hands. "I didn't have any."

"Are they expensive?" Jartz felt a little foolish when he caught others glancing their way.

"No, not particularly." Leuna had also noticed that they were attracting attention. "I'll keep some in stock from now on, alright?"

"It'll have to do," Jartz agreed grudgingly.

He brightened when a hand set a bowl of thick, steaming stew on the table in front of him. A platter piled high with golden rolls was placed in the center of the table, followed by small jars of honey and saucers with soft butter. His grievance temporarily forgotten, Jartz rubbed his hands together and dug in.

Leuna indulged herself in a juvenile eye roll, then picked up her own spoon. Neba's lips twitched, but he said nothing. The stew was good enough that they all had seconds. Jartz in particular enjoyed the rolls, smearing them with butter before dipping them into the honey in the jar he'd appropriated for his personal use.

Afaria brought damp towels to wipe their sticky

fingers on, then wished them well as she followed them to the door.

"Happy now?" Leuna asked Jartz, who was still licking his lips as he boarded the *Skimmer*.

"As a kaleko curled up on a sunny windowsill." Jartz nudged her with his elbow to let her know he wasn't really still mad about the potion.

Chapter 17

"I can't believe we're here," Neba murmured, leaning on the *Skimmer*'s rail. Unlike the *Morning Song*, the *Skimmer* was able to travel at night and Ilun was now barely visible in the dim morning light. Through the morning fog that drifted over the town from the river, he could see small, dingy buildings haphazardly strewn across a lazily cleared bit of wilderness. There were even tree stumps in the middle of the dirt roads, with the rut pattern showing that the townspeople preferred going around them to removing them.

"Mind your footing as you exit," warned Ainak, the *Skimmer*'s captain. "The dock's a shoddy bit of workmanship and has many a loose board." He hesitated, then offered, "I'll send a couple of the lads with you, if you like."

Leuna heard the implicit warning and gripped her staff a little more tightly. She hadn't expected Ilun to be that rough.

"Thanks." Jartz shook his head. "We don't want trouble."

"Trouble is the one thing you're sure to find in Ilun." Ainak folded his arms across his chest. "We'll wait for you."

"We don't know how long we'll be," objected Leuna. She'd already paid him, and anyway, money wasn't a worry for her. But supposing they decided to remain a few days?

Ainak's weathered face softened as he looked down at her. "We'll wait," he repeated. Afaria would ban him from her kitchen if he let anything happen to her favorite customer.

"Then we'll leave our packs. And our dragons." Neba set aside his bow as well and gestured to where Presa and Sparks were still snoozing beside the vessel. They'd entertained themselves at the river during supper the night before and played some odd game of touch-and-go during the first half of the journey, darting about on the water like fowl. When Neba and the others woke in the morning, they'd found the two dragons clinging to the *Skimmer* by their tails, drifting and drowsing.

Ainak chuckled. "Hope they like fish for breakfast." He'd heard from Marroi customers at his sister's inn that dragons favored fish, so on a whim he'd ordered his men to drop their nets shortly before Ilun came into view. It wasn't a good haul even by their standards and they weren't professional fishermen. But it should serve to keep the dragons happy, which seemed like a good idea to him.

"It's their favorite," smiled Leuna, relieved. She'd been so focused on finding Burua that she'd forgotten about the dragons.

Neba offered the captain his hand. They exchanged a firm grip, almost as if they were sealing a bargain, and Neba stepped onto the gangplank. Weaponless, for he'd left his staff behind, too.

"Town's not up yet," observed Jartz softly. They had a crude map of the town drawn by the captain, but if the businesses were still closed, how were they going to find this Burua person?

"Look." Leuna pointed. One house stood out from the rest. The board colors were mismatched, but the grass was evenly cut and the lawn in front of the house was flat and tree stump free.

"Kaze Tari, the newssheet interviewer, said the house where she lived had flower beds out front with a little piece of ground out back." She gestured at the town in general. "It's also the only house that I can see which is large enough for a spare bedroom."

"Smoke from the chimney," Jartz observed. "Whoever lives there is already up and doing."

"Wait." Leuna held up her hand when the others started to move forward. "Let me talk to her first. Alone."

"Not a chance," snorted Jartz. "She's as likely to manipulate your mind as offer a hot tisane."

"I need to talk to her before she sees Neba," Leuna insisted, frowning.

"Alright." Jartz took her by the arm. "We'll go in together. Can't get us both at the same time."

Neba opened his mouth to argue that it was *his* memories they were there to retrieve. Then his eyes narrowed and he glanced towards the back of the house. *Why not?*

Leuna looked over her shoulder to make sure Neba wasn't following and…he was gone? But where?

"Jartz, I don't see Neba." Warily, she changed her grip on her staff, but no attack came from the shifting, foggy shadows.

"Good." Jartz rapped on the door. "Then neither will whoever it is that lives here."

A cool breeze rattled a loose shutter somewhere and trailed its fingers across Leuna's cheek, making her shiver involuntarily. A moment ago the town had seemed simply lazy. Now she felt rather like a prey animal who'd just come face to face with the patiently waiting predator.

A tiny window in the door slid back with a clack of wood on wood and Leuna jumped.

"Who're you?" asked a voice so cold it brought goosebumps to Leuna's arms.

"Nob'dy important," Jartz returned just as coldly. "Heard tell we could find a…" He paused, grimaced, and continued, "Find help here."

"What kind of help?" snapped the voice.

"The kind we could talk to without a door bein' between us." Jartz let anger color his tone. Jingling his money purse he added slyly, "Was we told wrong?"

The window clicked shut without warning. Jartz scowled at the door and considered kicking it. Leuna was just opening her mouth to ask what he'd been thinking when they heard the scrape of a bolt being slid back.

"Come in," invited the voice. "And bolt that door behind you. I'll make a hot steep. You'll need it after your night boat ride."

Leuna and Jartz exchanged wary looks. They could hear the sound of someone walking away, someone who walked heavily and with a limp.

Jartz' hand shot out and blocked Leuna's way. Where there was one enemy, there might be two. Loosing his belt knife its sheath, Jartz entered the house first. It was dark inside, except for the room directly ahead. Finding nobody hiding in the shadows or behind the door, Jartz beckoned for Leuna to join him.

"Don't lower the handle," Jartz muttered as Leuna closed the door. "Might need a fast exit."

Leuna swallowed, but did as he instructed, leaving the bolt handle sticking out at shoulder height instead of nestled down between the metal braces.

A woman stood before a small hearth, working the wood with a poker and tongs. "Draw a kettle, dearie," she instructed, motioning vaguely towards a sink and the kettle sitting on the counter beside it. "A little mullein, I think, to keep away the cough." Leaving the fire, she walked over to a collection of jars and selected one.

"Thank you." Leuna had stolen a glance or two as the woman walked and decided that something must be wrong with her left leg or, more likely, her left ankle. Filling the kettle, she carried it over to the fire. The heat felt good as she hung the kettle from the metal arm and pushed it in over the flames, as its blackened bottom testified it had often done.

"Sit yourselves down," invited the woman, who was in the process of lifting down three mugs.

"Thank you," Leuna repeated. "But before you go to any more trouble, I need to know if you are Jabea Burua."

One of the mugs crashed to the counter, rolled, and was stopped by its handle before it could lurch onto the floor. The woman spun to face them, giving them their first good look at her. Leuna stifled a gasp. Jabea was Marroi!

"Who are you?" she bit out.

"There's no need for that," Jartz growled a warning, pointing at where her right hand was feeling its way towards a handful of sharp knives. "We're not here to hurt ya."

"You *are* Jabea Burua." Leuna stepped between them, drawing the woman's eyes to her face. If it had been written on the woman's face in large, block letters it couldn't have been any more obvious. "Aren't you."

The woman's shoulders sagged and she nodded.

"Come," Leuna invited, patting the chair beside her. "Sit down. I'll finish preparing the steep."

Sniffling and wiping at her eyes, the woman shuffled over and collapsed into the chair. For the first time, Leuna noticed the grey hairs in the woman's untidy brown braid.

"Don't weep." Jartz mustered as kind a tone as he could manage given how little he really knew about her. "We've not come to do you any harm."

She managed a teary laugh. "Yet harm you've done, just by saying that name. I was run out of two towns before I found Ilun and I've lived quiet here."

"You mean the people here don't know who you are?" asked Leuna, confused. That didn't match what Kaze had said at all.

"Eh, they know." Jabea shrugged. "An' they don't care. Iff'n I don't bother them, they don't bother me." The fire crackled and snapped at them, angry at being contained by the stone walls of the hearth. "Howsomever, havin' strangers come poking their noses in private affairs, claimin' to be hunting me? I reckon that counts as a bother." She couldn't help the fear that crept into her tone. If she were forced to leave here, would she even have the strength to start over again in some hostile new town?

"Sounds lonely," Jartz said after a minute.

"And what do you care?" Her guard was back up and Jabea was prepared for battle. "What evil d'you think you can buy from me?"

Leuna shook her head at Jartz when their eyes met. Picking up the prepared mugs, she came over by the fire. Jartz drew up a second chair for her, then found another one in the next room for himself.

"My name is Leuna Oneko," she began. "Master of medicines."

Jabea rubbed her palms on the legs of her britches. "So it's from Ibilia that you've come," she deduced aloud. "Can't they leave me be? It's been an age since I was a student on trial!"

"I'm here first and foremost because I have a patient who has suffered the loss of his memory."

"His?" Jabea leaned forward, her sad eyes suddenly gleaming with interest. "Not him?" she jerked her chin in Jartz' direction.

"Why...no, he..." Leuna stumbled over her words, but Jabea had heard all she needed.

"At last!" she exclaimed, rubbing her hands together. "I'd given up hope, but he's come back at last. Survived their plottin' to do him in and dump him off, good lad that he is," she chortled. "Where is he?" When they stared at her, dumbfounded, she demanded, "You've surely not left him off somewhere, thinking to bring me to him? Ha." She shook her head forcefully. "Too old to travel. Too old to live this close to the wet and wind of a river, but got no choice about that. Travelling, that I can choose and I choose not to."

Speechless, Leuna scrambled to figure out what had just happened. She'd expected evasion, outright lies even. It had never occurred to her that Jabea might outright admit she'd been practicing, let alone insist on seeing Neba. What was going on?!

A board creaked and they all looked up as Neba stepped out of the shadows. He'd slipped in the back door, undeterred by the bar mechanism.

"It is you." Jabea wiped uselessly at the tears streaming down her face. "I've been so worried!" Coming to her feet, she plunged towards him.

Jartz sprang to a standing position, reaching for his knife, and froze, stupefied. The strange woman had wrapped her arms around Neba and was sobbing into his chest.

"Couldn't bear it," Jabea whimpered. "No more harm. No more." She shook her head vigorously, smearing her tears on Neba's shirtfront. "I swore it."

Neba practically carried her back to her chair and eased her into it. He didn't bother trying to explain the rush of protective feeling for the woman now that he'd seen her, he simply acted on it.

"Shhh," he whispered, wiping away her tears with his fingers. "Ezagutzen dut zure bihotza da eskubidea." Jabea caught Neba's hand and pressed his palm against her damp cheek.

Jartz leaned closer to Leuna. "What'd he say?"

"That he knows her heart is right."

"He must know somethin' we don't." Jartz scratched his chin. "I'm real confused."

"Can you tell us what happened?" Leuna asked Jabea. "He doesn't remember."

Jabea frowned. Taking Neba's face between her hands, she tilted his head back and examined his eyes.

"When I met him, I did the same thing." Leuna met Jabea's gaze without flinching. "He had a small lump on the back of his head, but his eyes were clear."

"That's bad." Jabea released Neba and sat back, a thoughtful expression on her face. Ignoring the kettle, which began to whistle as she got to her feet a second time, she said, "I'll tell you everything. Come." Snatching a thick shawl from a peg by the door, Jabea wrapped it around her shoulders.

Leuna got up as well, automatically pulled the kettle away from the heat.

"Quietly," warned Jabea as she led them to her back door. "If they discover us, we're all dead." And with that, she slipped out into the rapidly lightening world.

They all scurried across a patch of open ground and into the woods. Leuna tripped on a vine and landed on her outstretched hands in the damp grass. Grumbling, she waved Jartz away and got up on her own. An indistinct form began to take shape in the trees ahead, the shack discernible primarily because it blocked the view of trees further on.

As they got closer, a door became visible in the near wall. Jabea entered first, producing a small but bright firestone from somewhere on her person. Constructed of gray grisa wood, the building had a plain dirt floor and just enough room for them all to squeeze in with the stacks of boxes. Jartz grunted in pain as he cracked his shin on a table leg and shoved two rickety chairs out of his way.

Neba clutched at his head and leaned against Jabea, who muttered something in a soothing tone of voice.

"What is it?" Leuna remembered too late that they were being stealthy and lowered her voice before asking, "What's wrong with him?"

"It's complicated." Jabea seated Neba in one of the chairs and faced Leuna. The firestone in her hand blazed so fiercely that it washed all of the color out of her face, making her look eerily like a character straight out of a scary children's tale. "We don't have time for this, but I need you to trust me."

"Then tell us everything," Jartz said from where he had his foot up on a box, nursing his bruised shin.

"As I said, we don't have time. And some of it would only interfere with his restoration." Jabea frowned, thinking furiously. "We had to come here because this is where I worked with him the first time."

"Why him?" Leuna asked abruptly. She needed to be sure Jabea was telling the truth about not using her logura skills.

"Because he got caught." Jabea scowled and spat on one of the boxes. "Those are dragon goods. Hides, teeth, claws, even preserved organs for the extremely superstitious in distant countries. This one," she pointed at Neba, "was investigating another storehouse in Ibilia and they captured him. Brought him here by dragonflight so I could question him." Gently, she stroked Neba's hair.

"That's when you used the mind manipulation," Leuna probed. A piece of her died with each of Neba's whimpers, but she told herself she had to ask. Her grandfather and the university board would need to know, to understand.

"Yes, to save his life." Jabea smirked at the skeptical look on Leuna's face. "He wisely refused to tell them who he was. I could have gotten the answer for them, but I already knew."

"You recognized him." His shin forgotten, Jartz stared at Jabea.

"I knew him," she agreed. Dipping her free hand into a pocket of her shawl, she lifted out a small sack and emptied it onto the table in front of Neba. Three painted ash stones rolled onto the table. Neba snatched them up and held them close. "I hid his most dangerous secrets in these ash stones."

"And replaced them with the story that he was Jerl Karruan, a Dragon Soldier!" That piece clicked into place in Leuna's mind.

Jabea nodded, pleased they believed her. "He was supposed to be released to me after the shipment went out. I would have restored his memories then, except..." She shrugged eloquently. "It did not go as planned."

"Because, like any good soldier, he tried to escape," Jartz guessed.

"By the time I found out what had happened," Jabea heaved a sigh, "he was gone. They planned to kill him and leave his body, but when they returned injured, I allowed myself to hope. I would've come for him, but where to go? And how?" She shook her head.

A dozen new questions formed in Leuna's mind. Why had *all* of Neba's knowledge of the Marroi nation been dangerous? How had Jabea come to work for the smugglers and poachers? And many more. Tucking the questions away for later, she decided the most important thing was that Jabea hadn't acted with malice.

"They dropped him a few days walk from Herrixka." Leuna put her hand lightly on Jabea's shoulder. "And now it is time to restore his memories."

"Yes." Jabea set the firestone on the table. "There must be no distractions, or it will not work." She looked from Leuna to Jartz, holding their gaze until they nodded meekly. Satisfied, Jabea motioned for Jartz to get her a chair. Seating herself across from Neba, she began emitting a soft, droning sound.

One, two, three. Again. *One, two, three.* Neba hadn't been able to think or do anything else but assure himself that they were all there. *Gray. Blue. Red.* He stirred the stones with his finger, preparing to count them again. Then he heard a sound. His memory of the first logura was still hazy, yet he knew that sound. Slowly, he looked up.

As soon as his eyes locked on hers, Jabea stopped droning. "Choose a stone," she instructed him, her voice void of intonation.

Without hesitation, Neba picked up the blue stone. It felt heavy, so heavy that he could barely lift it. He knew it contained an important memory.

Jabea held out a palm-sized block of heavy granite. "Smash the stone to release your memories."

Neba set the stone on the table, took the granite block, and brought it down on the stone. For good measure, he worked over the ash stone until only dust was left. Several silent seconds passed while he stared at the dust. Doors were opening in his mind and light was flooding in. And sadness. He blinked.

"Nire."

Leuna jerked as if she'd been stung. *That* was the memory he'd chosen to retrieve first? 'Nire' was a woman's name and one of the few words Leuna had picked out of his fevered babbling. Ever since then, the fear that she'd fallen in love with a married man had intensified.

Chapter 18

Slowly he began noticing his surroundings. The cramped room smelled of damp earth and wood. It was strangely familiar. Looking up from the stone dust on the table, he made eye contact with Jabea. And smiled.

"I remember." His smile faded. "My wife died. Terrible accident." He exhaled a slow, shuddering breath.

"Choose a stone," Jabea instructed again. She felt smug, but she didn't let it affect her tone.

"I…" He hesitated. "There's something I have to do first." Slowly, he uncurled his dark fingers from around the granite block, revealing indents in his skin from where he'd gripped the corners. "It's important."

Looking to his left, he saw a tan, wiry man leaning against the wall. A coarse off-white shirt hung off his narrow shoulders and was bunched around his waist by a thick leather belt. A money purse hung from the belt on one side and a long, heavy hunting knife from the other.

"Are you a poacher?" he asked.

The man's jaw dropped open and hung there. Then he straightened away from the wall and said indignantly, "You know durn well that I'm not! I'm your friend. Same as her!" He pointed across the room.

Following the direction of the impolite gesture, he saw a woman. Her eyes were wide with what looked like concern. *For him?* he guessed. *Why? Jabea was helping him.*

He rose and crossed the room to her. She looked *so* familiar! Taking a lock of her hair between his fingers, he let it slip through them, marveling at its softness. Tiny brown dots—freckles?—were scattered across her tan face, making her hazel-green eyes seem all the more vivid. Running the tips of his fingers down her cheek, he reached the point of her chin, tipped it up, and pressed his lips to hers.

Emotions assailed Leuna as he lifted his head and looked down at her, a puzzled expression on his handsome face. Nire—his *wife*—was dead. She was at once sorry for his loss and weak with relief and guilty for feeling relieved… It was a lot for her to take in.

His eyes flicked to hers, then dropped to her lips again. Her heart began singing like a Slarian bard at an uda festival, rejoicing in warmth and new growth as the seasons changed.

"I…don't even know your name," she whispered. Her breath caught in her lungs when he put both hands on her waist and drew her still closer to him. This time, she released her staff and came up to meet him halfway. Eyes closed, she breathed him in. Arms around his neck, she held on for dear life as feelings swept through and over her. It was like drinking a cup of rich, hot cocoa after a cold walk, warming her from the inside-out. And it was *so much more.*

He rested his forehead against hers, their breath intermingling. She was so beautiful. So strong and warm. Her answer to his kiss made him want more, yet he had to draw back because…

"I don't know your name, either." He stroked her

cheek and watched her enticing lips curve up in a lazy smile.

"Very funny," she murmured, shoving her hip against his.

"He's telling the truth," Jabea affirmed from where she'd been watching, bemused. "As his memories and identity are restored, they will assert themselves over the memories he has made since my first meeting with him."

"What?" Leuna stared at her, shocked. Then she looked up at Neba…who wasn't Neba. The eyes looking into hers were still gorgeous. But when he'd tried to kiss her before, there had been such intensity of purpose in those eyes, such promise. It was the closest she'd ever come to seeing her future.

"How long until his memories merge?" she asked hopefully.

"That is difficult to say." Jabea pursed her lips, then shook her head. "I am sorry. If I had realized you were in love, I might have been able to save that memory for him."

Leuna's stomach turned into a block of ice and her suddenly leaden arms slid from around his neck. She pushed against his chest when he tried to draw her close again.

"Go." Leuna nodded at the table. "We both need to know who you are."

"It is possible…" Jabea lifted a shoulder. "If we delay between each memory, a day or so, his past and present may knit together more smoothly." Then she cautioned, "But he must learn who he is again, soon. He is needed."

Leuna looked up and met his eyes.

"I know you would be worth the wait," he said firmly.

"Make up your mind fast," Jartz hissed. When they started kissing, he'd bolted for the door, only to stop stock still when he heard footsteps in the grass outside.

"If they are coming, you must retrieve your memories," Jabea blurted. "Now!"

Leuna pushed him towards the chair and put his hand on the granite block. It wasn't until a tear landed in the dust of the first ash stone that she realized she was crying.

"You know my voice," Jabea intoned. It was dangerous to continue after so many interruptions, but she saw no alternative. Those who were coming wouldn't believe the same lie twice. "Reclaim your memories!" She slid the red stone before him.

He hesitated. His love's hand—he knew not what else to call her—rested on his own. He would lose her if he smashed this stone. Yet he was needed. But by whom? He couldn't imagine their faces or their voices or the color of their eyes...

His face hardened. Just as he began to lift his hand, his love's tightened around it and began lifting as well. She, too, knew he had to do this. *He was needed.* Together, they brought the granite block down on the ash stone, obliterating it in a single move.

King Txoko turned with a roar as the door burst in. The man beside it was flung to the side by the force of its opening, where he struck a wall and stayed, dazed. Seizing the chair he'd been sitting in,

Txoko lifted into the air and hurled it over Jabea's head at the smugglers who foolishly tried to rush the tiny room.

A staff rested against a stack of boxes and he lunged for it. It wasn't his, it was too short, but it would serve. Striking and stabbing with the staff, he drove the poachers back out into the open, where he cracked their skulls and ribs until none were left standing.

"This way!" called Jabea, beckoning for him to follow her into the forest.

"Wait!"

Txoko whirled towards the man's voice, staff at the ready.

"Easy!" Jartz leapt back, both hands up and away from his body. "Friend, remember?"

"He does not," Jabea snapped, looking anxiously into the woods. Away from Ilun.

She'd dreaded this day. The sadness she felt at leaving miserable little Ilun was mostly due to the rough kindness of her citizens; which had also been a small part of why she agreed to help the smugglers. The temptation of her own house, well, that had been a slightly larger part, bur really…who cared if an inspector overlooked a crate or two? Who better than a logura to make sure they would? The smugglers in turn had brought the poachers, and before she realized it, she was bound in a loose web of thugs, ready to tighten around her at a moment's notice, like a trap around a wild animal.

"Come with us," Jartz urged. "We have a boat at the dock, the *Wind Skimmer*. She sails like a dream and we'll take you wherever you want to go."

"You will take me to Ibilia," ordered Txoko, still wary of a trick.

"We will," agreed another voice firmly. It came from a woman who stood in the doorway of the shack. Though her hair was awry and there was blood on her pant leg, there was a strangely serene expression on her face.

"They're telling the truth, Txoko." Jabea broke the silence. If she had to flee, Ibilia was the last—and worst—place she could think to go. But the king's safety was more important than her own, so she tarried. "Go with them."

"I'll go where you do," Txoko declared stoutly.

"Here." Leuna stepped forward, tugging her belt purse free as she came. She couldn't think of anywhere Jabea was less likely to want to go than Ibilia. "Take this," she pressed it into Jabea's hands. "If you have nowhere to go, travel to Herrixka and wait for me at the home of the doctor. You'll be safe there, I promise."

Jabea stared at her in shock. Her escape plans involved long, hard days and nights of travel with only the hope of escaping a violent end. She hadn't dared plan past that. As she accepted the purse, she pressed the final ash stone into Leuna's palm.

"Can you ride?" Jartz held up the reins of a horse he'd found tied nearby. "This is a smuggler's horse. He'll run all day and night without stopping. You'll be miles away before you can blink." He patted the animal's muscular shoulder confidently.

Jabea made her decision in an instant. "I can ride."

"And how shall I keep my promise to protect you

if we go separate ways?" Txoko demanded even as he stepped forward to check the saddlebags. They held no feast, but she wouldn't starve.

"If I keep your promise to keep her safe, then you can consider yourself in my debt," suggested Leuna archly. "Now let's be done quibbling and get moving. This," she gestured at the groaning smugglers and poachers, "can't have gone entirely unnoticed." With that, she scooped up her staff and headed towards the dock. "Are you coming?" Inwardly, she reasoned that whether Txoko—as Jabea had called him—was the Marroi king or just a Marroi man with the same name, which she privately calculated at about a mila to one odds, it was imperative that they leave.

"Yes, ma'am!" Jartz passed the reins to Txoko and took after her at a trot.

"Go with them," Jabea advised, preparing to haul herself into the saddle. With some help from Txoko, she settled her old bones in the surprisingly comfortable saddle on the first try. It'd been a long time since she rode bareback in her father's fields, yet she found herself looking forward to the trip now that there was hope at the end of it. "Trust them. They will do right by you." Taking the reins from him, she nudged the horse with her heels. "Come on, Sinful." She clucked at the animal. "Let's see what you've got!"

Txoko's eyebrows went up and he chuckled as he watched her duck under a branch on her way to what might've been an old, old trail. One of his would-be assailants started to sit up and he kicked him. The man hadn't finished folding back to the ground before

Txoko selected a discarded sword and spun on his heel to follow the others.

His pride goaded him to stalk angrily down the center of the street, shouting a challenge to all comers. Discretion mildly suggested that was about as stupid a course of action as it had ever heard and bade him look to where the others were slipping quietly along ahead of him.

Leuna's hand on Jartz' arm slowed him. Was it her imagination or…

I'll be hanged a'fore I'll let you on my boat!" bellowed Ainak's voice. "This is my own property, free and clear and you've no business aboard." A chorus of grunts indicated that his crew was prepared for trouble.

"You don't seem to understand." A much softer, smoother voice carried faintly to where Leuna and Jartz were listening, a single building between themselves and the dock. "I'm the city inspector. I must be permitted to board all fishing vessels at my request."

"I'll be sure to warn any fishermen I meet," barked Ainak in a laugh. "This here's a commercial vessel, licensed to carry passengers and freight."

"May I see the license?"

Leuna couldn't help frowning. The voice was completely wrong for a town like Ilun. Only a hint of an accent marred his Lurrakian pronunciation, it was true. But the words he chose, the way he implied a threat without raising his voice…

"He's lying," she whispered to Jartz. "He's no more a city inspector than I'm a plume-tailed scuriday!"

"Agreed," murmured a deep voice from beside her.

She swallowed her yelp of surprise and nearly choked on it. She hadn't heard Neba, um, *Txoko* approaching.

"About time you got here," snorted Jartz quietly. "Got a weapon?"

Txoko flashed him a grim smile and held up the blade he'd taken.

"That'll do." Jartz nodded approvingly. He was more comfortable with his fists than any other weapon, or he would've picked up a sword for himself. "We go up peaceful-like. If they don't let us pass, we're ready."

"Ainak won't leave without us." Leuna bit her lip, mentally taking stock of her travelling medical case. "I hope no one gets seriously hurt." Cuts and bruises she could handle. Anything much worse than that would require some ingenuity to care for.

"C'mon." Jartz jerked his head towards the dock. He stepped around the corner of the building—and found four men waiting for them.

"You." Leuna couldn't tear her eyes away from the man nearest her. He had a wide, pink scar that ran across his face. "You were in the forest."

The man sneered at them, then made a kissing sound in her direction. There were no bows here and she was only carrying a staff. Things were going to turn out very differently this time!

"Brought reinforcements, eh?" Jartz taunted, bringing his fists into position. "Still doesn't look like enough to me!"

Inexplicably, it was Txoko that started it. The

scarred man danced out of his way when Txoko lunged forward, but two of the others closed the gap. They stayed wide of each other, trying to flank Txoko for an easy capture.

Leuna somehow was left opposite her...victim while Txoko took on two of the thugs and Jartz traded punches with a broad brute of a man. In anticipation of the inevitable, she tucked Txoko's gray ash stone into a small, secret pocket of her belt.

"What's the matter?" jeered the man, closing the distance between them. He'd waited too long to rush things now, so he wriggled his eyebrows and shoved his head forward as if about to say 'boo!' "Scared?"

"Not of you." Twirling her staff for show, she settled into a semi-comfortable position. "You're a coward. That's why you brought reinforcements."

Stepping rapidly forward, she thrust one end of the staff at his middle. Unexpectedly, he grabbed the staff with both hands and pulled hard. She ran two steps forward before she was able to let go of the staff, which put her dangerously close to him.

"C'mon, girlie," he invited, grinning evilly. "There's lots more fun t'be had."

He reached for her and she dodged, then rammed her shoulder hard against his. She managed to retrieve her staff, which was small comfort as she tripped over his well-placed foot and landed face down in the damp grass. As she sat up, she became aware of the nearest fracas. A few feet to her left, Jartz bobbed under a crushing swipe from the other man and landed four solid blows to a tree-trunk-like gut before dancing back out of the way again. At least he'd managed to keep his feet!

Rolling out from under her enemy's descending boot heel, Leuna came up to a kneeling position and landed a solid blow to the back of his knees. He yelped and danced away, giving her just enough time to scramble the rest of the way to her feet. Her left wrist ached from her fall, making it difficult for her hold the staff properly.

"All right." He pointed at her. "I'm done playin'."

As he strode confidently forward, she realized he'd taken the bait. Sure she was injured. But not so badly that he could just walk off with her. Shifting her weight, she whipped her staff up over her head and brought all of that momentum into contact with the side of his head. Sickened by the dull *thud* of its landing, she turned away as he folded up like an old skeleton from one of her anatomy classes.

"At 'em boys!" Ainak's voice shattered what little peace was left in the village.

Leuna grimaced. They would be lucky to get out alive if the villagers decided to get involved. She gasped at the sounds of sharp teeth clicking, which were immediately followed by the flare of dragonfire and frightened shrieks. She opened her mouth to shout for Sparks and Presa to be careful, then swallowed hard. Probably best if she didn't distract them.

Txoko heard the dragons as well and grinned. Had Zain or one of his officers found him? Whoever it was—he parried and lunged with a reverse slice that finished one enemy—he was glad they were there! He'd obtained information about the poaching ring that would smash it! Following a feint with a rush, he ran his second opponent through. Looking anxiously for the next problem, he found himself face to face with the young woman from the shack. She stood loosely, mind and body still at the ready. Surrounded as she was by vile intent, he was surprised to see only sadness in her eyes. It made him want to comfort her. Under other circumstances, he would have smoothed her hair so that it matched her unruffled air. His grip on the sword tightened.

"Shall we?" Txoko spoke mostly to excuse the fact that he was staring at her. Comparing her to Nire, for whatever reason. Nire had been a pulsepounder, reckless, but never careless. She would've loved this little dust-up. He could picture her where the stranger stood, amber eyes glowing with excitement, searching for someone else to challenge.

Leuna glanced over her shoulder at Jartz, who'd gotten a choke hold on his man and was slowly riding his shoulders to the ground. Striding over to them, she lifted a vial from a pocket and slid it under the brute's nose. He was struggling for breath and now whatever he got would be permeated with lotan oil.

"He's done," she announced, capping the vial and returning it to her pocket. "We have a ship to catch."

Jartz' jaw hurt badly enough that he didn't answer. Planting his feet, which had finally reached the ground, he let go and watched his massive foe sag down in a heap. Taking a deep breath, Jartz fell in with the others. Thankfully, Ainak and his boys had stayed mostly aboard the *Skimmer*, concentrating their efforts on the men trying to commandeer the ship.

An occasional flash of fire made him think the dragons were doing the same.

The sun was up enough that they were able to see Ainak and his men in action. Boathooks and fists flew. One man was wielding what looked suspiciously like a large frying pan, and with great efficacy. The broken dock hampered the progress of the attackers, at least one of whom crashed through a weak spot and landed in the river with a cry. He was running scared from gleaming dragon teeth when a scaly yellow tail wrapped around his waist and dunked him. Leuna laughed aloud. They thought it was a game!

"Jartz? Can you make it?" She nodded at the bow of the boat, the nearest point to shore. The river was deep enough here that the dock was mostly a formality. Or a trap, depending on how one looked at it. The *Skimmer* had swung in bow-first, which she hadn't noticed until now.

Jartz nodded. The three of them jumped from the shore into the bow, Leuna using her staff as a pole to give her extra lift.

"Shove off, Captain!" shouted Txoko, dumping one of the last few would-be boarders into the water.

Chapter 19

"Thanks." A sailor grinned up at Leuna while she finished doctoring the cuts on his knuckles. Ordinarily, he'd have shrugged them off, or worn them as badges of honor. Since only a fool would turn down a pretty doctor, he respectfully touched two fingers to his cap before resuming his post on deck.

"Where's his majesty?" Jartz asked, stuffing the last of the trash into a bag for disposal at Auzo. Forgetting his question almost immediately, he shook his head. "Had me a real live king for a friend. That's one from the storybooks."

Leuna laughed a little and peeked at herself in the mirror. She'd been too busy to care until then. In short, she looked like she felt—as though someone had picked her up by the ankles and shaken her till the contents of her pockets fell out. *A little knowledge goes a long way*, her father used to say.

"It explains a lot, though." Taking her hair down, she ran her fingers through it and tamped down on a small sigh. Could she truly be in love with him if she'd rather stay in Herrixka where she was comfortable? If she'd rather not go to Marroi and become queen? Assuming that they would let her. She supposed they might be satisfied with a king and not need a queen…so long as said king and queen continued the bloodline. Which raised all sorts of questions about their laws on…a dozen matters.

Jartz looked around when she sighed. He almost joined her in it. He'd just lost a friend, a good one. She'd lost the man she hoped to spend the rest of her life with, judging by the way she'd behaved towards him. Nope, Neba was gone. Likely wouldn't return, given that he—as Txoko—had begun questioning Ainak about the fastest way to the nearest Marroi embassy before Ilun had finished fading from sight.

Still, Jartz had no words for Leuna. So, he wrapped his arms around her shoulders, drawing her in for a short, warm hug.

"Thank you." Leuna blinked back the tears in her eyes and managed a smile for her old friend. "I needed that."

"I need some fresh air," grinned Jartz. "C'mon."

Since she'd already done most of what she could to improve her appearance, Leuna allowed herself to be coaxed up the companionway and into the sunshine. She hadn't realized how cold she was until the sun's rays began to warm her.

"What's he up to?" Jartz frowned at where Ne...*Txoko* was messing with the dragons.

"I'm not sure," Leuna admitted, her pulse picking up when she saw him at the bow.

Txoko was on the wrong side of the railing, hanging on with one hand, his heels firmly planted on the last couple of inches of deck while he reached out to Sparks with his free hand. He spoke softly to the blue dragon, who came closer. Easing himself down onto the dragon's broad back, Txoko switched his grip to the raised ridges on Sparks' scales.

"No!" Leuna reached out as if to touch Txoko's shoulder, but at his urging, Sparks rose into the air, water glistening and dripping from his scales and claws. Looking desperately around, Leuna sprang towards Neba's pack. Cutting through the knots with the medical scissors she'd forgotten to remove from her belt, she yanked out the deia and brought it to her lips.

Txoko was just waving a jaunty farewell when a whistle sounded. The dragon beneath him twisted towards the boat and Txoko saw the woman from earlier. Both feet planted on the deck, she had what looked like a deia in her hands and was blowing with all of her might. It wasn't even an...anything. Not a command, not an imitation of a dragon cry. It was just one note that she held for as long as she had the wind. What was going on?

Angrily, he tried everything he could think of to turn the dragon back upriver, but Sparks ignored him. When the dragon did move, he plunged them both into the water. Txoko held on while Sparks took them under the keel of the *Skimmer*, but he knew he was just being stubborn. A dragon could hold its breath far longer than a human.

Releasing his grip on the dragon's scales, he lightly pushed off. The dragon used its mighty tail to turn its entire body to face him and they rose slowly together. He detected no animosity in the creature. It was young and, according to the captain, gentle but not trained.

As his head broke the surface, Txoko threw back his head and laughed. She was the first one he saw and the expression on her face indicated fear, then relief. Had she thought he'd drowned? Perhaps he could use that to his advantage. Convince her to part with the dragon for a short time. It was urgent that he return to the embassy at Ibilia as quickly as possible.

One of the *Skimmer*'s sailors threw him a line as the boat slid past and he hauled himself aboard, muscles straining against the current.

"Explain yourself," he ordered as soon as he had both feet on deck. He didn't have time for delays! He had vital information on the poaching ring that he had to pass along. *Now.* The woman—Leuna?— braced her fists on her hips, hazel-green eyes snapping with indignation. On the other hand, she'd taken her hair down and it fell in soft waves about her face. The stains on her blouse reminded him that she'd been below decks, tending to the wounded, and he felt a modicum of guilt over his decision to leave without telling her. "I have important business to attend to in Ibilia." Taking a quick look around, he waved his hand dismissively. "If you're worried about being rewarded for your assistance in my escape, you needn't be. Just come to the…"

"I think it's time we were properly introduced," she bit out before he could finish insulting everyone. "Ainak, will you do the honors?" She calmed down slightly by reminding herself of an old axiom of her grandfather's. *When people react strongly to something and you don't understand why, try to remember that they probably do.* In this particular case, that meant that if he immediately jumped to the conclusion that they were all in it for money, well, he probably had a bad experience to back the assumption up.

Amused and confused at once, Ainak scratched his head. "Doctor Leuna Oneko, this is your friend, Neba." Granted, Neba had been acting strangely since they came back from Ilun.

Txoko looked around for this Neba person. Every eye on the boat was turned to him. "What's the meaning of this?" he asked sharply. "I am Txoko Erantz, king of the Marroi." Water was still running down his face, so he reached up to squeeze some of the river out of his hair. Despite how ridiculous he felt, he held his place defiantly.

"If you'll hold still for a minute, I'll tell you," Leuna retorted. "What's the last thing you remember before finding yourself in the storage shack just now?"

His pride protested, but he answered anyway. How dare she speak to him like that? "Being held prisoner in an even smaller shack."

"In Ilun?" she clarified, keeping her gaze pinned carefully on his face. She'd seen Neba shirtless twice and it still seemed like an entirely new experience to see Txoko with his shirt plastered to him, defining every muscle and accenting the difference in the way he stood. This man carried himself like a king and it was far more than posture. It was as though he bore the weight of the world on his shoulders while keeping them boldly squared.

"Of course." Irritated, he looked over at where the dragons were frolicking in the river. Perhaps if he'd taken the yellow dragon, he could've gotten away.

"So you were captured in Ibilia just a day or two ago and brought to Ilun by dragonflight. Right?" Leuna ignored Jartz' snort and watched Txoko

"Yes, obviously! I've given you the benefit of the doubt up till now," Txoko returned impatiently. "If you have a point, make it quickly."

Leuna held up her hand when the men started to

grumble. She didn't need anyone getting new cuts and scrapes in the name of her unwounded pride.

"Captain, what day is it?" She looked at Ainak.

"Uh." He stared blankly. "It's the fourth day of ziren, the eighth lunar."

"What game is this?" Txoko's glare was hot enough to take in Leuna, Jartz, the captain, and the entire crew. "Do you think I will be so easily deceived?" He nearly choked on what would've been a threat when he saw what Leuna was holding between two fingers.

"You left this behind," she said conversationally. Confident that she had his attention now, she continued, "I've known you for six weeks as a man I called Neba. You saved my life." She felt a flicker of amusement at the way his frown relaxed a bit at that information, as if to say, *Of course I did.* "Jabea told me something about this ash stone that I will tell you when we reach the embassy."

"I command you to give me that stone." His tone had evened out admirably. He hated that he had no idea what she was talking about. The very idea that he couldn't account for six weeks of his own life was ludicrous. Except...without remembering why it was so, he knew that he desperately needed that ash stone.

"Sorry, Your Majesty." She closed her hand around the stone and held it close to her body. "I'm going with you to the Marroi embassy. I'll give it to you there and not before."

Txoko considered his options. He had nothing with which to bargain. Taking it by force was out of the question, if only because the crew looked ready to pounce. He exhaled slowly. If she was truly willing to turn it over at the embassy, well and good.

"Then come along." It was half challenge.

She narrowed her eyes at him. "After you change into something dry."

For the first time, Txoko looked down at himself. *Where did I get these clothes?* he wondered.

"Your things are in that pack," she offered quietly, pointing.

"I ain't so sure this is a good idea," objected Jartz. "Sparks isn't full-grown yet. What if he can't carry you both clear to Ibilia?"

"It isn't as far overland," Leuna started to explain.

"No, he's right." Txoko lifted a dry shirt out of the pack and held it up curiously. His servants wore better quality cloth than this! "Neither dragon could carry us that distance."

"You're confident that Sparks could've carried you, though?" Leuna clarified.

"Sparks? That's what you call the blue one?" At her nod, he nodded back. "Riding him I could be there in a few hours instead of a few days." Txoko dug around for a pair of pants and finally came back to the pair he'd found at first. Suppressing a sigh, he started towards the companionway.

"You'll need a bridle. Somethin' to hold onto. Won'tcha?" Ainak studied him carefully. Neba, as they'd called this man at first, would've died before letting anything happen to Leuna. Txoko? Well. Ainak remembered a set of identical twins that he'd grown up with, one of whom was given to pranks. It had taken him years to be able to look into the same face and see the difference in the eyes that told him which man was which. And right now, he wasn't sure of Txoko.

"Sparks hasn't been ridden much," Leuna admitted. "And Presa hasn't been ridden at all."

"Then we'll figure something out," Txoko sighed. "Since Sparks," his tone indicated disdain for the name, "likes you so much, I'll ride the yellow one."

"Presa," Jartz supplied.

"Yes." Txoko hurried below without looking back. It was a relief to slip into the dry things, though he begrudged every moment he spent doing it. *Six weeks?* The ambassador must've gone gray by now, wondering where he was.

"Easy, Presa." Leuna stroked the scaly yellow neck soothingly. "It's new, isn't it, girl?" She looked over to where Jartz stood, ready to lower the 'saddle' onto Presa's shoulders, and shook her head. "If we take her by surprise, it'll just prove she's right not to trust us."

"Allow me." Txoko took the saddle and looked it over. Someone on board must've sacrificed a few blankets and rope. It was an extremely amateur effort, yet he could tell what they were trying to accomplish. Adjusting the rope loops, he commented, "It's a bit thin, but it should help. However, you're trying to put it on the wrong dragon."

"If you're thinking of trying to ride her yourself…" Leuna began.

"What else?" he asked. "You've never travelled by dragonflight, correct?"

"That's true," she conceded. "But Presa doesn't really like people much."

"Ah, and she likes you better than she liked me?"

Txoko smiled. "It won't be the first time I've ridden a reluctant dragon."

Leuna shrugged slightly to prevent Jartz from voicing the opinion on his face. "If you're sure."

"Coax Sparks over, please."

In a matter of moments, Txoko had slipped the front loop over Spark's head and settled the saddle on his shoulders. The dragon didn't even look around from where Leuna was tickling his ear feathers. "I think they both like you better," Txoko laughed, allowing himself to relax a little. It wasn't how he'd planned it, but they would be on their way soon. "Now, if you'll climb aboard, Miss?"

"Doctor," corrected Jartz.

"Yes." Txoko bore the correction as well as he could. "Doctor."

Leuna took his hand and allowed him to steady her as she swung her legs over the railing.

"Here I come," she told Sparks. Stepping onto his back, she wobbled a little due to the movement of his muscles as he worked to keep his place at the bow. "You don't mind, do you, fella?" She knelt, letting go of Txoko's hand. As always, Sparks' scales were warm under her hands as she situated herself. There was no belly-strap on the saddle, so she sincerely hoped he didn't try anything, um, exciting.

"How about it?" She patted the smaller, smoother scales on his neck. "Shall we give this a try?"

As if he understood what she was saying, Sparks swam away from the boat, spread his wings, and lifted off. Leuna took a deep breath and clung to the ridges on his scales as he rose several yards into the air, then relaxed a little as he leveled out. She'd left her pack for Jartz to wrangle, but had a few things tucked into her belt just in case.

"How're you going to get on Presa?" Jartz asked Txoko curiously. She'd moved further away from the boat and it looked like she was getting ready to follow Sparks, like always.

Txoko answered by lifting the deia. A melodic trill issued from it, drawing Presa and Sparks' attention. She was just coming in range when Jartz spoke again.

"Thought you might want to know," Jartz said in a low voice, "that you're in love with that woman."

Txoko nearly fell overboard.

"Everything alright?" Leuna called, eyeing Jartz suspiciously.

"Fine." The men said at the same time.

Txoko gave Jartz one long, searching look, then stepped off the boat and onto Presa. Though she hissed and rattled her scales in displeasure, Txoko successfully transitioned to a seated position.

Leuna couldn't quite catch what he murmured to Presa in Marroi, but she was amazed at how quickly Presa calmed down.

"See you in a few days!" called Jartz, waving as Presa joined Sparks in the air.

Leuna waved back, then hastily gripped the scale ridge again. As they gained altitude, Txoko and Presa leading the way, the saddle wobbled a bit with Sparks' wing flaps. Her stomach lurched with each wobble.

"Relax." Txoko nudged Presa up a little so that they were even with Sparks and Leuna. "Loosen your knees and get more of your leg around him," he suggested. "Dragons don't mind a heel in the ribs the way horses do."

"Thanks." Leuna managed a tight smile as she followed his advice.

"That's it. Now, let's try going a little faster." Txoko signaled Presa, who responded immediately.

Leuna gasped when Sparks followed suit, then ordered herself to relax again.

"I'd feel better, I think," she swallowed and looked ahead instead of down at the treetops that raced along beneath them, "if this saddle was more secure."

"I understand," Txoko assured her. "We'll take it easy, alright?" He watched her nod. She'd prudently put her hair back up in a braid, but the wind was already teasing wisps of it loose. "If you hold on tight like that," he indicated her white-knuckled grip on Sparks' scale ridge, "you'll lose feeling in your fingers." That brought color to her cheeks and he admitted to himself that she was pretty enough. Hardly enough information to assess that fellow's assertion of a romantic relationship, though. He perked up when an idea occurred to him.

"Talk to me." He smiled when she looked at him, eyebrows up in surprise. "It'll take your mind off the flight."

"What can I say?" She shrugged and felt a hair less tense.

"How did we meet?" He frowned at her answering laughter.

"You saved my life." As she recounted their short time together, she found that it did help to have something else to focus on. Concluding her story with their arrival at Jabea's, she turned the tables on him. "Your turn." She lifted one hand to her mouth and blew into it to warm it. "How did you get from Ilun to anywhere near Herrixka?"

She was instantly sorry she'd asked. His handsome face lost its friendly smile. In less than a wingbeat, it had changed so that it looked carved from the dark coastal stones.

"Give me your word that you will tell no one else." This was the last thing he wanted to talk about, for several reasons. However, they still had over an hour to travel, possibly two. And, if she agreed not to tell, she could hardly endanger his investigation into what had to be corruption in his court.

"You have it," she answered at once.

Their eyes met across the distance and he felt as though he could reach out and smooth away the worried crease on her forehead.

"I…only remember up until meeting Jabea." With an effort, he turned his mind back to her question. "I was following a clue in Ibilia, where I found a hidden storeroom." She nodded, so he kept going. "And was ambushed. They were just thugs, but they were smart enough to figure out that I knew too much. They argued for a while about whether or not to kill me," he lifted an indifferent shoulder, "then decided their boss would want to talk to me first, figure out how I knew where to look. So they blindfolded me and flew me to Ilun."

"Where they took you to Jabea?"

"Yes." He laughed harshly at the memory of the hours of interrogation he'd endured first. "I think their fists were finally getting sore. At any rate, they wanted her to manipulate my mind so I'd tell them whatever they wanted to know."

"Why didn't she?"

"She's Marroi." He smiled slightly. "She left our country as a young woman to study in Ibilia, but she knew her king by sight. Rather than doing as they asked, she offered to replace my real memories with safer ones." From the corner of his eye, he thought he saw Leuna wipe a tear from her cheek. "What is it?"

"Oh." Leuna sniffled and considered blaming the tears on the wind. Except that she couldn't lie to him just to save face. "We…" She cleared her throat. "I came here expecting to find a traitor to the service of mankind. To find that Jabea had twisted your mind for her own purposes, her own benefit." She exhaled heavily. "This makes *so* much more sense. Instead of King Txoko, you became Jerl Karruan, Dragon Soldier of the First Order." She laughed and shook her head. "Who couldn't even remember what color his dragon was."

Txoko found himself smiling despite the bleak outlook of his immediate future. Meetings, debriefings, audiences, and so on until his world balanced back out. Ending this poaching ring wasn't going to be simple, even knowing who was in charge.

"I wish I remembered." Their eyes met and she smiled.

"I think I can give this to you now." She'd tied the ash stone in a corner of one of the sailor's bandanas and she offered the bandana to him. It was her last excuse to see him, to be with him. It broke her heart to give up the ash stone, and the tiny sliver of hope she'd been holding onto, but her heart had been broken before. At six, when her pet kaleko died. Again when her own mother died. And many times since then as she hurled herself against the limits of medicine, striving uselessly to save a patient.

From her seat on Sparks back, though, she felt she could see the future. There was simply no reason to hold onto the ash stone. He didn't know her—or love her.

Txoko coaxed Presa to fly enough below and behind Sparks for him to reach her. The wind from Sparks' wings buffeted him, making it hard to remain astride Presa. Nevertheless, he was tempted to go on holding Leuna's hand once he'd touched it.

"Thank you." As he'd suspected, the bandana contained a hard lump the approximate size of an ash stone. He slipped it carefully inside his shirt and let Presa resume her original course and speed.

"I should've given it to you sooner," Leuna half-apologized, looking down at her hands. Funny. She'd forgotten to be afraid of how high they were and how fast they were going. "I just wasn't ready to let you— I mean, Neba—go."

He studied her a moment. "And you are now?"

"I have no choice." She pointed with her chin. "We're almost there." Good timing, too. The cramp in her left leg from holding on for dear life was only getting worse.

Startled, Txoko saw that she was right. While he couldn't yet make out individual buildings, no other city on all of Jatorri could boast that its edge was a perfect circle around its center. He wasn't quite sure, but he thought he heard her murmur to herself, "*A job well done.*"

Chapter 1

Leuna and Sati burst out of their rooms at almost the same moment and stood, staring at each other in the hallway. Sati's gleeful adaption to some parts of city life was abundantly evident in the frilly, lacey nightgown she wore, while Leuna's no-nonsense soft britches and shirt marked her as the country doctor she was. And had been, for the past ten years.

"Is the house afire?" Sati asked, still rubbing the sleep from her eyes.

"I don't smell any smoke." Leuna shook her head and looked downstairs to the front door, which rattled under a fresh barrage of knocking. Spotting herself in the hallway mirror, she grimaced. She was modestly dressed, but she'd foregone her nightly braid and her brown hair stuck out every which way.

"Should we answer it?" Sati eyed the door with trepidation.

"At this time of night?" Xelebre, Leuna's grandfather, stood in the doorway to the master bedroom, pulling the sash tight around his dressing robe. "Never. Let the servants get it."

Gently, he took the young women by the shoulders and pulled them back to where they couldn't be immediately seen from downstairs. Merezi, his wife, was just joining them when whomever was pounding on the door began shouting as well.

"Jaurle Izan! Open in the name of King Txoko!"

Leuna's chest constricted painfully and her hands dropped to her sides from where they'd been smoothing her hair. Up until five days ago, she'd known the Marroi 'King Txoko' as Neba, her amnesic patient with intense golden eyes. His dark skin had been their only clue as to his identity when he turned up on the outskirts of Herrixka, her town and arguably the middle of nowhere.

"Open in the name of King Txoko!"

"He'll rouse the entire quarter," muttered Xelebre, formally known as Jaurle Izan. He didn't have to look at a clock to know it was dark outside and that all sensible people were fast asleep.

"Darling." Merezi caught his hand, stopping him from going down. "What if it's a ruse?" As one of the more practical jaurles in Ibilia, he drew both admiration and ire from those who worked with him.

"To what end?" Xelebre squeezed her hand gently. "The few enemies that I have are all too smart to call this much attention to themselves."

Leuna winced as the door shook again, almost coming loose from its hinges. Stepping forward, she swung onto the stairway banister and slid down to the house's first level. Some of the tension left her as she saw a bleary-eyed footman approaching from the servants' quarters.

"Open it," she instructed, pointing at the door when he hesitated. Moving back into the plentiful shadows of the house's sitting room, she waited to learn what was going on.

"Enough of that racket!" barked the footman as he swung open the door.

Ignoring the footman, the knocker shouldered his way inside. "Jaurle Izan! Show yourself!"

Leuna allowed herself a moment to assess the messenger. Dark-skinned and on the burly side, he nevertheless carried only a short dagger at his belt. No other weapons were in evidence and he was breathing heavily, as if he'd run all the way from the Marroi embassy.

"How dare you come here in the middle of the night and demand audience with the jaurle?" She stepped out of the shadows, letting him get a good look at her. Not that there was much to see. To her extreme surprise, the man had barely gotten a glimpse before he dropped to one knee.

"Doctor Oneko." His right arm across his chest, he lowered his eyes. "Prince Zain begs you to come at once."

Leuna's eyebrows raised so far so fast that she almost didn't have to look up the stairs to see her grandfather and the others descending. She flung up a hand to stop them.

"Why?" The one-word question brought his eyes to her face.

"The king is not well."

"Has the embassy no physician?" His lips tightened and Leuna got the distinct impression that she was dangerously close to being tossed over his shoulder and taken to the embassy whether she liked it or not.

"You have been called for."

She sucked in a breath, easily reading between his words. As Neba, King Txoko suffered from incapacitating mind fevers. That was part of how she'd come to diagnose his condition, to realize his mind had been intentionally manipulated. His old memories had recently been restored by the logura, or doctor of mental health. In the process, he'd lost all of his new memories. So unless King Txoko was up in the middle of the night calling for a woman he'd barely met, some small part of Neba's memories must've surfaced.

"Sati." She looked up at her former apprentice. "Please bring me my medical case."

"Are you sure that's wise?" Xelebre asked Leuna. He frowned and came down the stairs, ignoring the glare of the massive messenger. Xelebre had never met the Marroi king, but he'd liked Neba—for the two or three days that he'd known him.

"At the moment, I probably have a better understanding of the king's situation than any doctor in Ibilia," Leuna reminded him gently.

"More than a logura?" Xelebre countered quickly.

"Perhaps not," Leuna amended, smiling at Sati as she accepted her medical case. "But under the circumstances," they'd all promised the prince that they'd keep the bizarre events of the last lunar quiet, "I'd like to examine him myself before I recommend bringing in another doctor."

"If you are ready?" The messenger's words were half-question, half-command.

Leuna saw her grandfather's face begin to settle into a familiar, stubborn expression, and hurried to wrap him in a hug. "I'll be back as soon as I can," she promised.

"Wear this." Merezi caught up her cape from where she'd left it for cleaning after the concert they'd gone to. The tiny smudge of dirt on the hem didn't seem important as she slipped the cape around her granddaughter's shoulders.

"Thank you." Leuna hugged her as well, then followed the messenger out the door, where, much to her surprise, a dragon waited.

"I'm told you've flown before?" The messenger tossed the words over his shoulder as he stepped aboard.

"A little." Leuna hated how timid she sounded, but this wasn't Sparks or Presa, the dragons she was used to and had even—sort of—helped to train.

"Nothing to it." Anxious to be away, he offered her his hand. "Just hold on and we'll be at the embassy before you can blink."

She tried to smile bravely as she clambered onto the back of the black and gold striped dragon. Its spiked tail rattled against the stones of the street for an instant; then, as soon as she had her arms wrapped securely about the messenger, they were off!

The creature's massive wings beat so furiously that they raised columns of air about its sides, buffeting her until she hid from them against the unperturbed man's back. She seemed barely to have gotten her breathing under control before the muscles and scales underneath her stopped moving. Her arms tightened spasmodically around the man, though not yet enough that her hands could touch. Were they going to fall out of the sky? How many of Ibilia's fine buildings would be crushed under the weight of the dragon? Would the dragon be alright or was there some small chance it would be injured in the crash?

"We've arrived."

Leuna jerked upright and looked around, blinking. Her cheeks burned as she realized that they hadn't just arrived, there was a small audience in attendance. Most of them wore knee-length batas with the royal crest on each sleeve, indicating their role as house servants, but that didn't make it any less embarrassing.

"Thank you." Forcing herself to let go of him, she decided to slide off the dragon's back as she would have either Spark's or Presa's. Only this was a much longer, much bumpier ride. This dragon must've been kneeling or lying down at her grandfather's, because it hadn't seemed nearly so far up as it now was down.

"Are you alright?" asked a woman, separating herself from the others and coming closer.

"Close enough." Leuna winced, then sighed, her legs and back thoroughly bruised from her experiment. She didn't miss that the woman spoke in slightly stilted Lurrakian instead of Marroi. "Can you take me to my patient?" A tall, thin man with a long, thin nose, stepped forward.

When he spoke, his words were deliberate and heavily accented, as if he spoke Lurrakian only grudgingly. "I will take you to the king." The short Lurrakian woman's messy hair and the battered medical case on her hip did nothing to reassure him about the prince's decision to send for her. A sleeping tonic would have soothed the king's frenzied mind just fine. He bowed stiffly. "Follow me."

She did her best, though he made no effort to adjust his stride to hers. The marble rooftop where she'd landed gave way to a marble staircase—no banister. Gritting her teeth, she placed one hand on the wall and tried to ignore the way the man's embroidered, silk bata swirled around his knees as he rapidly descended, making it seem almost as if the steps were in motion. Finally, on the third level down, the man turned to walk down a hallway where every window that would've let in fresh air and sunshine during the day was shuttered, the only light coming from the firestones embedded at intervals in the walls. That seemed odd given that the first of Jatorri's three moons was entering its full stage and its soft, orange light would've lent the dim hallway a cheerful air.

Her step faltered at the first sound of shouting. A glance at her guide showed that his face had gone even blanker and stiffer than before. The voices continued to rise and she recognized one of them. It was coming from behind a heavy door, which a muscular guard opened at a signal from the man beside her. She started to rush in, but the man spoke.

"Wait here." The man was resigned to announcing her, but he hoped to make one more argument against her interference.

Hearing the almost-sneer in his tone, her lips tightened. Brushing past him, she dodged the startled guard's grasp, and plunged into the room. She stopped abruptly, taking in the scene before her. There was a fire burning in the large fireplace on the far side of the room. Luxurious chairs were strategically scattered throughout, their elegant brocade and stiff backs clearly of Lurrakian design. Perhaps that was why the room's only two occupants, remained standing.

"I told you!" Fully clothed, Txoko half-stood, half-leaned against a wall to her right. "I want nothing to do with that cursed stone!"

"Your Majesty." Prince Zain ran his fingers through his hair, the action causing the muscles in his bare back and side to visibly ripple. "You're right. That stone is worthless. Less than that. It should be destroyed."

Leuna's eyes followed Zain's gesture to where a small, gray ash stone sat in state on a marble table. A brick sat beside it, ready and waiting to smash the stone, releasing the secrets stored there by Jabea Burua. It was an old trick of logura, or mind manipulation.

"He's right." They both swung around to look at her as she came further into the room. Something medically unnamed flared in Txoko's eyes, almost knocking her back a step.

"Ah, Doctor." Zain smiled tightly, unhappy at having to involve a stranger. "Kolo found you."

"Leuna." It was more sigh than word, and Txoko was suddenly in motion. Vaulting over a table that stood between them, he crossed to her in an instant. She barely had time to raise her hands to the height of his chest before he'd taken her in his arms. Without waiting for permission, he kissed her. Tenderly. Possessively.

Leuna forgot about the others in the room as she curled her fists in the soft, silky material of Neba…Txoko's shirt to keep from wrapping her arms around his neck. The same arms, the same lips. She'd only had the pleasure once before, but her senses screamed that it was Neba, though she knew it wasn't. Her heart, still grieving her loss of Neba, threatened to explode in rebellion as she struggled not to kiss him back.

The pain that pulsed through her with every erratic heartbeat was reflected in his golden eyes as he slowly released her.

"Don't you love me anymore?" He didn't understand. Not her, not himself. Kissing her had seemed as natural as sunlight. He'd expected more of a response, though. Had he misunderstood his memories of their trip together from Herrixka? Why was she staring at him like he was a stranger?

Confused and disoriented, Leuna willed her hands to unwind from his shirt so she could step back, breathe a little Txoko-free air. I have to remember he's Txoko, even if he doesn't! She had to clamp her lips shut to keep from saying, I loved Neba. And he wasn't real.

"Thank you for coming so quickly."

She swung around to find Prince Zain staring at her, his thick, dark eyebrows drawn in so far that they looked like a single, fuzzy caterpillar. Licking her traitorous lips—for she had kissed Txoko back, at least a little—she nodded.

"Of course." Maybe she was still reeling from the effects of Ne…Txoko's kiss, but she had to remind herself that Prince Zain was Txoko's cousin. They were so similar! Zain's piercing amber eyes were only a shade more orange than Txoko's. He had the same firm jaw and straight nose. Even the way that he stood, shoulders back and hands quiet at his sides reminded her of Txoko.

Txoko stared back and forth between them for an instant before he strode to the marble table, his handsome features twisting in anger. Snatching up the brick, he brought it down hard on the ash stone. Abruptly, he was wholly absorbed in what he'd just done. Lifting the near edge of the brick, he peeked at the dust underneath it. Slowly, he straightened, his free hand rising to cover his eyes as he swayed. The brick slipped from his fingers and bounced twice before coming to rest on the plush carpet.

"No, no, no!" Leuna rushed forward, catching him about the waist and easing him onto the couch behind him. "Get his feet," she ordered.

To his credit, Zain leapt to obey, lifting Txoko's sandaled feet onto the expensive brocade without hesitation.

"What is wrong?" he asked in flawless Lurrakian.

"So many things," she muttered under her breath. She reached for her medical case, but it wasn't there. Zain must've followed her bewildered gaze to where she'd dropped it in the middle of the floor, because he retrieved it before she could ask.

"Stand aside," ordered the tall, thin man, appearing at her elbow.

Leuna didn't even look up from what she was doing. She'd completely forgotten the man existed and wasn't about to give place to him now.

"Hold these." She handed him three glass bottles from her case. The next time he spoke it was in rapid-fire Marroi and she only caught the gist of it. Something about how he was the royal physician and how dare she—she missed a few of the adjectives he used to describe her—presume to do what she was doing?

"He called for her. Not you." Prince Zain's response was delivered in a perfectly calm tone, but still in Marroi.

Leuna surreptitiously wiped a tear from her cheek and bit her lower lip to keep it from trembling. Neba's transition to Txoko had happened so quickly and so completely once he began regaining his memories in Ilun that she'd never expected to see him again. His face would taunt her from every Marroi coin that passed through her hands, but the man she'd come to know and love? Replaced by a stiff, formal stranger. So what could possibly have happened to make a few weeks of memories take precedent over a lifetime of identity?

"Mind fevers are dangerous," she said aloud. "If you know more about them than I do," she lay a square of gauze flat on Txoko's chest, "then stop stalling and get to work." She took the bottles back from the physician and shoved her chin in the direction of the door. "If not, we need water. Quickly."

Deftly she poured a drop each from two of the bottles onto the gauze. Much to her relief, Prince Zain remained while the physician stomped off to get water. Deliberately, she worked the oils together until they had soaked through the gauze. It had all taken less than a minute, yet she was worried as she held the gauze to Txoko's nose. Patting his open-front bata until she found a handkerchief tucked into the wide gerri he wore wrapped around his waist, she began gently dabbing at the sweat that had broken out on his face.

"How can I help?" Zain dropped to one knee beside his king's head and looked up at her.

She almost dropped the bottles she was corking. The resemblance between the two men was absolutely uncanny.

"Hold these?" she suggested timidly. He smiled as he took them and she tried to focus on the gauze. "If we're lucky, this," she nodded at the gauze, "will force a redirection of his thoughts and King Txoko will resurface."

Zain frowned. "I had no idea that smashing the stone might harm him."

"I don't think it did. He was already behaving strangely, remember?" Then, answering the genuine regret she'd heard in Zain's voice, she tried to smile. "Logura is as much an art as a science. Perhaps if he hadn't been so upset," she felt a slow heat rising from beneath her shirt collar and did her best to ignore it, "it would've gone much more smoothly."

Zain's eyes dropped to her neck, widened almost imperceptibly, then rose to meet hers again. He knew so little about her. Much more now that he'd witnessed the passionate exchange of a few minutes before. He admired her efforts not to participate, sensing strength if not fully understanding it. All he was sure of at the moment was that this Lurrakian doctor was very different from King Txoko's first wife, Nire.

"You know the logura who did this to him."

Leuna closed tired eyes. Now that she was semi-comfortably perched on a non-flying seat, it was all starting to catch up with her: the shock of being woken in the middle of the night; the unadulterated fear of riding a strange dragon; Txoko's devastating kiss.

"I know her name, yes." She opened her eyes and looked directly at the prince. It might've been too bold; she had next to no idea how the Marroi culture worked, but she needed to know he believed her. "As I told you before, I gave Jabea Burua some money and suggested she go to Herrixka, the town where I serve as doctor. We were under attack from the poachers and she was afraid to return to Ibilia."

"Because of her prior offenses."

"While a student at the university, yes. Her offenses, her logura experiments, were what drew my attention when I was trying to help him regain his memories." Absent-mindedly, Leuna put two fingers on N…Txoko's neck to check his pulse. It was still racing.

"Yet you believed her when she said she only took his memories to protect him." Zain's carefully modulated tone was the only thing that kept the sentence from being an accusation. "Do you still believe her?" He gestured at the king, then laced his fingers together and leaned forward slightly, one elbow propped on his elevated knee. "Could this not be the work of an enemy?"

Txoko groaned and stirred. "Enemy?" he rasped. "Where?"

"Not here," Leuna soothed, patting his chest. Prince Zain watched her closely as she lifted the gauze from Txoko's nose. "Take a deep breath, please." The acrid scent of the mixed oils had roused him before he could slip fully into the mind fever and now he needed to clear it from his lungs. "Good. Another." Her hand, still on his chest, rose and fell with his breaths. "How do you feel, Your Majesty?"

"Like I've been hit with the clubbed tail of a kisket dragon." Lifting his hands to his head, he blinked up at her. "I...know you."

"Not really." Leuna busied herself with returning the two bottles to her case. Where was the physician with the water??

Zain's head tilted to the side as he watched her reaction when the king sat up. Txoko didn't actually touch her, but that was largely because she leaned clear of him while he moved. Having seen the way she responded to the king's kiss, Zain found that very interesting.